THE NIGHT
IS DEEP

— A LIAM DEMPSEY THRILLER —

ALSO BY JOE HART

Novels

Lineage
Singularity
EverFall
The River Is Dark
The Waiting
Widow Town
Cruel World
The Last Girl (The Dominion Trilogy, Book 1)

Novellas

Leave the Living
The Exorcism of Sara May

Short Story Collections

Midnight Paths: A Collection of Dark Horror

Short Stories

"The Edge of Life"
"The Line Unseen"
"Outpost"
"And the Sea Called Her Name"

THE NIGHT IS DEEP

— A LIAM DEMPSEY THRILLER —

JOE HART

THOMAS & MERCER

Published by Thomas & Mercer, Seattle

www.apub.com

Amazon, the Amazon logo, and Thomas & Mercer are trademarks of Amazon.com, Inc., or its affiliates.

ISBN-13: 9781503935877
ISBN-10: 1503935876

Cover design by M. S. Corley

Printed in the United States of America

To my family. Your love and support is the lighthouse that guides me.

CHAPTER 1

He ran down the alley, gun clutched in one hand, feet pounding the familiar concrete.

Abford sprinted away from him, long, dirty hair bouncing against his shoulder blades, scrawny legs pumping. The alley seemed to elongate as they ran, light filtering between the buildings like bladed things that would flay skin if touched. Liam squinted, the adrenaline rolling through his veins in a white-water current. He could still hear the gunshots, their ringing clear like a tolling bell over the hill. He poured on more speed, sure that he wasn't actually moving, that neither of them were. Abford's body jerked as he began to turn, hair swinging, cruel face coming into view. The gun he held came up slowly, as if the alley were full of drying amber, each of them encased. And now Liam couldn't feel the ground beneath his feet, couldn't see the buildings anymore, because he knew what was happening, knew what would come next.

No, God, no.

His arm snapped up, mirroring Abford's, as the other man planted his feet, soles sliding to a stop, shoulders hunched. The pistol rose up, its muzzle like a dark sun staring with blind violence. Liam's gun sights flooded his view, their three dots leveling with one another, only Abford's grimacing face above them. Now he could shoot. Now before everything happened.

Pull the trigger.

Pull the trigger.

Pull. The. Trigger.

He tried as hard as he could but the gun resisted him, its will separate from his own, until he saw the flash of dark hair sliding into view, covering his target. Her face turned toward him, mouth opening in a question.

Why?

The gun bucked in his hand.

"No!"

The cry came from him like something alive trying to escape. He sat straight up in bed, tearing the sheets and blankets with him. Sweat dripped from the back of his hair, coursing rivers down his spine as he trembled and looked, wide-eyed, around the room.

His bedroom. He was in the farmhouse outside Minneapolis, his home. It was early, he could tell from the dimness that barely lit the windows, how the dark hadn't fully given way to morning yet. It was his hour, the hour before dawn that he always awoke to. Sometimes drifting upward to peaceful consciousness.

And sometimes like this.

A warm hand traced its way up his back as his breathing gradually slowed. Fingers grasped his bicep and drew him gently back to the bed. Dani's face was barely visible in the cool morning light, the curve of her cheek and tip of her nose only suggestions. She stroked his face and the side of his neck.

"It's okay," she murmured. "It's okay. Just breathe."

Her touch and the words were enough to slow his heart, his sweat cooling as he lay above the blankets. The house creaked around them, a gust of wind coming off the fields to the east making its bones shift, sounds he'd heard all his life.

"Was hoping I'd make it through the week," he said, staring up at the ceiling.

"It's coming less and less."

"Yeah."

"But no easier when it does."

"No."

They lay there for a time, watching the shadows of the room shift and shrink. From down the hall drifted the rustle of Eric turning over in bed, a soft snore, then quiet.

"I think it helped going and talking to him," Dani said.

"Yeah. It was one of the hardest things I've ever had to do. To look him in the eyes and say I'm sorry for taking away his wife and son." His voice shook with the last three words. Dani moved closer to him, wrapping a leg over his, and he could feel the scarring below her knees. It had faded in the last year so that the burns were now only pale patches of flesh, rippled in the places where the fire had lingered longest. She kissed his shoulder.

"He forgave you," she whispered.

"But I can't."

"Not right now, but someday you will. You'll realize it wasn't your fault and that burning inside you will go out."

"What if I don't want it to?"

"You don't deserve this. I know you feel like her blood is still on your hands, but it never was. It's not about holding on to the guilt and self-hatred, it's about letting it go."

Liam pulled her closer to him, turning on his side to face her. Her dark brown hair fanned across the pillow behind her and she gazed at him unblinking. He kissed her, filling it with everything he couldn't say, his gratitude that she was simply there beside him. When their lips parted, he stared at her until she began to smile and turned her head away.

"I hate it when you do that."

"I know."

"It's not polite to stare."

"Don't care, you're too pretty."

She giggled as he nuzzled her neck and caressed her hip and stomach. "Don't get me going," she whispered. "The door's open."

He kept his face buried above her shoulder. "Then close it." She laughed and pushed him away, but only a few inches before kissing him lightly again.

"Big day," she said.

"It is."

"Ready for it?"

"Yeah. I think I am. Are you?"

"Of course. Just a little jealous, that's all."

"Jealous?" he asked, drawing back from her. "About what?" She untangled herself from him and slid out of bed, tugging one of his old T-shirts over her head.

"Just that Eric's getting your last name before I do, that's all." She gave him a taunting smile over one shoulder and strode to the bathroom. He issued a sound of mock exasperation as the shower came on and Dani began to sing.

⌣

"Eric Daniel Shevlin, is it your wish to be adopted by these two people, Mr. Liam Patrick Dempsey and Danielle Margaret Powell?"

Liam glanced down at Eric, who looked at the judge sitting behind a deep-red mahogany bench. An expression bordering on terror tightened the boy's face, and the empty right sleeve of his dress shirt was shaking.

"Yes."

The court stenographer's keys tapped quietly along with their answers as the judge asked them each questions. Liam's head was light with the knowledge that within minutes the young boy beside him would be fully, and irrevocably, Dani and his responsibility for the rest of their lives. The thought both thrilled and frightened him, but the overwhelming love he felt every time Eric hugged him good night, or asked him to play catch in the yard, diminished the fear to an undercurrent. He was sure that every parent felt some form of it, fear's twining with love unavoidable. He and Dani were Eric's protectors now. There would be no going back.

"Do any of you have anything else to add?" the judge said, breaking Liam from his reverie. He glanced at Dani, then at Eric. Both of them wore tentative smiles.

"I don't think so, Your Honor."

The judge flashed them a small grin. "Then we're all finished. Be good to one another."

They stepped from the courtroom together and entered the long hall outside. There was a large wooden bench there and Eric walked to it, sitting down on its edge. Liam gave Dani a look before they sat on either side of him.

"Hey, are you all right?" Liam said, placing a hand on Eric's back. The boy nodded, then smiled sadly.

"Kinda weird, that's all."

"Remember what we talked about, you don't have to give up your last name," Liam said.

"I know. But it wasn't really my last name anyways. Not really. And besides, every time I write it down I think of what they did." He gazed up at Liam, brushing away a streaking tear. "I still love them, but I don't want their name anymore."

Liam shot a look at Dani who was biting her lower lip. They had been honest with Eric about what had transpired in Tallston the year before, why his adopted parents had been slain along with Liam's brother and sister-in-law. He would've eventually found out through the media, or worse, from another child at school. Besides, they agreed Eric had a right to know why he had lost most of his arm, and nearly his life.

"Okay, it's your choice."

"That's what I want." Eric leaned into Liam and hugged him. Liam brought an arm around his shoulders and then it was his turn to swipe at his eyes. Dani embraced them both. When they released one another Liam squeezed Eric's shoulder.

"Let's go to lunch."

They dined at Eric's favorite restaurant, a small Mexican joint that served a burrito that could melt the roof of a person's mouth, and the best guacamole Liam had ever eaten. As they finished up their meal, Liam sat back from the table and rubbed his stomach, washing the heat from his mouth with ice water.

"That was delicious," he said. "But I'm not sure I should've had something so spicy for my last meal."

Dani rolled her eyes. "I told you not to order two enchiladas."

"Yes you did, but if I'm going to die I want to do it on a full stomach."

Eric laughed. "You can chicken out if you want to."

"Yeah, you still have time," Dani said.

"Listen you two, I've dealt with some of the most dangerous people in the state, looked death in the eye without blinking." Dani made a blabbing gesture with her hand to Eric and he pealed with laughter again. Liam raised his eyebrows and sat forward. "It'll be me urging you guys on, not the other way around, just you wait."

"Holy shit, I'm not doing this," Liam said, gazing down at the two-hundred-foot drop. He edged back an inch and bumped into Eric.

"*Buuuuck, buckbuckbuckbuck,*" the boy mumbled under his breath. Dani joined in on Eric's other side making the clucking sounds a chorus. Liam closed his eyes and exhaled. The bridge they stood on seemed to sway beneath his feet, but he knew it wasn't the concrete and steel moving, it was his resolve. Why the hell had he agreed to this?

"Okay folks, whenever you're ready," the man wearing reflective sunglasses and a too-large smile said.

"Ready," Dani said.

"Ready," Eric echoed.

"Shit," Liam muttered as they stepped to the edge.

"On three," Eric said, his arm tightening around Liam's waist. "One, two, three!"

They leaned out as one and plummeted into nothing.

The air ripped past them and he heard Dani and Eric scream in unison. His own cry was locked behind clenched teeth that threatened to crack, as he stared down at the ground flying up to meet them. The velocity was a living, breathing thing around them, its shriek that of the speeding wind.

The lashings on their ankles suddenly tightened and all the blood in Liam's body rushed to his skull. They halted at the end of the bungee cord, pausing in time, the three of them clutching each other, then they shot back up. Eric whooped and Dani laughed. Liam tried not to vomit. Losing his lunch now might have very unpleasant consequences for them all.

After they'd come to a stop, they were reeled back up and helped onto the bridge. The smiling man Liam had hired for their jump clapped him on the back.

"Nothing like it, eh buddy?"

Liam gritted his teeth. "Nothing in the world."

"Can we go again?" Eric asked, his face lit up beyond happiness.

"I've got an extra twenty minutes on my schedule, so it's fine with me," Smiley said.

Liam swallowed his enchilada for the second time and tried to resist punching the man's sunglasses off his face.

———⌣———

They got home as the sun was nearing the western horizon, the fields beyond the farmhouse still an emblazoned green of alfalfa in the early October light. They'd stopped at an ice cream parlor on the way home. Liam, barely holding on to his lunch as his stomach kept insisting that they were still hanging from the end of the bungee cord, declined the offer of sweets, while Dani and Eric both partook in large banana splits. As they pulled into the garage, and Liam shut off the pickup, Eric sighed in the backseat.

"What's wrong?" Liam asked.

"Just remembered there's school tomorrow. I wish it was still summer vacation."

"It flew by, didn't it?" Dani said, turning to look at him.

"Yeah."

"You know, it won't be too long until baseball starts up again. I think practice begins in February or March," Liam said.

"It's like four months away."

"But we've got Halloween coming up and then Thanksgiving and Christmas," Dani said.

"That's true," Eric replied, brightening. "Hey, wanna go play catch for a little bit?"

"Sure, you need help with the gloves?" But Eric was already scrambling out of the truck and running to the house. "Guess not," Liam said.

"How's your stomach?" Dani asked.

"I'm more aware of it than I've ever been before, thanks."

She laughed and reached out to hold his hand. "Today meant a lot to him. A lot to me."

"Me too."

"You sure we're up for this?"

"Yes."

"Good. I am too."

"Just no more bungee jumping, okay?"

"Okay." She leaned in to kiss him as her door was wrenched open and Eric threw Liam's glove to him. It landed on his lap and Eric bounced in the space beside the truck.

"Quit kissing and come on, Liam, it'll be dark soon!"

"Okay, okay. Wait, hold on," Liam said, pulling Dani into an exaggerated embrace.

"Yuck!" Eric cried.

Dani and Liam laughed as they climbed from the vehicle and Dani headed toward the small, newly completed building set behind the garage. They'd had the studio built not long after she and Eric moved into the farmhouse. Dani hadn't had to take a web design job in almost six months. Now she concentrated solely on her art and the various shows that she sometimes helped curate in Minneapolis.

"I'll be in the studio finishing up that print," she said.

Liam nodded as he and Eric took up positions behind the house in the well-trimmed grass. Eric paused, situating his left-handed glove beneath the stump of his right arm, readying it for the moment after the ball left his fingers.

"Okay, remember now, we're not going for speed, we're looking for accuracy, right?" Liam said, slowly dropping into a crouch. "Slow is smooth—"

"Smooth is fast," Eric finished. "It's starting to feel normal throwing with my left."

"That's good. I can tell even in the last few months that you're getting better." The boy shuffled his feet and arranged his mitt one last time before rotating through the pitching positions; leg rising, arm drawing back, ball flinging from his fingertips, as he fluidly finished the throw. The ball zipped across the space between them and made a satisfying snap in Liam's glove.

"Nice!" he called. Eric had already shoved his mitt onto his hand and was crouched, ready for a return grounder. Liam marveled at how he'd adapted to losing the use of his right arm. Not only in his favorite sport, but in every aspect of his life. And the way that his arm had been taken from him, with the violent stroke of steel by a brother he never knew he had—the boy was a phoenix.

Liam tossed the ball back and Eric scooped it up, resetting himself for the next throw. They played until the sun had dropped below the land, setting fire to the rim of the world. When it was too dark to make out the baseball, they headed inside, Eric to the bathroom to get ready for bed and Liam to his study.

He shut the door behind him and sat at the desk built into an alcove in the wall. Bookshelves flanked the desk, their spaces filled with true crime novels, law tomes, and fiction by Lee Child, Stephen King, and Blake Crouch. Above the desk was a corkboard. Articles cut from newspapers hung from pushpins beside witness statements and official police reports. Each row was headed by a different picture. Most were of men and women, but there were several of children. The cold cases were his filler when requests for an investigative consultant were slow. And they'd been slow for nearly three months. In truth, he was comfortable with the pace of his career. Since he'd decided in the aftermath of Tallston to keep the life insurance money left to him by his sister-in-law, they were financially secure now. The farmhouse was paid off along with Dani's vehicle and his own. There was plenty of money in the bank, and some earning interest in investment accounts. The security was something he was unaccustomed to—like having forgotten some crucial duty each day only to find out it had already been completed.

He opened the folder he'd been working on the day before. A man by the name of Dennis Sandow had been found in a drainage ditch outside a small town called Crenshaw five months ago. He'd been cut twelve times across the chest with a very sharp knife and then shot four times with a large caliber handgun. He'd been a husband and a father of two boys both under five years old. His killer hadn't been identified.

Liam pored over the case: the facts, suspects, interviews, timelines, and statements all coalescing in his mind until it was a story without an ending. The tire tracks found leading away from the ditch were the most promising evidence since there had been zero DNA recovered from Sandow's body and clothing. The tracks had been matched to a specific line of Toyo tires and the investigators had determined the wear of the treads belonged to a set that had been on the highway for less than three months, but a search of sales at local retailers had turned up no leads. Liam stared at the names and numbers until they began to blur. There was something beyond the tires that he was missing, that everyone had missed. No murder was perfect because the people committing them were just that, people. Everyone made mistakes whether they were taking an exam or planning the end of another's life.

He was so deep in thought that he didn't hear the door open or Dani enter the room until her hands touched his shoulders. Liam jerked, then exhaled, settling back into the chair as she rubbed the tense muscles in his neck.

"Sorry, didn't mean to scare you," she said.

"It's okay. Just lost." He gestured at the material before him.

"No headway?"

"None. How about you?"

"Got the print done. Cindy's going to pick it up tomorrow. And we've got to finish school shopping for Eric. He's still coming home with requests for different classroom materials."

"Don't they provide anything for kids anymore?"

"Budget cuts."

"I guess. I can run tomorrow if you've got a list."

She squeezed his shoulders and then slid her hands down his chest. "Suburban dad. How's the first day feel?"

"Really good. Very right. How about you?"

"Same. Like it's all falling into place." She paused for a moment, kissing him on the neck before slipping onto his lap. "Are you happy?"

He smiled. "Yes."

"Really?"

"Unbelievably. This is . . ." He looked around the room as the sound of Eric running down the hallway to his room echoed to them. Music blared and quieted. ". . . exactly what I wanted," he finished. Dani kissed him long and deep, giggling as he began to run his fingers up the back of her shirt. She stood, slapping his hand away.

"It's time to tuck him in."

"Mmm, can I be next?"

"Come on."

"Okay, I'll be right there."

Liam sat for another minute at the desk after she'd headed upstairs, scanning the information one last time before staring into the smiling face of Dennis Sandow. It was a family photo, his petite wife by his side, their two boys, now fatherless, standing in front of them in matching sweaters. Liam sighed and stood, flipping off the light to let darkness reclaim the office.

He and Dani tucked Eric in together and Liam left to shower, while Dani finished reading a chapter out of Eric's latest young adult adventure book. The scalding water was intoxicating and he closed his eyes as it loosened the muscles he'd used to play catch. Sometime later the shower door slid open and Dani stepped in behind him, her clothes piled beside his on the floor. He turned to her and they embraced, their bodies melding beneath the spray of water. They took turns washing one another, lingering on certain areas longer than necessary, and when Dani turned the water off and took him by the hand, he nearly picked her up and carried her to the bed.

They made love in the solid darkness, the half-moon beyond the window the only light. It pooled in silver puddles on their bodies, and when they finished they lay entwined, looking up at it, their afterglow surrounding them like the moon's rays.

He slipped into sleep without meaning to, Dani's breath steady and warm against his neck, the memory of her heat following him down into dreams.

The buzzing of some enormous insect woke him in the early morning hours. His eyes cracked open, almost expecting a swarm of hornets to be circling their bed. Instead, the cell phone drew his attention to the bedside table, its vibrating dance only visible by the border of light from its down-turned display. He fumbled and brought it before his squinting eyes, the number on the screen vaguely familiar. It was not yet four o'clock.

"Hello?" he said, voice thick with sleep.

"Liam?"

"Yeah?"

"It's Owen." The man's voice on the other end was more ragged than his own.

Liam sat up in bed, scrubbing the sleep from his eyes, the immediate sense that something was very wrong settling over him. He and Owen hadn't spoken in the last year, their sporadic calls having grown further and further apart in the wake of everyday life. "Owen, what's wrong?" There was a sound like a cough that became a stifled sob.

"Someone took her."

"Took her? Took who?"

"Valerie," Owen choked out. His voice shook again. "Someone took my wife."

CHAPTER 2

Liam finished packing the last of his clothes as the smell of coffee wafted to him from the kitchen.

He zipped his bag shut and tucked his father's folding razor into his front pocket. He gave the room a final look and walked down the hall, stopping outside the last door. Cracking it open he gazed at Eric's curled, sleeping form, his chest rising and falling beneath the blankets.

"See you soon, buddy. Love you."

Liam eased the door shut and climbed down the stairs, setting his bag by the entry before moving to the kitchen. The sun was beginning its ascent, only the red edge of dawn slicing the darkness away in the east. Dani stood in her robe at the sink washing dishes. A protein bar sat beside his travel mug, which steamed like a chimney.

"I'm sorry you woke up," he said, running a hand up her arm before sitting to put on his shoes.

"It's okay. Just an early start on the day, that's all. So how do you know him, again?"

"He went to the academy in Minneapolis and did a few months of field training after we graduated. We lived together for about five months before he dropped out of the program," Liam said, lacing up his tennis shoes. "He loaned me some money a few times to get me through when things were tight. Great guy, one of my best friends back then. We had a lot of fun while we were in training."

"Why'd he quit?"

"I think it was more of a rebellious stunt against his parents than a real career choice. His folks were rich. His dad was a judge; mom was an attorney. They had bigger things in mind for Owen than being a cop. He went to the academy to piss them off. When they were sufficiently angry, he dropped out and went to law school. He was a lawyer for five years and ran for the senate in the last election."

Dani leaned against the counter, sipping her own cup of coffee. She tilted her head. "What's his last name again?"

"Farrow."

"Yeah, that does sound familiar. He didn't win, though."

"No. He went back to being a lawyer in Duluth and worked on a ton of community action groups. The last I talked to him, he was contemplating running for mayor up there." Liam finished tying his shoes and stood, pacing to the counter and taking a drink from his travel mug.

"So he didn't say what happened, only that his wife was taken?"

"He just kept saying he needed me to be there. All I could get out of him was that someone came into their house last night, knocked him unconscious and when he woke up, Valerie was gone."

Dani stepped forward and kissed him. "Then you better get going. Be safe and come back to us, Mr. Dempsey."

Dawn crept over the land in a film of gray, slowly pulling everything from beneath the blanket of darkness. Liam drove five miles over the speed limit on the freeway, stopping only once to fill up on gas and replenish his coffee. The gas station brew was disappointingly bitter after the smooth taste of Dani's French press. He grimaced, swallowing another mouthful.

As the miles fell away the land began to change. The familiar fields and rolling hills gradually closed in, their edges hemmed with growths of trees. Soon the forests were broken only by the occasional town or home nestled within their folds, their shapes alien against the rural backdrop. The temperature fell the farther north he traveled. A sign appeared and faded that told him he was only a few miles from Duluth. Most of the trees along the road held armfuls of blazing leaves, some already-fallen foliage littering the ground like a thousand drops of fire.

The city of Duluth appeared opposite piles of iron ore and a littering of ships in the large harbor on his right side. The sun brandished its early light across Lake Superior's surface in rippling waves that stained the water red in a blood-slick that yellowed closer to shore. Homes and businesses grew from a steep hill on the left, their shapes like the blunted teeth of some giant's jawbone left to rot.

He knew Superior was much more lethal than it looked, the water having been the demise of many sailors over the years. He had heard its temperatures were so cold the bacteria that made bodies bloat and rise to the surface were slowed, earning the lake the oft-referred-to phrase, *Superior doesn't give up its dead.* But Liam knew little more about the shipping industry that was the heart of the city's commerce, other than if a person wished, they could travel from the Duluth harbor all the way to the Atlantic without ever leaving their ship.

He wound his way through the city, brownstone buildings sliding past the windows, the sidewalks beginning to crawl with those on their way to work. Traffic was light on the highway leading out of the north side and he followed the GPS set in the dashboard to the address Owen had given him.

The homes grew progressively larger with more intricate designs the farther he drove. The gates and fences became higher, their tops pointed, entrances locked securely shut. Ahead two police cars were pulled to the side of the road near a sprawling estate. The gate was open onto the paved drive, revealing several more vehicles stationed in front of a large home overlooking the glaring surface of Superior. The house itself was three stories and painted a deep shade of blue with white trim. A door that would have been at home on any English castle, complete with iron knocker, was partially open and two figures stood inside the house, their heads turning toward his truck as he pulled to a stop behind the last SUV. Liam climbed out as a woman stepped down from the porch and held up a hand.

"Sir, I'm going to have to ask you to leave, this is an emergency scene."

Liam nodded. "I know, that's why I'm here. My name is Liam Dempsey. Owen called me this morning regarding what happened." He put out his hand. The woman stared at him for a moment before shaking his hand. She was short and solidly built with dark auburn hair and a round face that hovered above a black pantsuit. Her brown eyes assessed him in less than a second, recording and categorizing as she released her grip.

"I'm Detective Denise Perring. Mr. Farrow mentioned you'd be coming. Are you with the state police?"

"I was a homicide detective in Minneapolis. Now I'm a police consultant."

She squinted at him. "You're the cop from the Tallston incident, aren't you?"

"Yes, but like I said, I'm not a cop."

"Well, I can assure you, Mr. Dempsey, we have the situation under control at this time."

"I'm sure you do, but Owen requested that I come."

Perring opened her mouth to reply but a voice from the house cut her off.

"Liam, so glad you're here." Owen Farrow trotted down the steps and hurried to them. He hugged Liam tightly before standing back, holding him at arm's length. Owen hadn't aged a day since Liam had last seen him. His sandy hair was still parted to the side, though now a white bandage clung to the back of his skull, and there wasn't a spare pound on his runner's frame. The only other difference was the slight growth of stubble on his chin and cheeks and the watery quality of his bloodshot eyes. He'd been crying. "So good to see you."

"You too, Owen. I'm sorry it's not under better circumstances."

Owen's fingers tightened on his shoulders and his jaw clenched, but he managed to nod. "Thank you for coming." He turned to Perring who was watching them both. "Detective, I want Liam given all the authority of an investigator on your team."

"Mr. Farrow, I can assure you—"

"And I can assure you, Detective, that if Liam is not allowed to help find my wife, the chief will receive a call from me immediately."

Perring swung her gaze between the two men, then nodded curtly. "Understood. Can I suggest that we move the conversation inside?"

"Of course," Owen said, leading the way.

They followed him into the towering home, passing several uniformed police officers who studied Liam with the same curiosity and distrust that had been in Perring's eyes.

The house was immaculate inside, just as Liam remembered it from his brief visit three years ago. Rich hardwood floors ran everywhere throughout the home and each wall was adorned with minimalist paintings. Owen led them into a dining room that would have encompassed Liam's entire first floor. A command center was being set up on the immense dining table. Half a dozen men and women were stringing cords to outlets, and computers sat on almost every available surface. The room smelled of coffee and warm electronics.

"Listen up," Perring said, and everyone in the room paused amidst their tasks. "This is Mr. Liam Dempsey. He's going to be helping us out on this one. Everyone will treat him as a fellow investigator, is that clear?" There was a murmur of assent from the task force and Liam felt his skin prickle as dozens of eyes focused on him. "Okay, that's all. Carry on," Perring finished. A middle-aged man in a smart, gray suit approached Perring, murmuring something Liam couldn't hear before turning to him.

"Detective Rex Sanders, I'm Denise's partner. Nice to meet you, Liam."

"You also," Liam said, shaking hands with the detective.

"Owen tells me you're the best cop he's ever known, but I won't hold it against you." Sanders smiled, revealing square, even teeth. Liam returned the smile then turned to Perring and Owen.

"So what can you tell me so far?"

"I'd like to sit down, if that's alright with everyone?" Owen said. Perring nodded and they followed him past a high-ceilinged kitchen lined with expansive windows that provided an epic view of the lake. Waves rolled into the shoreline, breaking on the sand before sliding away again, their movement tireless. Two people wearing masks and latex gloves were kneeling beside a set of French doors leading to a covered porch. Neither of them looked up as the group passed.

Owen brought them into a spacious living room that held even more windows than the kitchen as well as a flat-screen TV that Liam at first mistook for a doorway into another darkened room. Owen sat on a white couch and motioned to the chairs opposite him. A low table separating them held four half-finished cups of coffee. Beside the table Liam spotted several dark splotches that had soaked into the tan rug. He shot a glance at Perring and saw she was watching him as they took their seats. Owen seemed to melt into the couch, his thin form becoming even more insubstantial as he settled into the cushions. Liam studied his friend, watching his hands, his eyes, the trembling of his lips.

"I've told this so many times it's starting to seem like it isn't real, like a story I heard from someone else," Owen said, not looking at any of them.

"Just start at the beginning," Liam said gently. "Tell me about last night."

Owen sighed and glanced out the windows at the lake.

"I got home from work late, about eight or so. Since I officially threw my hat in the ring for mayor I've been working a lot of late nights. Val had dinner waiting, she usually does. We ate together and then sat down to watch some TV." He paused and put a hand to the side of his skull, closing his eyes. "I'm sorry, but I need something," he said, rising to his feet. He moved across the room to a set of oak doors set into the wall and pulled them open, revealing a liquor cabinet. He poured himself half a glass of amber liquid and returned to the couch. "That pill the paramedic gave me this morning for my head isn't doing anything for my nerves." He took a long pull from the glass and rested it on his thigh, staring at a spot on the floor.

"You were watching TV," Liam prompted.

"Yeah," Owen said. "We were watching and then Val got up for something, ice cream I think. She asked me if I wanted some and I said no. Maybe if I had offered to get it for her things would be different." He turned his glazed eyes to each of them, the hand holding his drink shaking.

"Keep going, you're doing good," Liam said.

"I heard something, a thump like someone falling, and I started to turn to ask if she was okay, but then it was like a car hit me. I remember seeing this table turn sideways as I fell. Then I was on the floor and I knew I was going to pass out, I couldn't even lift my head. But before everything faded . . ." He bit into his lower lip and blinked away the solid layer of tears. "I heard her scream, and there was nothing I could do to help her." He made the same coughing sound Liam had heard on the phone hours before, and covered his eyes with one hand. Liam rose and rounded the table to grip his shoulder.

"Hey, we're going to find her and bring her home, okay?" Owen nodded, not pulling his palm from his face. "You sit here a minute while the detectives show me around." Liam squeezed Owen's shoulder one more time as Perring and Sanders moved out of the room and into the kitchen. Liam joined them and glanced around the space as the two forensic specialists pulled off their gloves and approached. One was an Asian man in his early thirties and the other was a woman who barely looked out of her teens. Both of them eyed Liam before turning to Perring.

"Anything?" Perring asked.

The man shook his head. "Besides the blood, only some hair but I'm guessing it will match both of the Farrows. We got some steel shavings outside on the porch but we think it's from the door lock itself."

"Blood?" Liam asked.

"A small amount near the hallway off the kitchen. We think it's Valerie's," Perring said.

"It appears that she was coming into the kitchen from the hall when whoever it was grabbed her. The edge of the counter has some hair and blood on it too. Looks like the intruder slammed her against it, then carried her out after knocking Owen unconscious," Sanders said. The two detectives filled in details like a married couple telling a well-worn story.

"Owen said he heard a thump before Valerie screamed," Liam said.

"Could've been anything," Perring said. "The intruder moving in the kitchen, Valerie being attacked . . ."

"So the intruder must have hit Valerie before attacking Owen," Liam said.

Sanders shrugged. "That's what we're thinking, right Toshi?"

The male forensic tech nodded.

"What was used to gain entry?" Liam asked.

Toshi glanced at Perring, who nodded. "Some type of thin pry-bar, maybe a screwdriver, jammed in at the top of the doors and then in the center locks. They weren't gentle, no finesse."

"Thanks. Keep us posted if you turn up anything else. Otherwise send me a report this afternoon," Perring said. Toshi and the young woman both nodded and returned to their examination of the kitchen. Perring and Sanders moved into the dining room where most of the task force was seated at the table, tapping on computers. Liam followed them, glancing at several screens as he passed. There was a complex city grid on one and a spreadsheet on another. Two of the investigators were on their phones scribbling notes on legal pads.

"Can I speak to you for a moment?" Perring asked. Sanders kept walking across the room.

"Sure," Liam said, following her to the vacant entryway.

"I just need to establish a few things before we go any further here, okay?" Perring said once she'd pushed the door to the rest of the house partially closed.

"Go right ahead."

"I've been an investigator going on twelve years, before that I was on the road for four. I've seen some shit. Right now I'm the lead of my unit and let me tell you, as a woman, that was not an easy position to rise to. Do not think for a second that I'm weak or will let you bully me around. It's never happened in my career, not for lack of trying on others' parts, mind you. This is my investigation and if your toenail so much as encroaches on improper conduct regarding this case, I will throw your ass in jail for obstruction of justice. Are we clear?"

"Abundantly," Liam said.

"That's good. Hopefully we can work together in a manner that brings Mrs. Farrow home safely." As Perring turned to open the door, Liam stopped her.

"Just so you know I have the utmost respect for cops, and it basically doubles for women who choose to go into law enforcement. I'm here to help and lend ideas, not to take over."

Perring watched him, her gaze keen and unwavering. Liam wondered how many confessions had been given under that cold stare.

"Glad we're on the same page," she said.

They reentered the dining room and found Sanders standing at its far end.

"So what's been done so far?" Liam asked as Sanders poured himself and Perring a cup of coffee from the pot that had been set up in the corner of the room. Sanders didn't offer him one.

"The neighborhood's been canvassed already, neighbors questioned. No one saw anything, though that's not surprising. This is a quiet neighborhood; rich, respectable, low incidence of crime. Most of the people around here are in bed by ten p.m." Perring sipped at her coffee.

"Some of the team is going through a list of anyone in the area who has a record. Peeping Toms, burglary, assault, anyone that might've seen this place and gotten ideas about stepping into the big leagues," Sanders said.

"But there's been no contact with the kidnapper yet?" Liam asked, moving toward the coffeepot. He picked it up. It was nearly empty.

"Not yet," Perring said, "but from how everything looks here, I'm betting that it won't be long before we hear something."

"Has Owen's insurance company been contacted yet?" Liam poured a thin drizzle of coffee that barely covered the cup's bottom. When he looked up both detectives were staring at him. "Sorry, I'll make another pot."

"Why would we call his insurance company?" Sanders asked.

"Because Owen ran for the senate awhile back. I'm assuming that when he did he took out ransom insurance. It's pretty common for public figures. I'd wager he kept it since he's running for mayor. I would add anyone who was aware of the policy to the list of suspects." Liam drained the coffee in one swallow, then glanced between the two detectives. "If it were my case," he added.

Sanders squinted at him, then moved to the closest task force member, murmuring something that Liam couldn't hear.

"I'd have to disagree on a suspect that was aware of the insurance," Perring said as Sanders returned.

"Why's that?" Liam asked.

"Because of the door. If he'd taken his time to do his homework on the couple, I would guess the entry on that set of doors would've been cleaner, more calculated rather than messy. Doesn't fit the profile."

Liam shrugged. "Only throwing out ideas. Do we know what Owen was hit with?"

"Not yet. It was blunt, though. His scalp was lacerated by something dull," Sanders said.

"While we're chatting, how well do you know Mrs. Farrow?" Perring asked.

"Not well," Liam said. "I popped in unexpectedly a few years ago and she was sitting in the living room. When Owen brought me in there she shook my hand then went upstairs, and I didn't see her again before I left. From what I understand she has several mental disorders that keep her partially housebound."

"Severe agoraphobia paired with disabling panic attacks," Perring said. "Mr. Farrow told us that she hadn't been out of the house in over two years."

"You're kidding," Liam said. "Owen never let on it was that serious."

"Apparently only a few people were aware of the severity," Perring said. "She worked from home as a freelance web content developer and hired a delivery service for groceries and household items. The nearest neighbor said that the farthest he had ever seen her from the house was down on their beach outside, and that was years ago."

Owen stepped into the room holding his glass, which had been refilled. His face was pale and he moved like arthritis plagued every joint in his body.

"Anything yet?" he asked.

"Nothing," Sanders said. Liam moved to his friend's side and gently took the whisky from him as Owen tried to sip from the glass.

"What are you—" Owen started.

"You need to be sharp right now. I'd want to drink too, but this isn't the time," he said in a low voice. Owen looked as if he was about to argue, then his face fell.

"You're right, I'm sorry."

Liam patted him on the shoulder and shared a glance with Perring as raised voices began to filter in through the front entry.

"I'm her father, goddammit!"

"Sir, I need to check with the lead detective."

"Get out of my way, son. Now."

Liam along with Perring and Sanders walked to the front door where a uniformed officer was trying to placate an older man wearing a tweed suit. The man was built like a bull, his shoulders wide and neck thick above his collar. His white hair was falling over his ruddy brow, and his hands were clenched into meaty fists.

"Can I help you, sir?" Perring asked, stepping behind the uniformed cop.

"You can tell me who's in charge here, lady, and get this punk out of my way before I move him myself."

"I'm the lead investigator, Detective Perring. Who are you?"

"Caulston Webb. Valerie is my daughter."

"Let him through," Perring said.

Webb pushed past the officer on the steps and stopped inside the door. He was shorter than all of them but gave off an air of superiority as thick as the smell of his cologne.

"Well, have you arrested him yet?" Webb asked, turning his heated gaze on each of them.

"Arrested who?" Perring asked as Owen entered the room.

"That bastard Dickson Jenner."

"Caulston," Owen said, reaching out to place a hand on the older man's arm. "Calm down." Webb shook his son-in-law's touch off.

"I'll calm down when that black sonofabitch is in custody, not before!"

"Mr. Webb, you'll need to control yourself," Sanders said.

"My daughter was taken, right from this very house, her husband attacked, and you want me to calm down when I know damn well who did it?" Webb's eyes had taken on a sheen of moisture. His fists opened and closed like beating hearts.

"Who is Dickson Jenner?" Liam asked.

Webb fixed him with a stare and blinked, his Adam's apple bobbing. "He's the man responsible for Alexandra's death."

"Who's Alexandra?" Liam said, glancing at Owen who looked stricken and pale.

Webb's voice dropped to a low growl. "Valerie's sister."

CHAPTER 3

They sat in the living room and Liam offered Owen's hijacked drink to Caulston Webb who accepted it with a grunt before perching on the edge of a chair.

Liam studied Webb, watching the expert toss of his head as he threw back the whisky without so much as a grimace.

"Would you like another?" Liam asked.

"No," Webb answered, shooting more poisonous looks at them all. "I want my daughter back."

"We're putting everything we have into finding her, sir, I assure you," Perring said.

"Then why the hell aren't you out busting Jenner's door down right now?"

"Mr. Webb, we are aware of who Mr. Jenner is and sent an officer to his premises this morning to speak with him. He had a solid alibi for the time period that Valerie was taken."

"Where was he? Down at that stinkhole bar near his place?"

"As a matter of fact, he was. He arrived at seven p.m. and didn't leave until closing time. The bartender corroborated his story."

"And you're going to believe him? He was probably drunk or in on the whole thing." Webb's voice rose and he banged the empty glass down hard on a nearby table.

"Sir—" Sanders began, but Webb cut him off.

"No. I trust you people about as far as I can throw you."

"Mr. Webb, I didn't work your daughter's case and neither did anyone else in this room," Perring said, her voice taking on an edge that cut the air.

"If I could interrupt," Liam said, glancing between the two of them. "Sir, if it's not too difficult for you, could you tell us a little about your other daughter and why you believe this Jenner is responsible for Valerie's disappearance?"

Webb gritted his teeth and his lips drew back as if tasting something rancid.

"My Alexandra was eighteen when she was taken from me. It was the summer after her graduation and she'd been dating Jenner for over a year. She'd even mentioned marriage." Webb shook his head. "I told her over my dead body. Of course that only encouraged her."

"Was your relationship with your daughter strained?" Liam asked.

"No. I loved both my girls and we got along just fine until *he* came into the picture."

"And by he you mean Jenner?"

"Yes."

"And you didn't approve of your daughter's relationship with him because he's African-American?"

Webb's eyes hardened as he stared at Liam. Liam gazed back, unflinching, waiting.

"She went to a party that August," Webb continued after a long silence. "She and Jenner were on the rocks and she wanted to have some fun without him. I knew they were drinking at the party; you'd have to be a fool to think they weren't. She disappeared around midnight from her friend's house and they found her the next morning on the steps of Saint Peter's Sovereign Cathedral. She—" Webb's voice caught for a moment and he closed his eyes. Owen stood and moved to his father-in-law's side, placing a hand on his shoulder.

"She jumped from the church's bell tower," Owen said. "She had gotten in through an unlocked door at the rear of the building and climbed up the tower steps." He grimaced and shrugged.

Webb shook on the edge of his seat, his entire body trembling, though there were no tears in his eyes now.

"You mark my words," he said, pointing a finger at all of them. "If she hadn't been dating that bastard, she never would have done it."

"Was he abusive in some way? Manipulative?" Liam asked.

"He got in her head. Filled it up with nonsense. She wasn't the same person after she started dating him."

"I guess I'm unclear as to why you think Jenner is responsible for Valerie's disappearance, Mr. Webb," Liam said.

"Valerie went to speak to him the day after Alexandra was found. She wanted to know why her sister had died and Jenner got enraged and pushed her. Said if she ever bothered him again, he'd kill her."

"And Valerie told you this?" Liam asked.

Webb nodded. "I need another drink," he said, standing and going to the liquor cabinet.

"Alexandra's death was ruled a suicide?" Liam asked.

Owen nodded. "They questioned Jenner and even held him overnight, but in the end there was no evidence that pointed to Alexandra being murdered."

"Was Jenner brought up on charges for the threat against Valerie?"

"No," Owen said. "Caulston filed a restraining order against him. Jenner's been out of work and a drunk ever since Alexandra's death. He's been the local pariah for the last sixteen years."

"Has he ever contacted you or Valerie since then? Ever seen him on your street or close to your home?" Liam said.

"No. I saw him coming out of a liquor store about a year ago, but that was on the other side of town." Owen reached back to touch the bandage covering his head. "I never told you about all this, but Alexandra's death is what caused Val's agoraphobia. We knew each other in high school, and before Alex passed away Val was vivacious, really outgoing. About a year after it happened, she became withdrawn. We started dating six months after Alexandra died and she was already having trouble leaving her apartment. She dropped out of college shortly after that but she got her degree online. She found a job with a placement company that hired freelance content developers and after using her for a year they hired her on full-time. It worked perfectly for her, but it was probably the worst thing for her disorder."

"She didn't have a disorder," Webb barked from beside the liquor cabinet. "She was horrified about what Jenner did to her sister and that he'd gotten away with it. She was terrified. I'll tell you, if this had happened fifty years ago there would have been another kind of justice." Webb nodded and sipped from his glass. Owen opened his mouth and then shut it before gazing down at the floor.

"Do you think it's worth going to visit Jenner again?" Liam asked Perring.

"The officer that went out to his place said he didn't think the man was in any condition to have kidnapped Valerie, especially after he found out how much he'd drank at the bar the night before. Plus, we have the bartender saying he was there until closing time," Perring said. "Unless we get some type of lead, we have no right to get a search warrant for his home."

"You're all gutless," Webb said. "You know what needs to be done but your hands are laced up with bureaucratic bullshit."

"That's enough, Mr. Webb." Perring stood. "Until you can maintain a civil tone, I'm going to have to ask you to leave."

"This is my daughter's house, you can't tell me to do shit, lady."

"Rex?" Perring said. Sanders crossed the room and held out his hand toward the doorway.

"Mr. Webb, please step outside."

"Owen, tell these bastards that I have a right to be here."

"Caulston, we need to keep calm, right now more than ever. Please, for Val," Owen said, his voice worn and pleading. The older man wavered and Liam readied himself to leap from his chair in case Webb's fist came up and connected with Sanders's jaw. After a long moment, Webb's shoulders sagged and he set the glass down.

"For Valerie," he mumbled, moving to a chair and dropping into it.

The same uniformed officer that had blocked Webb's entry to the house stepped into the room.

"Uh, Detective Perring? We have a report of a breaking and entering along with an assault on the south side of the city. Could be our guy."

Perring and Sanders were already moving. "Do they have him in custody?"

"Pursuit's just ended on thirty-five south. No shots exchanged but there's been reports of a gun in the suspect's possession."

Perring glanced back at Owen who had risen and followed her across the room.

"Mr. Farrow, you need to stay put."

"But this could be him."

"Which is exactly why you need to stay here until we have this sorted out. The moment we know something, we'll contact you."

Owen began to speak but Perring and Sanders left the room with the officer, and a moment later they heard the sound of several engines roaring away along with the wail of a siren. Owen stared at the entryway and jerked when Liam placed a hand on his back.

"I know you want to be there, but there's nothing saying that this is our guy. We need to sit tight. Perring's good, she'll handle this," Liam said. Owen nodded and shot a look at Webb who had risen to refill his glass.

"I've never felt so helpless." Owen rubbed the stubble on the side of his face. "Not even when Val . . ."

"When Val what?"

The other man lowered his voice. "When Val tried to kill herself four years ago."

"You never told me that."

"It's not something we wanted to broadcast. It was more of a cry for help than anything else. She swallowed half a bottle of muscle relaxants one afternoon when I was at work. I found her passed out in our room. I got her to the hospital and they pumped her stomach in time. She told me when she woke up that it was getting too hard to go on the way she was."

"Was she seeing a therapist?"

"Yeah. For a while he came to the house, but slowly Val couldn't stand to have anyone here besides me or her dad. After that they switched to phone consultations four times a week. He was the one that had prescribed the relaxants to help her sleep, along with two or three other kinds of antidepressants and anxiety meds. When she had her . . . incident, he changed her prescriptions and she seemed to get better. I didn't let her out of my sight for a week afterwards. I was terrified she'd try it again." Owen glanced out of the window at the white-capped lake. "But now is worse, so much worse."

"Do you have a picture of Val, maybe with Alexandra?" Liam asked.

"Yeah, she has everything of Alexandra's that she kept in her office upstairs."

"Show me."

Owen frowned, glancing at Webb who had refilled his glass and wandered into the dining room. He motioned in the opposite direction and led Liam out of the living room, away from the command post, and into a hallway that ran the width of the house opening onto other spacious rooms decorated with a practiced hand. At the far end of the hall, they climbed a set of stairs to the second floor and passed two closed doors before Owen entered a dormered room with birch flooring. A single window looked out over the lake and below that a glass-topped desk held two laptops along with a desktop computer. A vase of wilted roses sat on the desk's corner, dropping a circle of petals around it like dollops of dried blood.

"She didn't keep much after Alexandra died: her diary, some of her perfume, pictures, and a couple of T-shirts," Owen said, walking toward a short set of doors set into the wall beside the desk. "Truth be told that was all she could save before Caulston had almost all her belongings hauled away. He said he couldn't stand to see Alexandra's face everywhere and in everything." Owen opened the doors and drew out a cloth-lined wicker box. He set it on the desk.

Two T-shirts, one tie-dyed and the other white with an abstract drawing of a horse on its front, lay on top. Beneath them was a bottle of perfume, almost completely empty, a paperback copy of collected Robert Frost poems, a neon pink diary with a swooping embroidered design across its front, and at the very bottom a well-worn envelope. Liam drew out the diary first, setting it aside before thumbing open the envelope, exposing a dozen glossy photographs. Most were of a young woman at different ages, her face cherubic and smiling, with a missing bottom, front tooth in the first and slowly progressing through the years. The very last photo was of Valerie and the little girl, now nearly grown. They were carbon copies of one another; blond hair, long and styled to the side, their eyes dancing blue above identical smiles. The only discernible difference was in Valerie's gaze. It told of experience beyond her years, a dull worrying like that of a stone exposed to millennia of moving water. In the picture their arms were around one another and they sat on a bench with greening grass and budding trees in the background. They were both beautiful and so bursting with life, he thought he could almost hear their intermingled laughter.

"They look like twins," Liam said.

"They were only a year apart," Owen said, lowering himself into the office chair like a man twice his age. "They probably could have passed as twins Alexandra's senior year. That picture was taken right before her graduation, in the park down the street. I only knew her a little since Val and I ran in the same circles in high school, but didn't start dating until college. She was a sweet girl. It was the one thing Val could talk about without getting bound up. She would tell a story about Alexandra and laugh the whole time until she got to the end." Owen blinked and his eyes glazed. "I wish I could've gotten to know her."

"Do you mind if I keep this for now?" Liam asked, holding up the picture.

"No, go ahead. What do you want it for?"

"It might come in handy." He picked up Alexandra's diary and opened the simple, brass lock on the cover. Inside were numbered pages highlighted with a date at the top of each entry. The script was generous and looping with an elegant lean to the letters. She had dotted each and every lowercase *i* with a heart.

"I'd find Val reading that a lot," Owen said. "I didn't know if it was healthy or not, so I asked her therapist about it and he said if it wasn't causing a disturbance in her mood then to let it go. He thought maybe it was a way of coming to terms with the loss."

"Death's a cheat. You don't come to terms with it." Liam glanced at his friend, saw him wince. "Sorry."

"It's okay."

"We're going to find her, Owen, you know that, right?"

"But will she . . ."

"We're going to find her alive and safe, you got me?"

"Yeah."

"Now I do need to ask you, were you drinking last night?"

Owen frowned. "I may have had one. Why?"

"Just one?"

"Maybe two. Don't think for a second I don't remember what really happened, I can't get it out of my head."

"I believe you. Keep it under wraps today, all right? I was serious downstairs. Val is going to need you in good condition." Owen looked as if he were going to say something, but only nodded. "Now, can you call Val's therapist and have him drop by sometime today?"

"Sure. You think this has something to do with her treatment?"

"I don't know. But I want to get as clear a picture as I can."

"Okay, I'll call him in a minute." Owen stood, looking out at the lake, which had lost all its color since Liam had arrived. It was an indifferent gray now, matching the sky above. "Thank you for coming. You don't know how much it means to me."

"You're welcome. You helped me out a lot back in the academy."

Owen waved his hand dismissively. "It was nothing."

"It was something to me."

"You were one of the first people I thought of when I realized she was gone. You're the best investigator I've ever met. You being here is a whole lot different than lending you some cash for your car payment."

"Like I said, I'll do everything I can to help."

The two men moved out of the office and Liam paused in the hallway where a frame containing three pictures hung. The first was a snapshot of Owen and Valerie on their wedding day. They were on a small dance floor holding one another close, the lights low around them. The second was the two of them sitting on the rear deck of the house Liam stood in now. The couple's hands were linked between their chairs, their eyes looking past the photographer out at the lake. The third was the most recent. Owen was seated at the end of the dining-room table that was now holding multiple computers and sophisticated electronics, his hand gripping a glass of wine. He was staring at Val who looked directly into the camera, a faraway quality to her eyes. She barely looked five years older than the version Liam had in his pocket, definitely not sixteen.

"I'm going to take a quick ride," Liam said, continuing down the hall to the stairs. "Call my cell and let me know when Val's therapist can stop over."

"Where are you going?"

"I'm going to shake the past a little and see if anything falls out."

CHAPTER 4

Liam turned off the paved highway onto the county road, gravel crunching beneath the truck's tires.

The sun was only a shining gray circle behind the clouds and the fall colors had dimmed. The wind spun discarded leaves into the air like a playful child and the breeze smelled of smoke and shifting seasons. Instead of the day warming, the temperature had fallen, forcing him to turn on the truck's heater for the first time since April. He shivered, sipping at the dregs of his cold coffee and watched for the address he'd pulled from the Internet.

The mailbox he was looking for appeared after he'd crested a gentle hill overlooking a pond skimmed with ice. The house number stuck out at a broken angle from the side of a narrow drive trailing into a stand of oaks twisted with time. A layer of gold leaves paved the trail through the property and he let the truck idle most of the way in. When the house appeared after the second turn in the drive, his jaw tightened.

It looked more like a junkyard than a home. The yard was dotted with wrecked vehicles and piles of scrap iron. Rotted lumber leaned in a towering heap toward the north end of the property and in the clear spaces, dried weeds poked up in solitary stalks like survivors in some apocalyptic wasteland. The house itself was two stories, its paint faded from a vital blue to milky gray. Scrawls of graffiti ran in tattooed lines across every available surface, racial slurs colliding with curses intertwined with threats. The upper windows were boarded up and two slats of siding hung askew revealing tattered plastic sheeting beneath.

Liam pulled the truck up behind a rusted Ford flatbed and an old but clean Volkswagen Bug. He shut the engine off and climbed out to a series of barks coming from the muscular hunch of a pit bull that stood on the porch steps, white canines catching the cold light.

"Hey buddy, you're okay. You're a good boy, aren't you?" The dog responded with a growl that could have come from a diesel engine. "You wanna bite me, don't you?" Liam said in the same soothing voice. The dog cocked its head and licked its chops before settling onto its haunches. A moment later the front door eased open and an aging black woman in hospital scrubs stepped onto the porch. She was heavyset but moved easily, her sneakered feet creaking on the old boards beneath them. Her face was lined around the eyes and mouth, suggesting more scowls than smiles.

"Good morning," Liam said.

"We already had our visit from the police for today, you can get yourself right back in that truck and head on out." Her voice was clear and strong without a hint of hesitation or fear.

"I'm not a police officer."

"Well detective then. I don't care what you call yourself. We've dealt enough with you people. You want to make yourself useful, how about you find who put the latest paint on the side of my house."

"Actually ma'am I'm a police consultant, I have no jurisdiction here. I only wanted a few words with Dickson if he's home."

She studied him then motioned to her dog. "If you aren't a cop then what's stopping me from sending Fletcher here down to take a piece out of your hide?"

"Nothing. Only he'd be very disappointed with the taste. I've been told I'm stubborn and would assume that would make me tough and gamey." He waited, ready to run if she sicced the dog on him. A flutter of something came and went in her dark eyes and she screwed up her mouth as if she were thinking.

"I guess it wouldn't do much good. Damn dog doesn't listen to me anyway. What's your name?"

"Liam Dempsey."

"Wow, could you get much more Irish?"

"I try every year on St. Paddy's day."

Another flutter. Amusement. "My name's Tanya. I'm leaving for work but Dickson's inside. I'll hold you to your word that you only want to talk to my son, Liam, otherwise I'll be calling the police."

"Just a few questions, that's all."

"You're trying to find that woman, aren't you?"

"Yes. I am."

Tanya glanced from him to the steely sky and then at her overrun yard. She studied it as if seeing it for the first time before looking at him again.

"It's like a curse or something," she finally said. He didn't know how to respond so he said nothing. "Fletcher won't bite you, but I can't promise anything about Dickson."

Without another word she rubbed the dog's head and strode down the stairs to the Volkswagen and climbed inside. When she'd backed around his truck and disappeared down the driveway, Liam approached the house. Tanya was right. When he reached the top of the steps, Fletcher began to wag his tail and pant, first smelling, then nuzzling at Liam's hand. He scratched the dog's brindled hide.

"I am the dog whisperer."

"Who the fuck are you?"

Liam stood up, facing the man standing inside the screen door. Dickson had lighter skin than his mother but they shared the same eyes. He had a handsome face with a prominent jawline although a harsh growth of whiskers partially obscured it. He wore a sleeveless T-shirt and even though a formidable paunch protruded before him, the set of his shoulders and muscled chest told Liam that at one time the man had been a force to be reckoned with. Perhaps still was.

"My name is Liam Dempsey, I—"

"Yeah I heard you talking to my mother."

"Then you know I'm here regarding the disappearance of Valerie Farrow."

"I already told that cop who was here this morning that I didn't have anything to do with that. I was at the bar last night 'til closing. Go talk to Jim down there and he'll tell you the same."

"I believe you."

Dickson appraised him. "Then why are you here?"

"I was hoping you could answer some questions about Alexandra."

"Man, you're about sixteen years too late. I answered all the questions I'm ever going to answer about her." Dickson began to shut the door.

"If you could save her sister's life, would you?"

The door stopped. Dickson glared at him, his gaze flicking to him, then to the floor. He let the door swing wide before pushing the screen door open, holding it for Liam.

"Thank you," Liam said, stepping inside.

Dickson walked away from him down a narrow hallway and into a kitchen, his strides smooth and powerful. There were echoes of athleticism in his gait, possibly the remaining effects of a stern football regimen. Liam glanced around as he followed him farther down the hall. The house was the exact opposite of its exterior. The walls were a warm yellow with white trim. The floors were clean, and when he entered the kitchen the air of order remained, everything in its place. Dickson stood behind a breakfast counter and pulled two coffee cups from a cupboard before filling them from a steaming pot.

"We're out of cream," Dickson said, motioning toward a round table beside a window that looked out into a backyard that was even more cluttered than the front. Liam sat and accepted the cup of coffee as Dickson drew out a chair opposite him and settled into it. Liam sipped the scalding drink and watched the other man through the steam that rose from his cup.

"You read my file?" Dickson finally said.

"No."

"Bullshit. All you cops read the files before you come out here."

"Like I said, I'm not a cop."

"Yeah. Consultant, right? You were a cop. I know that just by how your eyes move. So what'd you fuck up? Steel some meth from the evidence locker? Fuck the chief's wife?"

"I killed a pregnant woman and her unborn child." Liam let the words roll out naturally even as they tried to constrict his throat. A bead of sweat formed on his temple.

"You're serious, aren't you?"

"Why would I make something like that up?"

Dickson shrugged. "Wouldn't be the first cop that made some shit up."

"What do you mean?"

"I mean I'm acquainted with your tactics."

"You're referring to Alexandra's death."

There was a hesitation before Dickson spoke again, a softening of his eyes.

"Yeah."

"Tell me about it."

"What does it matter?"

"It might matter a lot."

"No one seemed to care before."

"Try me."

Dickson sighed and rubbed the beginnings of a beard.

"When she died they came right to me. First thing. No witnesses, no DNA, nothing, but they still came right to my door. They told me straight off that they had me at that church the night she died, that I should just come clean and confess to throwing her off the tower."

"That's a common interrogation tactic."

"Yeah? How about threatening to burn down your house if you don't tell them what they want to hear?"

"What?"

"The two detectives that came here were real hard-asses. Tossed me around a little, slapped the cuffs on me, that type of thing. But then they started saying that it would be so easy for a place like this to burn down if I didn't confess to having something to do with her death. They said that maybe it would happen in the middle of the night and my mom wouldn't wake up and get out of the house in time."

"You're kidding."

"Why would I make something like that up?" Dickson smiled without humor. "Of course it didn't happen because they had nothing on me. Alex killed herself but they still tried to pin it on me somehow. I know the threat to set fire to our house came down from the top, right from the chief. Old man Webb needed to lay his guilt and grief somewhere and who better than the poor black boy that was dating his rich, white daughter. He just couldn't get over the fact that she'd done it."

"So where were you the night Alexandra died?"

"What does that have to do with Valerie being taken?"

"Maybe a lot."

"You saying I had something to do with either case?" Dickson set his cup down and leaned forward. The muscles in his neck rose beneath the skin.

"No, but I'm trying understand who Valerie is. I need to paint a picture so I can figure out what this all means. Valerie became disabled after—"

"I know what she became. Don't you think I would change everything if I could? Don't you think I'd go back and be waiting for

Alex at that church? Try to stop her?" Now there was a sheen of moisture on Dickson's eyes. "I loved her."

"I don't doubt it, but I need you to tell me where you were."

"I was here at home. My mom wasn't working that night. We normally spent the evenings that she had off together, after my dad left us."

"Why weren't you at the party with Alexandra?"

"Because we'd argued the week before and she said she wanted some time to think. But you already knew that, didn't you?"

Liam ignored the jab. "What did you argue about?"

"Stupid shit. She'd mentioned marriage, partially to piss off her father, and I wasn't a hundred percent on the notion so she threw a fit. She wanted me to propose so bad. But it was more than that." Dickson paused and shook his head.

"What?"

"It was like she'd changed over the weeks before she died. She started having a little less time for me when I didn't pop the question the moment she suggested it. I almost got the feeling she was seeing someone else but I couldn't be sure."

"Did you mention this to anyone else? The cops?"

"No. Didn't seem important when I was worried that they were going to murder my mother." Dickson lowered his gaze to the floor and turned his coffee cup in a circle. "I told Valerie a few days before Alex died. She said not to worry, that Alex loved me and she'd get her head straight." He swallowed and blinked, looking away out the back window. "But she didn't."

"Did you notice anything other than that? Strange behavior? Did she say anything that might've hinted at what she was planning?"

"No."

"Can you remember—"

"I don't want to remember!" Dickson's voice was suddenly hard, all the sadness replaced by anger in an instant. "I really don't know what your game is. Valerie's missing, not Alex. I know where Alex is. I can show you her grave."

Liam brought his hands up. "Calm down."

"Don't tell me to calm down. You come out here rehashing shit that I try to forget every day and then expect me to be happy about it? Look out that window, look at all that shit in the yard. You know what that is? My career. I haul junk and scrap metal to the dump for cash. I fix cars up and try to sell them, but who wants to buy one from the nigger that drove a lovely white girl to her death?"

"Dickson, I'm here to help. I'm just—"

"No. If you want answers, go outside and read the writing on the wall. There's your answers. That's all I'll ever be." Dickson stood and bunched his fists. Liam tensed and slowly rose to his feet. "It doesn't matter what I say! Do you get it? People don't forget, they just pass the hatred down to the next generation."

"Dickson, please."

"No. You're barking up the wrong fucking tree. I'm at the end of my rope and if one more cop comes calling, there's going to be hell to pay."

"Valerie—"

"She hated me," Dickson said, poking a thumb into his chest. "Val was one of my best friends and the day after I lost the love of my life, she told me it was my fault that Alex was dead."

"If you really loved Alex, you'll help me now," Liam said, knowing his words would tip the scale one way or the other. Dickson didn't hesitate. His head and shoulders lowered and he rushed across the space between them. Liam had a split second to register how fast the man was, along with the fact that he'd definitely played football.

Dickson's shoulder caught him in the stomach, shunting the air from his lungs. He felt the other man's arms wrap around him, driving him toward the counter at the closest wall of the kitchen. Liam slipped his forearm beneath Dickson's throat as they collided with the countertop. The pain was a hot bed of nails in his lower back but he kept his hold on Dickson, sliding the guillotine choke in deeper. Liam brought his arm up, cutting off the blood flow in the man's throat. Dickson started to panic, trying to lift him up and slam him to the ground, but Liam pulled harder and felt the fight drain from him like water. He waited another beat and just as Dickson's body began to slacken, he released him.

Dickson tried to remain on his feet but his eyelids fluttered and he fell to the floor. He sat there sucking air, arms wobbling as he tried to hold himself up. Liam drew the photo of Valerie and Alexandra out of his pocket and tossed it on the floor between Dickson's splayed legs.

"I believe you loved Alexandra. But if Valerie dies and you refuse to help me, then you had a hand in her death."

Dickson coughed and rubbed his throat. "Fuck you."

Liam turned and walked out of the kitchen. "I'm staying at the Farrows' if you have a change of heart." He shoved the door open and stepped outside, running a hand over Fletcher's head as he passed. "Good boy," he muttered and continued to his truck.

CHAPTER 5

He stopped at a café atop a hill overlooking the nickeled surface of Superior.

Despite the chill weather, he ate outside, letting the cool air gust against his face as he spooned steaming bites of clam chowder into his mouth. The cold always helped him think. It crystallized thoughts into tangible things he could almost touch. He kept his office at home a brisk sixty-five degrees despite Dani's constant complaints about the draft from beneath his door. He finished his soup and fished his cell from his pocket.

How's shopping? he texted.

Only seconds until a reply flashed on the screen: Bought the whole store.

Better not have.

Haha. How are you doing?

Okay. Nothing concrete yet.

How's Owen holding up?

```
Not bad considering. He's partially in
shock but he's a strong guy.
```

Hope you find her soon.

```
Me too. Hug Eric for me.
```

Done! I love you.

```
And I you.
```

He stood and gazed out at the lake, the frosted waves rising with the wind like folding pages. The land on the far side was a curved dagger of purple fading to gray the farther north he looked. How cold would that water be today? How would it feel to slide beneath it and have it close over your head?

Superior doesn't give up its dead.

Liam shivered and zipped his coat up tighter before paying for his meal.

When he arrived back at the Farrow home, there were fewer squad cars on the street. Perring and Sanders's vehicle was still gone as was Webb's. When he entered the home every person on the task force looked up at him before going back to monitoring their computers. An officer speaking on the phone in the corner of the room gave him a curt nod as he passed. He found Owen standing with another man in the kitchen, their voices low over two cups of coffee. Owen spotted him and an air of relief appeared to wash over him.

"You're back, good. I was just about to call you," Owen said, setting his coffee down.

"Did something happen?"

"No, not yet. But this is Dr. Frank Reilly, Val's therapist." The other man stepped forward offering a hand, which Liam shook.

Reilly was a bear in a suit. He was easily four inches taller and fifty pounds heavier than Liam with long arms and fingers like jointed sausages. He had ruddy cheeks above a thick, red beard that parted enough to reveal a warm smile. His grip was like shaking hands with a vise.

"Nice to meet you," Reilly said.

"You also," Liam returned. "Could we sit in the living room?"

Owen nodded. "Sure."

They sat in three chairs, the low conversation of the task force rising and falling while the wind pushed against the windows, its voice hushed and hollow. Reilly barely fit in his chair but managed to retain his professional stature as he made himself comfortable.

"Doctor, I'd basically like you to tell me about your sessions over the years with Valerie."

"Well, Mr. Dempsey, I already mentioned this to Owen when he called me, but I'm really not at liberty to expound on details of Valerie's treatment. It would breach the doctor-patient confidentiality agreement. I can however tell you general information—"

"Doctor," Liam said, sitting forward. "Valerie, your client, this man's wife, was taken last night from this house. Right now we have no idea where she might be or who her assailants are. I don't have to tell you we're walking on thin ice here and I really need you to help us make some headway. It could literally mean the difference between finding Valerie alive or not." Out of the corner of his eye, he saw Owen flinch but he kept his gaze locked on Reilly.

"I understand the crisis but Valerie trusted me with the things we spoke about and I cannot—"

"Doctor, if something you tell us helps bring her home I can almost guarantee that she will be most grateful for the help you gave us. Am I right, Owen?"

"Yes," Owen said.

Reilly stared at Liam for a long moment before flicking his gaze to Owen. "I understand Mr. Dempsey is not an official investigator on this case."

"He's here at my request," Owen said. "And the lead detective has given him the same power as any official working to find Val."

Reilly stroked his beard and finally dropped his large hands to his lap but said nothing.

"Doctor, how long have you been treating patients?" Liam asked, staring out at the lake.

"Nineteen years."

"And how many have died under your care?"

A long pause. "Two."

"Both suicides?"

"Yes."

"How did you feel when you got those calls?"

"How do you think I felt? I was devastated."

"I'm sure you asked yourself what you could have done differently." Liam brought his gaze back to Reilly. "You can help Valerie now and hopefully that will be the difference in the call you receive when we find her." Reilly's mouth opened and it looked as if he were going to rise from the chair, but slowly he settled back into it, his overall presence seeming to shrink.

"I could lose my license over this."

"And Valerie could lose her life."

"Go ahead," Reilly rumbled after a moment.

"You've been treating Valerie since her sister's death, correct?" Liam asked.

"Yes, I first met her when she was nineteen. Her father hired me initially."

"And what was her emotional state when you started seeing her?"

"She was very emotionally withdrawn with flares of anger and violence, but those were short lived, only flashes in the darkness of her state. I diagnosed her with acute agoraphobia accompanied by chronic panic attacks at twenty years old. She complained of indigestion, ulcer-like symptoms, sleeplessness, hyperventilation, sometimes the feeling of drowning, and of course, the overwhelming fear of being in public, or even outside. Later that year she refused to see me at my office. Six months after that she wouldn't have me in her home. We continued our sessions via phone four times a week up until three days ago."

Liam sat forward. "What happened three days ago?"

"She didn't answer when I called at our appointed time."

"Had she ever done that before?"

"No. She called my office a few hours later and left a message with my secretary apologizing and saying that she'd been napping."

"Does that seem strange to either of you?"

Owen shrugged. "I know sometimes she napped during the day if she didn't sleep well. But it's not like her to miss one of her appointments."

"I'll be honest, it worried me somewhat," Reilly said. "But at the time I took it as a good sign."

"Why's that?"

"Because Valerie had been improving over the past two years. Her progress had been stagnant before then. We would take a step forward and then two steps back. So when she didn't answer the phone I thought that perhaps she had finally ventured out of the house or at least was attempting to. I'm not sure if Owen told you about the incident she had?" Reilly shot Owen a look and Owen nodded. "That was the anniversary of her sister's death, a particularly difficult time for her."

Liam looked at Owen. "I didn't know that was the date." Owen swallowed, his face darkening as he nodded again.

"I may have been able to discern more of the signs and warnings if I'd seen her in person. It's one of the drawbacks of strictly phone counseling. People can lie to you easier if they don't have to look you in the eye."

"But you say she'd been improving lately?"

"Yes, very much so. Her mood especially had risen. She actually laughed two weeks ago when I spoke to her."

"Did you notice a change in her behavior or mood?" Liam asked Owen.

"Not really. She may have been in a little better spirits, but it was always so hard to tell. She was sleeping better, I know that. Lots of times over the years I'd wake up and she would be in her office working or reading Alexandra's diary. But lately she would still be asleep when I'd leave for work." He shrugged. "I guess I was just thankful that she was getting more rest."

"How often did Dickson Jenner come up in your conversations?" Liam said to Reilly.

"Many times. He was an unavoidable subject."

"And what did Valerie say about him?"

Reilly sighed. "He was the cause of some of her angry outbursts. I had to be very careful when mentioning him. I approached speaking of him from angles if you will. We would talk about Alexandra and then I would ask her something about the days leading up to her death. Then I would broach the subject of Dickson. Most times she would simply shut down when his name came up. She felt he had attacked her on multiple levels. The first was that he was in some way responsible for taking her sister away from her, but another was she felt betrayed since up until then she'd counted him as a close friend."

"So she definitely thought Dickson had something to do with Alexandra's death?" Liam asked.

"Yes. For quite some time she confided in me that she was sure Alexandra had been murdered, though she mentioned the fact less and less over the years. I took it as a sign that she was beginning to rise past her fears and anger. You see many times when someone is lost, especially in cases of suicide, the survivors look for someone to blame other than the deceased. It's a coping mechanism of sorts, a way to transfer the pain and rage."

"Was there a change in her medication recently?" Liam asked.

"No. We adjusted her meds when she had her incident, but after that it was the same dosage and prescription," Reilly said.

"And as far as both of you know she hadn't left the house in some time?"

"Not in over two years," Reilly said, dropping his gaze to the floor. "It wasn't for lack of trying. One of the therapies I employ for agoraphobia is controlled exposure. The patient slowly exposes herself to certain fears or phobias under controlled conditions. For example, I tried repeatedly to give Valerie homework that involved leaving the house. The first step was unlocking the door. When she was able to do that the next action would've been turning the knob, then actually opening the door and so on until she could take a step outside. Of course this is all done over a period of weeks and months, but you get the idea."

"And how far had Valerie gotten?" Liam asked.

Reilly clasped his hands. "She never even unlocked the door."

Footsteps came from the kitchen and Perring entered the living room followed by Sanders. Both detectives wore sour looks that only deepened when they saw the therapist sitting across from Liam. Owen stood and moved toward them.

"Was it him?" Owen asked.

"No." Perring glanced past his shoulder at Liam and Reilly. "Completely unrelated domestic dispute that blew up. Who is this?" she said, motioning to Dr. Reilly.

"He's Valerie's therapist," Owen said. Perring's eyes narrowed and she tilted her head to one side, just enough for Liam to notice. He stood and made his way toward the kitchen. Perring followed him and put a hand on his lower back, guiding him through the French doors and out onto the porch. The wind bit into the thin shirt he wore and the waves were a constant hushing chorus. Perring snapped the doors shut behind them and turned, her index finger like a dagger pointing at his heart.

"Was I unclear in any way this morning about our arrangement?"

"No, ma'am," Liam said.

"Then what in the fuck are you doing interviewing without my permission?"

"I thought it would be helpful to hear what Valerie's therapist had to say about her condition." Liam crossed his arms, trying not to shiver. Perring didn't move, seemingly oblivious to the cold. "I was going to give you and Sanders a full report when you got back."

"I'll tell you one more time, Mr. Dempsey, do not try to work around us. I don't want to have to send you home since it will be trouble for all of us, but so help me God, if you step out of line again, I will."

"Understood."

"Good. Now what did you find out from her doctor? He was on my list of people to call this morning."

"That she was making progress over the last two years. It sounds like she was slowly coming around even though she still wasn't able to leave the house. Owen told me she'd been sleeping better also."

"And this pertains to her disappearance how?"

"I'm not sure yet. It could be connected to Alexandra's suicide. Or maybe someone's been watching her, keeping her movements under surveillance even while she was at home. Maybe someone who doesn't want Owen to become mayor."

"So you think Jenner did have something to do with this?"

"No."

"And why's that?"

Liam shifted his attention to a seagull that floated on an air current a hundred feet above the beach, its beaded eyes searching the sand and rock below.

"Jenner had an alibi for the night when Alexandra died, so that leaves the theory that he influenced her in some way. Caused her so much pain emotionally she decided to end it after a few drinks. But if that's the case, he's guilty of nothing. She did it of her own free will."

"What's your point?"

"Why would Jenner decide to act now? What would make him want to hurt Valerie after all this time? Even if she harbored suspicion of him or he somehow blamed her for how his life turned out after Alexandra's death, why now?"

"So what's the connection between them then?"

"Not sure. But Valerie's state of mind stemmed from her sister's death. At the very least it's worth looking over again."

Perring studied him for a long moment, then drew out a pack of gum. She popped a piece into her mouth and offered the pack to Liam. He took a stick.

"Thanks," he said.

"I quit smoking a year ago. I go through more packs of gum now than I ever did cigarettes." She tucked the gum away and crossed her arms. "You're making sense but I'm having trouble seeing how the suicide ties into what happened last night." She sighed and glanced at the lake. "Goddammit. I was hoping this would be simple. Some dumb-shit kid out to make a fortune who'd fuck up the first time he got in touch with us."

"You never know. Maybe that's how it will go down."

"Yeah maybe."

The door behind them opened and Sanders poked his head outside, making a face at the cold wind.

"You two frozen yet?"

"I am," Liam said, moving past Sanders into the warmth of the house. Owen was showing Reilly out, and when he returned he took Liam's arm and led him to the far end of the living room.

"What was that all about?" Owen asked.

"Perring wanted to speak in private."

"No, not that. The questions you asked Reilly about Alexandra's death affecting Val. Everyone with a brain knows that's what caused her condition. I'd like you to be more concerned about where my wife is instead of a suicide that happened sixteen years ago." Owen's voice rose, anger barely concealed beneath the surface.

"Listen, I'm trying to gather all the facts. Alexandra's death was a huge impact on Valerie's current state. Maybe there's something there that will help us find her."

"She didn't run away on her own if that's what you're suggesting."

"I know that."

Owen seemed to calm slightly. "So where did you go earlier?"

Liam hesitated, glancing at Perring across the room. "To speak with Jenner."

"I thought so. What did he say?"

"Nothing incriminating."

"So you don't think he's the one?"

"No."

Owen closed his eyes and touched the back of his head. "Caulston is absolutely sure that he's responsible."

"Where did Caulston go by the way?"

"He went home. He got really fired up again after you left and stormed off. I'm not sure he'll be back."

"That may not be a bad thing right now," Liam said, leading Owen over to the sofa. "You need to stay focused, and no offense but your father-in-law isn't helping at the moment."

"He'd lead a lynching party over to Jenner's in a second if he could."

"Yeah, I gathered that. I did want to ask you, and I'm sure Perring already did, but with you running for mayor is there anyone you can think of that would go this far to stop you?"

"No. Perring asked me that earlier too. I've had a lot of support from the community and I've even met with Mayor Wilson. Since he's retiring there's only one other candidate that I'm running against."

"And who's that?"

"A city council member named Grayson. Old guy, maybe in his early seventies. Not someone who could do this." Owen rubbed his face with both hands and Liam saw how bloodshot his friend's eyes had become.

"You need to get some rest."

"No, I'm fine. I want to be awake when we get a call," Owen said.

"You'll be exhausted and bound to make a bad decision if you don't get some sleep. Go lie down for a while, I'll wake you if anything comes in."

Owen finally nodded. "Okay, but if—"

"Owen," Liam said, placing a hand on his shoulder. "Don't worry, we'll take care of everything." Owen gave him a tired smile and shuffled out of the room, his tall form disappearing into the hallway and up the stairs. Liam watched him go, then turned and moved to where Perring and Sanders were talking with a uniformed officer. The officer finished speaking, nodded once to Perring as she said something Liam couldn't hear, and donned his hat before leaving the room.

"Anything new?" Liam asked.

"No. We had a few of our uniforms go shake down a couple of dealers and touch base with a narc we use from time to time. No one's heard anything about a kidnapping," Perring said.

"I'm surprised the press isn't banging on the door right now," Liam said.

"They were. The local paper and a news unit out of the cities both stopped by a couple hours ago but our guys headed them off in the driveway."

"So someone leaked something," Liam said.

"We think one of the uniforms that was first on the scene has loose lips," Sanders said. "He's gotten reprimanded for it before but there's no way of knowing for sure."

"This could turn into a circus, especially with Owen's public status," Liam said.

"Let's hope not," Perring said.

Liam gazed at the floor for a moment before saying, "Did forensics examine Owen's head wound?"

"And why would you ask that?" Sanders said.

"Curious."

"I'm surprised," Perring said. "You being his friend in all this."

"If I didn't ask it would bother me."

"Yes, we looked into the possibility that Mr. Farrow is somehow involved in his wife's kidnapping," Perring said, her eyes never leaving Liam's face. "Do you think we're that incompetent?"

"No, honestly I don't, but I'd like to know what you found."

"We had a paramedic examine Mr. Farrow's head wound along with a member of the crime scene team posing as an assistant. The force of the blow at the angle it was struck makes it pretty unlikely that Mr. Farrow did it himself. And I know that doesn't rule out his involvement, but judging from his emotional state today, I would say he isn't involved, or he could give De Niro a run for his money at the Oscars. Also we checked his bank accounts. The Farrows are not hurting for money."

"How about a witness corroborating his story about leaving work late?"

"We interviewed a secretary earlier over the phone who said he was at his office until the time he claimed."

Liam nodded. "I had to ask."

"We've got a stop to make uptown and then we're going to grab lunch for everyone here along with some more coffee. You want anything?"

"No, I'm fine. Thanks, though." Liam smiled.

"Just 'cause I offered you a sandwich doesn't mean you're my buddy," Perring said. But before she and Sanders left the room Liam could've sworn he saw a slight twitch at the corner of her mouth.

He stood for a second in the middle of the living room, then moved to the stairway leading to the second floor. Upstairs, the master bedroom door was partially shut and he glimpsed Owen lying flat on his back upon the bed, eyes wide, staring at the ceiling. He almost pushed the door open and said something to him, but instead continued past to Valerie's office.

He stepped inside and pulled Alexandra's diary from the basket before turning in a slow circle. He imagined Valerie here in the small hours of the night, gazing at her sister's handwriting. Maybe she even looked out the darkened window into the world she'd left behind, to the past she kept locked away except for the small basket holding only faded memories and pages written by a long-dead hand.

Liam returned to the sofa downstairs and began to page through the entries, eyes hovering on scribbled out words, the names of Alexandra's friends, everywhere, but without a pattern.

May 11, '93
I hate Val! She caught me playing in the ditch near the house and told Dad. She said I shouldn't be playing out near the street because of stranger danger. I told her I'm old enough now that I can take care of myself. She's not Mom no matter how much she wants to be.

December 26, '94

I got such a beautiful bracelet from Dad for Christmas! It's solid gold inlaid with a cross and it's SO pretty! I can't wait to wear it for the New Year recital at school. Jenny Taylor is gonna be so jealous! Val got a really nice ring that used to be Mom's. Dad said that I can have something of hers when I'm older. Wish I was older.

June 23, '95

Val just saved my life! We were out riding bikes and I hit a pothole and took a bad digger on the road. I scraped up my knees and elbows, but that wasn't the worst part. When I fell my bracelet hit the blacktop and it scratched the gold! I wasn't supposed to be wearing it. Dad said it was only for special occasions. I was crying and saying how Dad was gonna kill me and Val took the bracelet off and reversed the cross so that the dented side was toward my skin instead of facing out. You can't tell it got hurt at all! Val's a genius. She's gonna be something great someday like an astronaut or the president or something.

Liam flipped to the rear of the journal and read the last four entries, the leap in time like watching a life on fast-forward.

Feb 5, '99

It finally happened. Dickson and I did "it" in the sauna last night! It was so great and it didn't hurt nearly as much as Gracie said. Dickson was so gentle and I knew it was his first time too, since he was shaking so much. It was magic. I love him, I love him, I love him! Val would kill me if she knew, but deep down I know she's happy for me. Just the big-sister-protective thing kicking in. I can't blame her, she's had to stand in since Mom died. And Dad, oh God! If he knew what we did in the sauna, he would absolutely kill Dickson! He'd probably kill me too. Maybe I should tell him. Then he'd disown me and Dickson and I could run away together. We could start a family somewhere new and get away from all the small minds that give us looks in the halls. I wish things were different, but they're not. I can't wait to get out of this town.

May 17, '99
I told Dickson I loved him today. He got this surprised but happy look on his face and then said it back! He loves me! We're already making plans for college down in St. Paul even though dad's already forbidden it. He wants me to go to his alma mater here in Duluth but I'm done with this town. I'm tired of all the snide comments and "black on white" jokes. If I hear "once you go black, you never go back" one more time, I'm literally going to murder someone! But we have each other, and that's all I care about. I think he's going to ask me to marry him soon!

July 20, '99
What's with men anyways? It's like they can't ever make up their minds. I mentioned the "m" word to Dickson yesterday and he freaked! Like I was trying to give him some disease! I know his family life wasn't good while his dad was still around. Dickson told me he cheated on his mother constantly and she always knew about it but didn't say a word because she didn't want Dickson growing up in a broken home. Like it wasn't broken already . . . I think that's what he's afraid of. I told him he wasn't his father and he got really angry and yelled. I took it with a grain of salt because it's been really stressful trying to make plans for college without anyone knowing. We were able to slip away a week ago and look at apartments off campus. We found some cute ones but they're all

really expensive. Dad said again yesterday that if I insist on going to school in the cities that he's not going to help with tuition. I know he's bluffing but he gets so angry these days. I think he misses Mom. Like we all don't.

I know if we get married Dad will have to accept him. He won't have any choice. All I have to do is get Dickson to propose. If I can't think of anything else I'm going to have to do it! My friends would never let me live that down, haha!

August 1, '99
We broke up. I can't believe I just wrote those words. We've been dating for over a year and now we're not. We were in the middle of trying to plan for the first few weeks of school (we even had money put down on a tiny apartment) and I mentioned getting married again. Dickson flew off the handle. He told me to quit pushing him and that I needed to give us time. I told him if he really loved me then what was stopping him? I don't get it. I'm ready to spend the rest of my life with him. He's everything I want. He's my best friend, he's unbelievable in bed, and he's got the kindest heart out of anybody I've ever known, including Val (if you ever read this, sorry Val) I know we're not broken up for good, but it feels that way. I don't know what to do. I have to do something to get rid of this feeling. I want to die.

Liam flipped the page and saw only blankness from that point on. He turned back to the last passage, noticing several faint discolorations near the binding. Tears. The ghostly spots were where Alexandra's tears had fallen. He closed his eyes. Only days later she'd been found dead, smashed upon the cement outside the church. Liam shut the diary, his knuckles turning white as he pinched the covers together, thoughts coalescing in his mind.

Valerie had thought Alexandra's death wasn't a suicide at all. What had her basis been? Had she known or suspected something that ate at her through the years, gnawing away at her psyche like some carnivorous scavenger? The thought of someone tossing her off the church tower, this young girl who had written the innocent and touching words in the diary, caused a note of anger to toll within him. When he looked out across the lake, the waves had calmed to ripples. It didn't give up its dead.

As he watched the lake the anger slowly gave way to fatigue, the constant din of low conversation coming from the task force almost like a lullaby. A cell phone rang. A door opened and closed. The wind nudged the glass and Liam drifted.

A strong hand suddenly grasped his shoulder, and before his eyes even opened he had the person's wrist in his hand and was yanking them forward.

"Hey, calm down!" Sanders said as Liam twisted the man's arm. Realization flooded him. He'd fallen asleep sitting up. His surroundings, which had seemed so foreign seconds before, aligned into recognition. He released the detective's arm and blinked, taking in the raised voices in the dining room.

"About broke my damn arm," Sanders griped, rubbing his wrist. "Come on, we just got an e-mail. This is it."

CHAPTER 6

The dining room lights had been turned on and it was only then that Liam saw evening had overtaken the afternoon while he slept.

The command center in the dining room now consisted of a half-moon group of people crowded around a large laptop. Two chairs had been pulled close. In one sat a task force member wearing horn-rimmed glasses, his hair raked back in an uneven wave as if he'd pushed his fingers through it too many times. In the other was Owen, eyes just as bloodshot as they had been hours ago. Owen spotted him as he entered and he gave him a quick nod before Perring began to speak.

"Okay people, listen up. About three minutes ago an e-mail arrived in Mr. Farrow's inbox. It was simply titled 'ransom.' Now from what Heller says it came from a burn site, which means that once we watch the video attached, the e-mail will be deleted from the inbox and then burnt from the site it was transferred from. We're ready to record it so there's no worry about not catching everything on the first go round, but it does present a problem for tracking an IP address. We'll talk about that more later. I want everyone to watch this and hold thoughts or opinions until after we've seen everything." Perring gave the small crowd a look, then nodded to the man in the glasses. He turned and tapped the laptop's trackpad twice. A few seconds later an e-mail screen opened. He clicked on the attachment's icon and immediately muffled sobs emanated from the speakers.

Liam flinched as the video screen blazed into life. They were looking at a basement, that much was apparent. The light was low and yellowed, illuminating only a portion of the room. The walls were cinderblock and stained partway up with blotches of mold. Cobwebs hung in tangled strands from the open joist above.

And in the middle of the floor Valerie sat in a wooden chair with a thick, plastic gag in her mouth.

Her hands were behind her, shoulders pulled back in accord with how tightly her wrists were bound. The video screen ended at her knees but by the way her legs were clamped together Liam assumed her ankles were tied as well. Crusted blood stained the waves of her blond hair above her right temple and ran down into the neck of the T-shirt she wore, coloring the collar a sickly maroon. She sobbed around the gag, white teeth biting into the blue plastic bit that was shoved so far back into her mouth little lines of blood drooled from the corners of her lips.

"Oh God, no," Owen breathed. He reached out to touch the screen but Perring stopped his hand and held it in her own.

The shot remained on Valerie as she cried, tears streaming down her cheeks. After nearly thirty seconds, the camera began to turn, smoothly panning the basement until Valerie slid out of view. It slowed, jiggling a little, then stopped, centering on a seated figure. The person was only visible from the shoulders up, their face completely hidden behind a hooded mask that gave no hint at any features. Liam noted the width of the shoulders, the definite masculinity of their shape.

"I think this is all the proof you need that I have your wife," the figure said. The voice was garbled and low, almost mechanical in nature. "Although I can send you one of her fingers if you need further verification. You will give me two million dollars in unmarked bills or she will die." Valerie's cries increased and it sounded as if she were trying to say *please* but it came out as *feez* around the gag. The kidnapper kept speaking as if he couldn't hear her. A faint methodic thumping rose in the background and fell away. "I will contact you again in two days. The countdown has begun."

The video ended, then disappeared from the screen, leaving the small symbol of a burning tree in its place. Owen began to cry in earnest and slumped forward over the table as if he'd been shot. Perring put a hand on the back of his neck and gazed around at the task force.

"Heller's going to send copies of the video to each of you. I want everyone to go over it. Watch it and then watch it again. I want a list from everyone in half an hour, anything pertinent you can think of, anything that stands out to you. Let's find her, people, clock's ticking." The men and women dispersed, returning to their computers. There was a rustling of fast food bags as they were cleared from the workspace, then the tapping of keyboards filled the room. Liam knelt by Owen's side, touching his heaving back.

"Hey, listen. She's alive, okay. We can quit worrying that she's not, right?" Slowly Owen raised his reddened face and nodded. "So now we've got a plan. That guy wants his money. He doesn't want her dead, otherwise she would be."

"Liam's right, Mr. Farrow," Perring said. "This is by no means a good scenario but it's much better than some of the alternatives. Now you need to decide how we're going to proceed. Are you willing to try and raise the funds for Valerie's release?"

Owen sniffled and squinted at her. "What? Of course. Of course I'm going to pay, what choice do I have?"

"We could try to extend the ransom time, call his bluff, use our resources in the meantime to smoke him out of wherever he's holed up with her."

"No, absolutely not. I won't risk her life over money. My insurance company will reimburse me. I already spoke to the necessary people this morning to acquire the money."

"Okay. I always have to give people options," Perring said. "So we'll go ahead with the ransom demands and when the kidnapper makes contact again we'll put a contingency plan into effect."

Owen nodded and Liam caught a faraway glint in his eyes, a fading of sorts. Owen's head continued to bob, and when he tried to rise from the chair, his legs wouldn't hold him. Liam steadied his swaying form until the other man could stand on his own.

"I think I'm going to throw up," Owen said, then hurried down the hall. They heard the slamming of a door that deadened the sound of him being sick. Liam stared after his friend before turning back to Perring.

"Can I have another look at the video?" he asked.

"Sure. Here. Heller, share your laptop with Mr. Dempsey."

The man in the horn-rimmed glasses scooted to the side, holding out a hand as Liam settled into a chair next to him. "Brandon Heller."

Liam took his hand. "Liam Dempsey."

"Good to meet you, Liam. Okay, I'm going to start the video over from the beginning if that's fine with you?"

"Perfect."

Heller opened the recorded file from his hard drive, but before he began to play it he handed Liam a set of ear buds. "Go ahead and listen first, I'll take the second round."

Liam plugged the buds into his ears and Heller hit the Play button. Valerie's sobs were much louder and so defined that it made him want to close his eyes to the pain and anguish that each sound brought. Instead he removed his focus from her form in the chair and began to study her surroundings: the stain on the cinderblocks, the mold, old spider webs, the lack of light. The camera shifted away from Valerie and he watched the shudder that ran through the video as if whoever was turning it had fumbled their grip for a moment. When the kidnapper spoke he listened for any phonetic markings: odd pauses, slurred speech, lisps, rounding of vowels, but there was nothing. Besides the obvious electronic masking of the man's voice, there was nothing peculiar or defining about it. When the thumping rose in the background, Liam turned up the volume one notch, replaying the portion several times. *Dunk, dunk, dunk, dunk.* A pause. *Dunk, dunk, dunk.* It sounded like someone was knocking on a door with a large piece of iron. When the video finished playing and reset, he pulled the ear buds out and handed them to Heller.

"What do you think?" Heller asked, twisting the cords in his fingers.

"Well we know it's a basement. Looks old, unused. I'd say it's either in an abandoned building or somewhere run-down, but that doesn't really narrow our search." Liam felt a flicker of amusement as Heller scrambled for a piece of paper and began to jot down notes. For the first time he noticed how young the man was, definitely not older than twenty-five. "The water stains are interesting. Looks like the building was flooded at one point."

"We had a really terrible flood here a few years back."

"That's right, I remember seeing it on the news. Was there anywhere specific in the city that got hit hardest?"

"No. Everything from the top of the hill down was partially underwater. There was less damage on the north and south ends of the city but everything in between got nailed."

Liam sat forward and stared at the computer screen. "That sound near the end, the thumping, it's really familiar but I can't place it."

Heller put the buds in his ears and ran through the video before drawing them out again. "Sounds like music from a passing car."

"I thought that too at first but if you listen closely there's no increase or decrease in volume like you'd have with a car driving past," Liam said.

Heller frowned. "You're right. Maybe it was someone playing a song upstairs or outside."

"Maybe, but it didn't sound like that. I think we might've heard some lyrics or melody alongside the bass with it that loud." Liam sat back in his chair, lacing his fingers behind his head as he looked out through the kitchen windows at the lake. With the falling dark the water had turned a lurid black draped with patches of the last light drifting on its surface. The sound in the video replayed in his head as clearly as if he were hearing it again. There was something exciting about listening to it.

Somewhere in the back of his mind he knew what it was.

Heller continued to take notes as Perring and Sanders circled the table, stopping at several computer stations to gaze at the screens. Owen appeared from the direction of the bathroom and Liam rose, walking beside him into the living room.

"You okay?" Liam asked.

"No."

"Stupid question. Would you like something to help calm your nerves? I'm sure Perring could have a prescription sent over from your doctor right away."

"No. If I could have a drink I think that would help." Owen's watery eyes met Liam's and then slid away.

"Go ahead," Liam said. Owen swallowed, then made his way to the liquor cabinet before taking his drink to the couch. From the dining room, Perring's voice asked for the task force's attention. Liam walked to the doorway and leaned against it.

"Okay people, what do we have?" she said, placing a digital recorder down in the middle of the long table. A slender woman with mousy hair stood up and held a notepad before her.

"Generally we all agree that Mrs. Farrow is being held underground, some type of old basement by the looks of it. It's been flooded to a height consistent with most basements and properties below the hill so that's where we think we should begin the search. As far as the kidnapper goes, I'm guessing age to be somewhere between twenty-five and fifty, and by the width of his shoulders over two hundred pounds. We didn't pick up any voice tags or any other significantly revealing speech patterns. Obviously he was using a type of voice distortion, but he sounds Caucasian with a Midwestern speed and cadence to his sentences. I would go so far as to say he's well educated by the way he structured his sentences. The sound that can be heard behind the kidnapper's voice three-quarters through the video could be the bass of a stereo or possibly a train passing nearby."

Perring waited. "Is that it?"

"Yes ma'am."

"Anyone else have anything to add?" A burly, mustached man at the far end of the table raised a hand. "Mills?"

"There's a possibility that there's more than one kidnapper. By the way the camera turned it looked like either someone else had moved it for the person speaking or he had it on a remote pan."

"Good," Perring said, scanning the group again. "Let's have the recording analyzed, see if there's any way of telling what type of camera he's using. If we find that out, we can do a check of local shops that sell them. It's thin but right now it's all we have to go on unless we can pull an IP address from the burn site."

Liam dropped his gaze to Heller's computer screen where the video was playing again. The portion where the beating noise came in the background passed, and something caught his attention. He stepped forward so fast that everyone glanced in his direction.

"Rewind that," Liam said, pointing at Heller's screen. The man did so without question. "Now turn up the sound as loud as it will go." Valerie's gagged cries came from the speakers as the kidnapper talked over her. The bass thumping started and Liam pushed a finger against the screen. "There. Something fell from the ceiling while that sound was going on."

Heller leaned in, squinting as he replayed the video. Several other officers rose from their seats and closed in around them. "You're right," Heller said. "It looks like a little bit of dust fell from the ceiling."

Liam looped the sound in his mind, letting it become a rhythm. *Dunk, dunk, dunk, dunk, dunk, dunk, dunk.* He closed his eyes. The first tinges of memory grew on the outskirts of his consciousness, a glint of sunshine off of a car's rear window being the first image that came to him. Heat, roasting within his clothes. A sense of impatience, his fingers drumming against a steering wheel.

All at once the memory surfaced clearly like a fish leaping into the air. He opened his eyes.

"It's a jackhammer," Liam said, looking around the group.

"Can't be, it's too slow for that," Sanders said.

"Not a handheld one, the kind that mounts on a payloader or a backhoe." Liam watched several officers frown, then begin to nod.

"I think he's right," the task force member who had spoken first said, looking at Perring. "There was some construction going on down the street from my house earlier this summer and they were using one of those to break up the pavement. Sounds exactly the same now that he mentioned it."

Perring looked at Liam. "Okay. I want a report of all construction activity utilizing this type of equipment within the city limits in my hand in the next ten minutes. This is definitely worth a look, people." The tap of keyboards rose in the room. Several cell phones appeared and in a matter of seconds officers were scribbling down notes. Perring approached Liam and gestured toward the kitchen. When they were in the next room she pulled out her diminished pack of gum and unwrapped another piece.

"Nice ear," she said.

"I heard that sound enough when I was on duty in Minneapolis. There always seemed to be construction going on somewhere."

"If you're right that's going to narrow down a search for us real quick. Owen will have a decision to make."

"What decision?" Owen asked, stepping into the kitchen. His drink was only half gone but Liam wondered if perhaps he wasn't still on his first anymore.

"Mr. Dempsey here may have identified the sound in the background of the video," Perring said. "We think it might be an industrial jackhammer and that would pinpoint the location Valerie's being held at." Perring gave Owen a long look, which he read correctly.

"If you figure out where she is you want to go in and get her, am I right?" Owen asked.

"Yes," Perring said.

"And you need me to okay it since she's my wife."

"Yes."

Owen sighed and rubbed the side of his face before leaning back against the counter. To Liam he looked like he'd aged ten years since that morning. "It's going to be dangerous for her." Owen said.

"It's dangerous for her now," Perring returned. Owen gazed at her, then at Liam. Liam nodded.

"We should move forward with this if it pans out," Liam said. There seemed to be a wavering inside Owen that Liam could see, as if a guttering candle flame was nearly extinguished.

"Okay. But I want to be there."

Perring chewed her gum harder. "You can be in a squad car out of sight." Owen began to protest but she shook her head. "That's the best you're going to get. Sanders wouldn't even agree to that most likely."

The mustached officer named Mills entered the room and handed Perring a sheet of paper. "Got ahold of the city administrator. She said there are three locations in the city undergoing street repair but only one that was utilizing a backhoe with a jackhammer in the last three days. It's over on West Seventh Street, south of the second intersection."

"You're sure?" Perring said, studying the note.

"Positive. Bigger city it would've been a nightmare to narrow down, but Duluth is small enough there weren't any other options."

"Good. Get SWAT's collective ass in gear. I want three teams of four ready to roll in the next forty-five minutes. Tell them I'll be in touch before then. Send them all the information we have so far as a briefing."

Mills moved out of the room, calling out to someone as he went. There was a bustle of movement from the dining room and Liam couldn't help the rusty feeling stretching its legs in the base of his stomach. The thrill of the chase still lived and breathed after its long hibernation.

"You'll be with Sanders and I if that works for you, Liam?" Perring said.

"That's fine."

"I'd like to be in the same car with you also," Owen said after a moment. "I need to be there when it happens. No matter—" He took a deep breath. "No matter what the outcome."

Perring flicked her eyes from Owen to Liam, then back again. "Okay, but you both do exactly as I say, no argument." Both men nodded. "Good. Let's get organized, it'll be dark soon."

CHAPTER 7

Liam moved down the sidewalk, head hunched low, the wind even sharper than it had been that afternoon.

He glanced up the street, the sodium halos of light pouring from the street lamps like dirty water. A row of run-down houses lined the north side of the road while the opposite held homes in considerably better repair. *Wrong side of the tracks,* he thought, trudging onward. Almost out of sight he spotted the blinking lights mounted to the tops of several sawhorses marking the beginning of the construction area across the intersection he was approaching. He neared a bus stop and ducked inside the glass alcove, glad to be out of the wind's direct fury. He pulled out a brand new pack of cigarettes along with a Bic lighter and blazed the end of the cancer stick with a flick of his thumb. He drew a small amount of smoke into his mouth and then blew it back out before looking around.

Many of the houses on the north side of the street were missing siding. A few had garbage strewn in the front yard, but all of them were occupied. Lights blazed in each of the windows and voices clamored from the third house down where the bass of loud rap music flowed out like a speeding heartbeat. Liam gazed at each home, examining the garages, the vehicles in the driveways, the signs of life. As he took another fake pull from the cigarette, the radio tucked behind his ear came to life with Perring's voice.

"What do you see, Liam?"

He turned away from the construction area before answering into the small microphone beneath his collar. "The houses on this end of the street are way too active to have someone like Valerie making noise in the basement. Someone from next door would hear her."

"So what are you saying?"

"I don't think she's in any of the homes. How does it look on the other side?"

There was a pause. "The same. Houses seem to be all occupied."

"I'm going to make my way up the side street that leads to the alley and see what I can see."

"Don't fuck this up, Liam."

"I won't."

He crushed out his cigarette and tossed it in the butt-can outside the bus stop before drawing his jacket tighter as the October night deepened around him. The heft of his handgun at the small of his back was comforting, like a thick blanket on a cold evening. He glanced once more down the street at the dormant construction equipment, forms of sleeping monsters in the ill light.

The side street led up one of the steep hills that seemed to be a constant feature everywhere on the east side of Duluth. There were no flat spots; you were either walking up or down. His thighs burned as he moved and a light sheen of sweat developed near his temples despite the cool air. When he came even with the alley running south, parallel to Seventh Street, he turned into it, making his movements seem as natural as possible to anyone who might be watching. He was simply a shipyard worker returning home, maybe a college student walking off a bender in the fresh air. He shoved his hands deeper into his pockets as the shadows of the alleyway swallowed him whole.

He moved behind the dilapidated houses, their two-story height seeming much taller now that he was beside them. To his right was a cleared parking lot, empty save for a pop bottle that chattered across the cement beneath the urging wind. Several gnarled trees grew beside the alley, their twisted branches naked and obscene in the darkness like arthritic reaching fingers. Ahead a deeper shadow took the form of a square building with several broken windows in its second level. Liam stopped beside the trunk of the last tree and studied the building for a time before speaking.

"Perring?"

"Yeah?"

"I think I might have something. There's a building midway up on the next street over. It would be right behind the construction zone, the only access being from the west."

"What's it look like?"

"Abandoned. It's made of brick and the windows are busted out."

"Can you tell if it has a basement?"

"No, not from this side. Don't see any ramps or stairs leading down. Can you get any info on it?"

"Sure. Sit tight."

He waited, almost lighting up another smoke simply for something to do. He watched the building for movement—a shadow passing one of the dark windows, a light bobbing around its corner, a vehicle parked nearby—but there was nothing. The wind tugged at the branches above his head and a flutter of dried leaves cascaded around him. One landed on his shoulder and he brushed it away.

"Liam?"

"Yeah."

"It's an old commercial rental property, closed down now. The upstairs had everything from law firms to small engine repair."

"Is there a basement?"

"Yes. It hasn't been used in years but the last occupant was a printing company."

"A printing company." Liam pushed away from the tree. "That basement would've had to have been soundproofed for the equipment."

"My thoughts exactly."

"That's where she is."

"We have to be sure, we get one shot at this. We do it wrong . . ." She let the last sentence hang.

"Do you see anything else promising? Anyone spotted anything on the other three sides?"

"Nothing like this."

"It's got to be that one."

Perring was silent for a long moment before coming back. "Okay. We already have a sharpshooter positioned on the two open streets. SWAT's going in in five minutes. We're going to follow right after that. You come in behind us, got me?"

"Loud and clear."

"Out."

Liam reached back and drew his pistol, checking that a round was chambered before slipping it into the holster once more. A tingling flowed through his muscles and his heart started to quicken its pace. *Here we go,* he thought absently as he readied himself for what was to come. He knew Dani would be terrified to know he was going into a situation like this. His consultant jobs over the past year had been confined to interviewing suspects, accompanying detectives to crime scenes, and sitting before a computer in too-warm offices that stunk of old coffee and crumbling linoleum. But here, tonight, with the wind kissing his flesh and the promise of action, the hope of reuniting Valerie with Owen, he was back in the worn groove his career had carved within him. This was what he was made for.

Two dark vans rolled down the street beside him, their lights off, tires barely making a sound. They pulled to a stop near the sidewalk and it was only a second before the doors burst open and figures dressed entirely in black swarmed out, short rifles gripped in gloved hands. They flowed around the building like water, securing the two visible entrances before the reverberation of the first door being battered inward met his ears. Cries of *"Police!"* echoed to him and he started to run.

He covered the hundred odd yards to the building quickly, not breaking pace as he drew his handgun. As he ran, he flipped down the Velcro flap on the front of his borrowed jacket, revealing the word POLICE in reflective block letters. More shouts came from inside the building, and over the sounds of his breathing he could hear another door being busted open. As he reached the side of the building, Perring's sedan pulled even with the curb and she leapt out with Sanders beside her, their weapons drawn, faces tight with anticipation. He followed them inside, throwing a quick look at Owen who sat in the rear of their car beside a uniformed officer, his friend's face pale in the wan dome light.

The building stank of mold. Water stood in puddles in a stripped concrete floor full of divots. The wind followed him inside and coursed past him as he turned with Sanders and Perring down a wide stairway that dropped into darkness. A SWAT member waited at the base of the stairs, rifle pointed at the ground, the flashlight attached to its forestock blazing a circle of white on the floor. He directed them straight forward and they moved in a line past darkened doorways and vacant rooms. Liam's heart double-timed now. There had been no shots but that didn't mean the silence would hold. Ahead an overhead light threw a septic glow onto the floor through a narrow entry and he recognized its yellowed tone from Valerie's video. His nerves sung beneath his skin. There hadn't been a single shot, she must be okay, she must be alive. Perring entered the room first and Sanders followed.

Liam had to pause in the doorway since the small space inside was so crowded with people.

The room was twenty feet across and fifteen feet deep, much like the others they'd passed. A tangle of cords ran down through one wall and hung like slayed snakes above a scarred worktable. The chair Valerie had been seated on in the video sat to one side, several dark blots dried beneath it. There were water-filled scratches and gouges on the concrete floor and the smell of mold lent a thick quality to the air.

Besides the five SWAT members and the two detectives, the room was empty.

"Goddammit!" Perring swore. "They're gone. We missed them." She turned to one of the SWAT members. "Clear the rest of the building. You find anything you come get me."

"Yes ma'am," the officer said and led his team out of the room. Liam stepped inside once they were gone and gazed around.

"How long do you think?" Sanders asked, sauntering around the space, thumbs hooked in his pockets.

"Since they were here? At least a few hours, maybe more," Perring said. Liam knelt beside the chair Valerie had been strapped to. There were worn grooves in its back where her hands had been tied. He leaned closer to the floor and studied the drops of blood near the chair. They looked like blackened pennies in the sickly light.

"I think it was longer," Liam said at last.

"Yeah?" Perring said.

"I'd put my money on early this morning by the looks of the blood."

"So she was held here for what, a few hours?"

"Just long enough to make the video. Then moved," Liam said, standing straight.

"Smart," Sanders said.

"More like reckless," Perring said. "Moving her like that, hundreds of things could go wrong."

The officer that had been sitting in the backseat with Owen appeared at the door, his eyes swinging around the room before looking at Perring. "Detective? Mr. Farrow wants to know if he can come inside."

"Yes, let him in. Then call forensics. I want a full sweep of this building. Have four or five units canvass the neighborhood surrounding this block. See if anyone in the area noticed anything suspicious about this place over the last few weeks. Don't tell them a word about the case. If they ask we're investigating a simple break in. Got it?"

"Yes ma'am."

"Go."

The officer's steps faded in the darkness and Liam looked at the single bare light bulb hanging from the center rafter. It was so yellowed he imagined he could scrape the light off its exterior with his fingernail.

"Back to the drawing board," Sanders said.

"Why would he bring her here?" Liam asked. "Why not just make the video in such a remote location that we wouldn't have any clue where they were?" He moved to the workbench and inspected its length. It was clean and dry. "Construction was going on outside when he made the video. This guy isn't stupid so why would he intentionally leave a clue like that for us to find?"

"He wanted us to come here," Perring said.

"I think so," Liam said. "He wanted us to see something. That or he's enjoying leading us on a goose chase."

Owen's long form darkened the doorway. He looked around the room, eyes hovering for a long time on the chair.

"We're sorry, Mr. Farrow," Perring said.

Owen nodded. "Somehow I guessed this is what we'd find. I didn't believe it would be that easy to get her back."

"This is a step forward, Owen," Liam said. "We're going to find her."

Owen finally brought his gaze up as if noticing them for the first time. "I want everyone to back off. I want to give the money to this person and get my wife back. No more SWAT teams, no more busting in doors. We do whatever he wants."

"Mr. Farrow—" Perring started, but Owen held up a hand.

"She's my wife. I won't lose her over trying to get this guy." There were tears at the edge of his voice and a moment later he turned and disappeared into the darkness of the hallway.

"Let's get him back home," Perring said after silence returned to the room. "There's no use standing around here."

They filed out but Liam lingered for another minute, his eyes traveling over the chair, the grooves worn in its wood, the blood on the floor. He gave the light bulb one last look, then followed the detectives out of the basement.

A new shift of the task force had taken over by the time they returned to Owen's house. They glanced up from their computers as Owen filed past followed by Liam and the two detectives. In the living room Owen slopped a glass half full of whisky and drank it in three swallows before refilling it. Liam put a hand on his friend's arm but Owen shrugged it off.

"Owen, you know if Valerie had been in that basement tonight, she'd be home safe right now," Liam said.

"No, I don't know that and neither do you. Any of you," Owen said, gesturing at them all with the hand that held his drink.

"Look, I know you're upset but—" Liam began.

"Upset? Do you really think that word describes what I'm feeling right now?" His voice rose until it rebounded off the high ceilings. "I saw a video today of my wife gagged and tied to a chair. She was bleeding and calling out for help, and there's not a fucking thing I could do about it!" He shook with rage. Tears spilled from the corners of his eyes. "That any of you can do about it."

"Mr. Farrow—" Perring said.

Liam held up a hand. "Could you give us a few minutes?" Perring opened her mouth to say something but then closed it and merely nodded. Sanders ambled into the kitchen while Perring retreated to the dining room. Owen drank half of the glass before staring after the detectives.

"They're going to get her killed," Owen said, his voice a cracked husk, all of the anger drained from it.

"Valerie's not going to die," Liam said. "We're all doing our best here. Everyone's working hard and I can't imagine how tough this must be for you, but it was the right decision going into that building tonight."

"What if she had been there and the guy heard the door break down? What if—"

"You can't worry about that. She wasn't there. No one was."

"But he's got her right now," Owen whispered, eyes gleaming. "He's got her tied up somewhere and . . ." His words trailed off. Liam guided him to the couch before returning to the liquor cabinet to pour himself a drink. He took a long swallow of the whisky. It was oaky with tinges of honey and smoke. He sat down opposite Owen and watched the other man eye his glass.

"Thought you said we needed to stay sharp."

"You deserve your drink and so do I," Liam said. This brought a tired smile to Owen's lips.

"Wish we could get wrecked like back in school and wake up to this all being a nightmare."

"It would be nice if things worked that way."

"But they don't."

"No, they don't."

They sat for a time, sipping their drinks. The wind was an animal that pried at the windows, seeking a way inside. On the black cape of the lake, a set of lights bobbed as a boat cruised past. Somewhere a foghorn blatted in the distance, mournful and dying out as fast as it came.

"I always thought I could make a difference," Owen said quietly. "That's really why I joined the academy. I know everyone thought it was to piss off my parents, that's even what they thought, but it wasn't. I wanted to help stop terrible things from happening. But the truth is, I couldn't hack the idea that someday I'd have to face situations that I couldn't handle. Not like you."

"You're still making a difference. You're part of the system. Justice doesn't end with cops."

"I know. That's what I thought. It's what I told myself when I decided to run for mayor." Owen laughed without humor. "But I was wrong. I was wrong to leave her here by herself so much. I should've done more. But sometimes I got angry with her. Angry for her being the way she was. I wanted her to just snap out of it. Isn't that terrible?"

"Raging at something you can't control is pretty normal. When I was younger I'd have bouts of anger at my mom for dying, and leaving me and my dad alone, even though she died giving birth to me. It's natural."

Owen nodded to himself. "You're wrong though about the system. Being a lawyer or the mayor isn't going to get Val back. Hell, I could be the president and it wouldn't matter. It's people like you that make the difference."

Liam tried to respond but couldn't find anything to say. Instead he finished the last of his drink, relishing the sting of its passage down his throat.

"Why?" Owen finally said, breaking the quiet.

"Why was she taken?"

"Yeah. I know he asked for money, but really, why? Why my Valerie? Why her, why now?"

"Because he thinks he can get away with it. But he won't."

"Who the fuck is this guy?"

"Someone who stepped over the edge." Liam sipped his drink. "Most people stand right on the line, barely hold themselves back. And the crazy thing is they don't even know it. They're one paycheck, one bill, one little nudge from dropping off the map. You can see it in their faces when you pass them in the streets. There's a delicate balancing act going on every day behind their eyes, and sometimes with even the slightest push, everything falls down."

Liam fell silent, staring into the darkness past the window. When he glanced at Owen the other man held the expression he had noticed before, a candle flame within him flickering in a high wind.

"Are you okay?" Liam asked.

Owen seemed to surface from a depth, eyes swimming until they focused on him. "No. But I'm drunk and that helps."

"Did you get any rest today?"

"I don't think so."

"Then let's get you to bed," Liam said, standing.

"I don't know if I can sleep."

"You should try. There's still a lot that needs to be done tomorrow." He hoisted Owen up and put an arm around his shoulders to steady him. Owen swayed and put a hand on the wall to keep his balance as they went up the stairs. By the time Liam got him in a sitting position on the bed, Owen was crying again, silent tears leaking from the corners of his eyes. Liam helped him with his shoes and covered him with a thin blanket, tucking him in like the world's oldest child.

"I just want her back," Owen whispered. "We're going to get her back, right?"

"Yes we are."

"I keep seeing her face all bloody and . . ." His voice hitched in his chest and he wasn't able to continue.

"Close your eyes and take some deep breaths. You have good people working on this and they'll be here all night."

"You're not going to leave, are you?" Owen resembled a child more than ever with the blanket below his chin.

"No. I'm going to stay. I'll be here when you wake up."

Owen nodded and shut his eyes, a long sigh trailing from him. Liam waited several minutes and when he thought that Owen was finally asleep he moved to the door but the other man's voice stopped him.

"Thank you for coming, Liam. Not many people would have."

"You're welcome. Get some rest."

Owen swallowed loudly, then rolled toward the opposite wall. Liam left the door partially open and made his way downstairs to the living room where Perring and Sanders waited.

"He sleeping?" Perring asked.

"I think he will be soon." Sanders drew out a pack of cigarettes and opened it, cursing at its empty interior. "Here," Liam said, holding out the nearly untouched pack he'd used before entering the abandoned building. "You can have these."

"Thanks," Sanders said, drawing a cigarette out and placing it between his lips.

"You really should quit those things," Perring said.

"And start chewing gum like a psychopath? No thanks." Sanders jerked a thumb at Perring. "She smokes like a chimney from the time I meet her and then climbs up on a high horse a year ago and now she's shouting at me from it."

"Go chip at your lungs, old man," Perring said, half smiling. Sanders rolled his eyes and headed for the French doors.

"You two complement one another," Liam said.

"We get by. Been partners for a long time." Perring rubbed her forehead and drew out the worn pack of gum.

"Long day for you."

"Long day for everyone," she said. "I was so sure we were going to get this guy tonight. I could feel it."

"Me too."

"I can't get over the fact that it looked like he wanted us to know where he'd taken her. It . . ." Perring gestured with one hand ". . . pisses me off."

"Maybe forensics will find something. Or a witness might come forward. Maybe the guy got sloppy moving her and someone saw something strange but didn't think to report it."

"You don't really believe that, do you?"

Liam licked his lips, then shook his head. "No."

Sanders stepped in from outside and motioned toward the command post and Perring nodded.

"Get some sleep, Liam. If you're going to keep helping us, we'll need you sharp." She moved toward the dining room but paused before stepping inside. "Good work tonight. Glad you were here." She didn't give him a chance to answer before disappearing into the room. After a moment he made his way to the bathroom and brushed his teeth, looking down into the dark hole of the sink drain. In the living room he found a blanket beside the couch and draped it over himself before drawing out his phone. A text message waited on the screen from Dani. She'd sent it almost an hour before.

Going to bed soon. Hope you're okay. I love you.

He began to reply, then deleted the text. He didn't want to wake her. Instead he imagined her sleeping in their bed in the old farmhouse, warm and safe and so opposite from the situation Valerie was in tonight, he nearly shivered. If he and Owen's roles were reversed, he didn't know what he would do. *You're kidding yourself,* he thought. *You know exactly what you'd do. You'd be hunting whoever took her, with or without the law behind you. And what would you do when you found the person that had her? What if she wasn't all right? What if she were already gone? You don't even need to ponder it. Not for one second. You know.*

He silenced the internal voice and sent up a thanks to the universe that his family was where they should be before setting the phone on the table beside him. He didn't need to worry about what-ifs. Too many times people wasted their lives stressing about things that would never happen.

Through the window the clouds were corroded piles of ash that gradually parted to reveal a half-moon suspended in the ocean of darkness. As sleep slowly stole over him, he tried to draw comfort from the moon's light, but no matter how long he looked at it the only thing he felt was a cold apathy within its gaze.

CHAPTER 8

Dade Erickson pulled into his two-stall garage and shut the car off, the clacking rumble of the garage door closing behind him the loudest sound he'd heard all day.

The offices where he practiced law were like different partitions of the same cemetery since several of his staff had taken the day off for various functions. His secretary, Gwen, was on an administration retreat in Florida, and Nancy—one of his two partners in the firm he started—was on vacation with her family in Hawaii. Her imbecilic husband had scrimped and saved up enough to surprise her and their two snot-nosed kids with the getaway, working double shifts at the shipyard to pay for it. If he only knew what Dade and Nancy did in Dade's private bathroom when the rest of the employees of Erickson, Bender, & Scott went out to lunch, he wouldn't have been so keen to have his wife come along on the trip. *Not so keen at all,* Dade thought, remembering their last rendezvous and how Nancy had moaned what a superior lover he was compared to her husband while he sweated above her.

Chuckling a little, Dade got out of the low shape of his Mercedes E250 and admired the car beneath the lights.

"You're fucking sexy," he said, running a hand along the fender before going to its front to admire the grille. He'd only had the vehicle a week and he still got a semi-erection when climbing into the leather interior in the mornings before work. Maybe next week when Nancy was back they would leave early from work and he'd screw her in its rear seat. She'd like that, he was almost sure of it.

Making a mental note to suggest it to her after her return, Dade climbed the single step into his house and shut the door. The cleaning lady had been there that day. He could smell the flowery potpourri she always set out in little netted bags throughout the house. She made the shit herself and insisted on leaving it, even though he'd told her more than once he wasn't paying for it. In the kitchen he opened the fridge and drew out the acai-carrot juice blend he made every morning. Half for breakfast, the rest for after work. He would've rather taken a pull from the Glenlivet that rested on the top shelf of the pantry, but the juice concoction kept him lean and alert.

"Feral! Where are you?" he called into the darkness of the living room and poured a glass full of the purplish beverage. He waited, listening for the jingle of the cat's collar and soon he heard it. The big tom came sauntering into the light, his movements displaying every ounce of the predator he was. He was a muddy brown with short fur and deep orange eyes that held the impression of laziness until there was prey in sight. He had earned his name as a kitten after chasing and killing a large mouse in the attached garage. People said that kittens wouldn't kill anything they catch, that they were merely learning or playing when they hooked their growing claws into a bird or mouse. But in Feral's case they were wrong. Dade had been shocked at the sight of the kitten eviscerating the tiny mammal on the bare concrete, its blood smudging the clean floor as the cat ate. Ever since, he'd had a solemn respect for the animal. You never could tell what violence resided within another creature.

"Kill and eat anything today, you evil fucker?" Dade asked before pouring a small handful of dry cat food into a plastic bowl beside the refrigerator. He'd been limiting the cat's food over the past week. Bastard was getting fat. Feral gave him a withering look, then hunched over his bowl, teeth cracking the nuggets loudly. "You're getting soft," he said, downing the rest of his drink. He almost poured another glass but didn't, although he was feeling lethargic from the lack of sex that day. He and Nancy normally partook of one another almost every day of the week. Without the release he was feeling slow and stupid, like his movements were tethered to a weight he couldn't see. His thoughts gradually slipped to the plastic baggie wedged in the back of the nightstand drawer between a copy of King James's bible and his Glock 21. Marshall had dropped the stuff off last week when his recent supply had run out. He didn't use too much cocaine but it was something he enjoyed on occasion, like some men appreciated an afternoon of fishing or sailing. Maybe he would do a line later and call Nancy. She could chock the call up to business. Maybe he'd talk dirty to her with her husband standing right next to her. She'd get excited about that.

Smiling, Dade set his glass down on the counter and went upstairs. He moved through his master bedroom, discarding his suit like flaking skin, dropping the expensive shirt and slacks on the floor for his cleaning lady to pick up tomorrow. He turned the water on in the shower and doused his hair with shampoo, singing the lyrics to a song he'd heard that afternoon, loudly and off-key.

Midway through washing his hair, shampoo running frothy rivers over his eyes, Dade heard a sound.

He stopped singing, the last echoes of his voice dying out against the wet tile. He turned his head toward his bedroom, eyes scrunched shut, blind to everything beyond his closed eyelids.

There it was again. It sounded like the bathroom door bumping against the wall.

Dade pawed at his eyes, letting the scalding water run fully on his face.

There was someone else in the bathroom. He could feel their gaze on him. They were standing inches from the mottled glass door beside him, watching, waiting for the right moment to rip it open and grab him.

He managed to clear the shampoo from his face and blinked through the watery haze, panic a living thing in his chest.

The bathroom was empty.

His breath cascaded from him and suddenly the shower was too hot. His legs trembled and the thumping of his heart overrode any sounds beyond the shower's patter.

"Hello?" he said. "Feral?" When the tom's usual low meow didn't come, he shut off the water, not caring that shampoo still coated his back and legs. He stepped from the shower and pulled an oversized towel from the rack near the sink. The bathroom door looked like it was in the same position as when he'd gone in, but he couldn't be entirely sure. He stepped around the corner, surveying the well-lit bedroom. His clothes still lay where he'd dropped them. His bed was made. The door to the hallway was open.

Dade shook his head. Water dripped down from his soaking scalp, icy fingernails running the length of his spine.

"Stupid cat," he muttered, beginning to dry off his head.

A squeal and a click came from downstairs followed by a soft thump.

Goose bumps spread across Dade's skin in a rolling wave. His eyes widened, his vision taking on a watery quality as he stared at the doorway, waiting for another noise or a figure to darken the opening. He realized he was holding his breath again and let it flood out. There was someone in the house. Someone was downstairs right now probably listening just like he was. Who the hell could it be?

A burglar? One of his friends? Even as the word "friend" crossed his mind, he knew whoever it was down there had something to do with Marshall. The bastard couldn't keep his mouth shut. He'd told someone about the coke and now they were here, wanting the little baggie in the drawer. His eyes went to the bedside table automatically.

The gun.

What the hell was he doing? He had a gun and this was his house. He had every right in the world to defend it.

Dade crossed the plush carpet and eased the drawer open revealing the flat black of the Glock beside the bible. He pulled the weapon out, its heft alone giving him another level of confidence. Whichever of Marshall's cracked-out friends was downstairs right now, they were going to have a few extra holes in them that they hadn't been born with. If it was Marshall down there, he'd be extremely tempted to aerate the bastard too.

Dade wrapped the towel around his waist and eased out of his bedroom, the Glock extended before him. The stairs were dark but the single kitchen light was on, throwing some illumination at their base. It would be easy for him to shoot anyone that stepped into his line of sight now so he moved quickly down the treads pausing at the bottom so he could glance in both directions before stepping into the open.

Somewhere in the house, Feral meowed.

Dade swung out of the hallway and into the dining room, circumventing the kitchen completely. Shadows lay in heavy blankets across the table and chairs as well as the tall china cabinet in the corner of the room. Pale moonlight streamed in through a gap in the thick curtains that covered the picture window. He saw no strange forms against any of the walls or crouching beneath the furniture. Moving quickly, he crossed the space and entered the front entryway. The massive oak door was shut solid, the dead bolt turned to the locked position. Only the outline of his leather jacket hanging from its hook near the closet gave him pause before he continued on. Glancing into the kitchen he saw that its space was empty. He placed his hand on the cold knob of the garage door before yanking the door open. His fingers flapped in the darkness for a beat, searching for the light switch. In the depths of his heart he knew that before he was able to flip the light on, a hand would reach out of the darkness and grasp his wrist in an unbreakable grip.

His fingers brushed the switch and light flared above the Mercedes.

The garage was empty save for the car and some cardboard boxes he'd been meaning to throw away. With a lunge he stepped down onto the freezing concrete floor, lowering himself so he could look under the car's chassis. Nothing there.

Dade stood up and sighed hearing Feral meow again inside. It had been the cat all along. The animal had made some sort of noise that was out of the norm and he'd freaked out. He leaned against the doorway, letting the cool October air leech some of the fear away. His muscles were weak with the spike of adrenaline and when he returned inside the house his stomach slopped sickeningly. A wave of dizziness crested in his skull and he nearly stumbled before steadying himself against the wall. What the hell was wrong with him? Was he coming down with something or was it the aftereffects of panicking? Nausea continued to slither in his stomach while he locked the garage door behind him and stepped into the kitchen.

White-hot pain lanced through his foot making him stagger to one side.

His eyes registered the shards of glass on the hardwood before the dizziness returned full-force and dropped him to the floor. He sprawled awkwardly, the Glock bouncing and cartwheeling away. Pain shot up his elbow as he tried to brace himself for the impact but his movements were sluggish and his arm folded, the side of his head banging off the floor. A sound like a struck gong filled his ears and all his air left him in a whoosh. He folded in on himself in the fetal position but through all the pain in his arm and head, the agony of his foot held his full attention. He managed to bring his eyes down and let out a feeble cry.

A long sliver of glass protruded from the soft skin of his sole. Blood drizzled from the end of it creating a strangely beautiful contrast to the otherwise flawless crystal.

Dade made a strangled sound and slowly sat up, holding his foot off of the ground. He blinked, taking in the shattered remnants of his juice glass on the floor, spread out in front of the doorway in a semi-circle.

The fucking cat.

The thought pulsed in his dazed mind. He was going to kill it. As soon as he was able to walk, he would corner the bastard and shoot it with the pistol, he didn't care if one of his neighbors called the cops. Somehow Feral had gotten onto the breakfast bar and knocked the glass over. That was the noise he'd heard in the shower, he was sure of it.

"I'm going to fucking kill you!" he shouted, bringing his foot closer for inspection. Another bout of vertigo swooped over him and he nearly fell backward beneath its weight. What the hell was going on? He was in pain but not so much he should be passing out. He gritted his teeth and grasped the edge of glass before drawing it free in a sickening motion. The shard slid out of his flesh and he saw that nearly an inch of it had been in his foot. He dropped the piece and was about to yell another threat when he spotted something across the room.

The door to the little travel cage he kept beside the fridge, for when he took Feral somewhere, was closed. Feral's blunted face looked out from behind the crosshatched wire. He meowed again.

Confusion buffeted Dade in a way he had never encountered before. He felt his head tilt to one side even as heavy hiking boots came into view from the next room, smashing the remaining pieces of glass into dust. Dade's vision took on a kaleidoscopic quality as he raised his head, looking up the length of the figure that stood before him.

"What?" he managed thickly, before the room's corners seemed to open to the night sky as darkness rushed in and wrapped him in its embrace.

CHAPTER 9

He chased Abford down the alley.

Each breath coated in razor wire that tugged holes in his lungs. His fingers wrapped around the handle of his gun, feet connecting with the ground in painful steps, mouth full of gelled spit. His partner had already been shot. Liam had left him bleeding beside the door Abford had fired through. And he knew what would happen next. She would come out of the salon, dark hair styled for an anniversary that would never come, hand clutching her belly as she moved down the stairs where the bullet meant for Abford would catch her in the throat and steal two lives away at once. Any second now she would move into his line of sight.

Sights.

He could see Abford past the sights of his gun. He would turn now, raising his own weapon, ready to end Liam's life.

Instead he ran on.

Liam paused, half waiting for Kelly to appear like she always had before. She would step out any second now and he would kill her with a shot to the throat.

The alley remained empty except for Abford's sprinting form.

Liam ran.

Wind burned past his face. His eyes watered. He seemed to be on a treadmill, the speed increasing with each step he took. No matter how fast he ran he couldn't catch Abford, who raced ahead unimpeded. The alley narrowed between two buildings that seemed to move inward, crushing the space between them as he closed in on the corner. Abford turned without breaking stride. Liam slowed, edging up to the wall before pivoting around it.

A stairway dropped into darkness before him.

The alleyway was gone, replaced by a wide set of stairs that disappeared into the grip of swirling shadows. The sound of footfalls filtered up to him and he hesitated on the first tread. A cold dread filled him as if he were being poured full of ice water. He didn't want to go down those stairs. Only horror and death waited for him, he could feel it. As he stood there, locked in the grip of indecision, a memory of his father came to him.

He'd been young, maybe seven or eight, and his father had been alive and healthy, still working long hours at his barber shop each day, taking only Sundays off completely. They'd been outside at the farmhouse, having a fire in the evening after dinner. It had been late November and it was full dark save for the leaping light of the flames from their fire pit behind the house. The time around the fire was a special one since it allowed them to catch up on the day they'd spent apart, and Liam had always cherished the smell of the wood smoke and the gentle heat that warmed his toes and fingers despite the cold. On that particular night the fire had grown low and there hadn't been enough wood beside the pit to keep it going, so his father had risen from his seat and moved toward the rear of the garage where they kept the ricks of wood leaning against two stakes and the building itself. The space behind the garage had been coated in darkness, the clipping of moon hanging in the cold sky providing little light. Liam had stood to warn his father not to go into the darkness, that something terrible waited there for him, its talons honed to an edge, a living bloodlust born from nightmare itself. He'd watched in abject terror as his father strode into the waiting mouth of shadows and winked out of existence. In the depths of his being, Liam knew that he wouldn't return. There would be a scream and then quiet so deep it would sound like the world had gone deaf. Then he would see it moving deep in the darkness. Something cold and without pity that watches with glee as parents are taken from their children, because death is filled up but never full. That's what he'd feared in the night, always when his father was sleeping soundly in the room that he would one day share with Dani. The unfathomable horror of death. The inevitable gnashing of geared teeth in the machine disguised as life. Yet it wasn't life. Life was only a mask for what waited at the end for everyone and everything that drew a breath.

And it was what waited for him now at the bottom of those stairs. He hadn't fired the shot that had killed Kelly. This time it had been different somehow, though he struggled with the implications of what had happened. The memory of her death was still fresh and raw as burned skin. But something had changed now. He needed to go back and make sure. He needed to see her face and watch her walk away from the salon, untouched by his bullet, unscathed by tragedy. He needed to see her go home to her husband and children. He was about to turn away from the inky depths when a scream rose from the stairwell, gutting him where he stood.

It was Dani's voice down in the darkness.

Her shrieks were faint and so full of terror he didn't realize he was running until he stumbled on the last step and fell to the floor of a wet corridor, his weapon spinning away into the shadows. He didn't wait for his eyes to adjust but simply rose and ran on, not caring if he collided with something in the black. Ahead he saw a yellow glow spreading like a stain and as several doorways flashed by on either side, he realized where he was.

He was in the basement of the abandoned building.

Dani's voice came from the room at the end of the hall, the room where Valerie had been held, and she was sobbing his name between breaths. He yelled for her as the light brightened and then he was in the room, bursting through the doorway.

Dani was tied to the same chair Valerie had been in but she wore no gag. Her beautiful face was covered in blood and Abford stood beside her, his gun pressed to her temple. Liam reached for him and Abford turned.

The other man's face had no features except for a widening smile that split his skull from ear to ear. Abhorrent laughter slid from between the brown teeth that lined the giant mouth, and even as Liam screamed Dani's name, the report of the gun drowned his voice out.

He sat up from the couch, tossing away the weight on his chest—the blanket, now heavy and sodden with cold sweat. His mouth opened to cry out, but the focusing of reality helped him shape it into a soft moan. He swallowed, his tongue dry as shale.

He swung his feet off the couch and steadied himself there. His stomach was a punch bowl of acid, churning on itself as the dream replayed over and over in his mind. He reached out a shaking hand and touched his phone to light the display. It was a little after six in the morning. He stood and made his way to the dining room where the smell of coffee was constant in the air. Only one task force member sat at the table, an alert young man with a growth of stubble on his cheeks.

"Anything new overnight?" Liam asked, hating the wavering of his voice.

"Nothing."

"When did Perring leave?"

"Around midnight. She said she'd be back by seven or earlier."

Liam nodded and continued to the bathroom. Inside he braced himself on the sink until the sickness in his stomach begrudgingly passed. Each time he began to feel better the image of Dani's bloodied face floated behind his eyes and he closed them, holding on to the contents of his stomach by sheer will. He moved to the toilet and urinated before running cold water into his cupped hands and dousing his face. The icy shock was enough to put some strength in his legs so that he was able to pause and pour himself a cup of coffee in the dining room before stepping out through the French doors.

The steady rush of the waves met him. He watched the horizon brighten, drinking long swallows of hot coffee even as the cool air chilled the sweat in his clothes. When the axe blade of sun cut its way above the opposite shoreline he pulled out his phone and dialed, a lingering fear hovering over him that the call would go unanswered. But Dani picked up almost immediately.

"Good morning." Her voice was thick with sleep.

"I woke you."

"No, I was just getting up."

"Liar."

"Guilty."

"I'm sorry, I tried to wait longer." He turned his back to the lake, glancing in through the windows to see several more task force members trailing into the dining room.

"Why, what's wrong?"

"Just a nightmare. Nothing new."

"Abford again?"

"Yeah."

"Wish I was there." He could hear the rustle of sheets on her end and imagined the warmth of her beside him in their bed.

"Me too."

"How are things going? Any progress?"

"You mean when am I coming home."

"You got me."

He smiled but it faded as quickly as it came. "We received a ransom demand. We're going forward with it in the next few days."

"God. Poor Owen. How is he doing?"

"He's getting by."

"And how are you, other than the broken sleep?"

"Fine. As always."

"You're full of shit, Mr. Dempsey."

"Maybe."

"Do you think it can be handled without you from this point on?"

"Why?"

"Because I do want you to come home."

"I'd love to but I need to stay for Owen."

There was a long pause and he thought he could hear the old clock ticking downstairs, its rhythm like a tired pulse.

"You need to stay for Owen or for you?"

"What's that supposed to mean?"

"I'm asking if you have other reasons for wanting to be there."

"I'm here to help my friend."

"And doing real police work doesn't hurt either."

The door opened and Perring stuck her head out. She saw that he was on the phone and nodded before retreating inside.

"Is there something you want to say?" he asked.

"No. Not now. But I want you to be careful. You're a consultant, remember? It's not your responsibility to go busting into houses, gun blazing."

Liam chewed on the inside of his cheek. It was like the woman was psychic.

"I know that. I'll be safe."

"You better."

"I'll come home to you soon."

"You better." Warmth seeped into her voice.

"I gotta go. Tell Eric hi and I love him."

"I will."

"I love you."

"Love you too."

He ended the call and shivered, the last vestiges of the dream lingering even after hearing Dani's voice. *She's fine. Eric's fine. They're safe,* he assured himself as he picked up his freezing coffee mug from the porch railing. It had just been a dream, a mingling of Valerie's kidnapping and fears he didn't want to think about brought to light. *The subconscious is a cruel place,* he thought before reentering the house. Perring and Sanders were sipping coffee in the kitchen. Both looked unkempt as if they had slept in their clothes as well.

"Good morning," Liam said, refilling his coffee cup.

"What the hell's good about it?" Sanders said.

"Our overnight guy said that Owen didn't wake up," Perring said.

"Not that I know of," Liam said. "Hopefully he got some rest. Anything back from the canvass of the neighborhood where Valerie was being held?"

Perring shook her head. "Three uniforms knocked on fifty doors last night. No one saw a thing. No strange vehicles, no odd people, no noises. It's like Valerie and her abductors were never there." She sipped at her coffee, eyes unfocused. "We'll have to respect Owen's wishes from here on out. Even if we get a solid lead, he might not want us to go in after her. Last night really shook him up."

"I can't blame him," Liam said. He watched the task force set up for their day in the dining room and then excused himself to go shower. The hot water was rejuvenating and when he'd dressed in a set of clean clothes the nightmare had softened, the sharp edges dulling so that when Dani's tortured face rose to his mind he was able to shrug it off and let it slide away. When he reentered the kitchen Perring was talking on her cell phone, her brow drawn and her mouth a flat line of displeasure.

"What about Link, where the hell's he at?" She paused, listening. "Oh for God's sake. How about Teller? The flu? Are you shitting me?" She noticed Liam standing at the edge of the kitchen and turned slightly away. "Yeah. Tell the chief I'll figure something out. It's only a few blocks from here. Yeah, okay." Perring hung up the phone then drew out a fresh pack of gum, ripping two pieces open before popping them in her mouth.

"That's like chain smoking," Liam said, trying a smile on her. She stared out the windows for a moment before glancing at him.

"I would kick a puppy right now for a cigarette."

"Sounded like one of those calls."

Sanders entered the room and immediately frowned seeing Perring's face. "What is it?"

"Homicide. Four blocks north. Chief wants me to go."

"What?" Sanders said. "Link or Teller can take care of that."

"Link's in Arizona on vacation, remember? And Teller's puking his guts out at home apparently. If I fucking find out that he was golfing like last time I'm going to kick his ass."

"There was a death only four blocks from here?" Liam asked.

"Yeah. Why?" Perring said.

"Home invasion?"

Perring chewed her gum for a moment. "Possibly."

"I'd say that's quite a coincidence having a death so close after Valerie's disappearance."

"Probably just that. Coincidence," Sanders said before turning back to Perring. "So they want us on that now? Who's going to run shit here?"

"We can't both leave." She glanced at Liam.

"I'll go with you so Sanders can stay here," he offered. "Until we hear anything else I won't be of much use. Owen might not be up for a while either."

"That's not procedure," Sanders said, an edge to his voice. "You're helping us on this case, not an unrelated homicide. That wasn't the deal."

"He can come, Rex. He's proven his worth so far on this one," Perring said. Sanders began to protest but she cut across him. "Look, unless you want to go against the chief's wishes and do the death by yourself, that's on you."

Sanders blinked, then sighed before waving his hand toward the front door. "Yeah, yeah, all right. I'll keep things rolling here."

"If Owen gets up have him finalize everything with whoever's he's getting the loan for the ransom from."

"I got this, Denise," Sanders said, turning away from them both. Perring jerked her head toward the door and Liam followed her outside, zipping his jacket as they stepped into the cool air.

"Didn't mean to step on any toes," he said as they climbed into Perring's sedan.

"Bullshit. You didn't care who you elbowed out of the way to come with," she said, backing out of the drive.

"No really, I—"

"Look, I know the score. I read about your case last night. The woman caught in the cross fire. Tragic thing to happen to any cop, and it looks like you were a good one. But most people, something happens like that, they drop it and move on. They take up bartending or drinking or origami. Unless that itch won't go away that makes you a cop in the first place." She glanced at him as she sped up an incline and blew through a stop sign. "And since you're here and not home drinking or folding paper cranes then I'm guessing you're still itchy."

"You don't know me or anything about me. No matter what you read," Liam said. His voice was flat in his ears and he kept his eyes straight ahead.

"That's fine if you don't want to acknowledge it. You can go home right now and go back to working on cold cases. I bet you've got an office full of them."

"Let's go see what we see."

"Fine. But just so you know, I'm more comfortable with you being here than before I knew your background."

"Great."

"I thought you'd appreciate that."

"That now you know what everyone else does? Do you think I can get away from it on a personal level? Do you think I need people bringing it up? I came here to help my friend any way I could and this is the only way I know how."

Perring seemed undaunted. "But you're not unhappy doing this. Police work."

Liam closed his eyes. "Let's just get there."

She was quiet for a long span and then made a quick right turn. "Fine. But I need something in my stomach if we're seeing a dead body. Can't hack the smell along with hunger pangs." She swung off the street into a parking lot and pulled into a drive-through coffee stand and ordered a sausage, egg, and cheese Danish. "Want anything?" she asked.

"No."

The smell of the greasy breakfast filled the car, making his stomach growl but he ignored it. As Perring wolfed the sandwich down he took her words apart and put them back together, trying to find a flaw in them, an inaccuracy. He couldn't.

Moments later they turned onto a side street that curved gently through a beautiful stand of trees alight with fall colors. Between their gaps large homes loomed above careful landscaping, their facades immodest with white balustrades and Greek columns. On the curve of the first corner two squad cars blocked a paved driveway and another sat before a two-stall garage. The garage was attached to a tall two-story brick house that sprawled on an acre lawn. Yellow "do not cross" tape spun in the breeze before the front door.

"What's the deceased's name?" Liam asked as they stepped out of the car.

"A Mr. Dade Erickson. He's a lawyer here in town. His cleaning lady found him this morning."

Liam turned in the drive and looked out at the view. The land dropped away in an almost dizzying slope, its side checkered with rooftops and blazing tree lines until it emptied out in the slate gray of Superior. "Hell of a view," he said.

"He could afford it. From what I know his parents were loaded before he started one of the biggest law firms in town. They owned a private shipping line or something."

They moved up the drive and past the running squad. A uniformed officer met them outside the front door.

"Charlie, what do we have?" Perring said.

"Body's upstairs in the master. The place is a mess. Forensics went through the kitchen first but everything's upstairs."

"You don't look so good," Perring said.

Charlie shook his head. "Seen a few bodies but nothing like this."

"Take five and head off any media out here, okay?"

"Yes ma'am."

They watched the officer walk away and Perring frowned before stepping inside. Liam followed her and they both stopped in the entryway, the smell meeting them immediately.

"Shit," Perring said.

"Smells like it," Liam said.

To the left there was a murmur of conversation. When they entered the kitchen a woman holding a digital camera glanced in their direction before continuing to photograph the scene before them.

A slick of dried blood six inches wide ran across the wood floor amidst the bright glitter of broken glass. Several shards were black with blood and an almost perfect crimson handprint stained the side of the breakfast counter. A bloodied bath towel was curled next to a Glock lying beneath a bar stool, a plastic bag beside it.

"Damn," Perring said. Another uniformed officer stood on the opposite side of the room, his hands on his duty belt.

"Something, isn't it?" the officer said.

"What are we looking at here, Tony?"

"Toshi can tell you better. He's upstairs. Just to warn you, it's a doozie."

Liam moved around behind the photographer and looked out to where the house joined the garage, then studied the blood trail and broken glass.

"Liam, this way," Perring said, motioning to the right. They wound their way through a large dining room and past a living room before entering a wide hallway that opened to a set of stairs. Drops of blood smeared the tread's centers and several specks of crushed glass were marked with small plastic evidence arrows. They moved up the stairs close to the wall, careful not to step on any of the glass or blood. At the top, the hallway opened into a large master bedroom with two curtained windows on its far side. Toshi, the lead forensic specialist, was on one side of the massive sleigh bed that took up the majority of the room. He was looking down at what was strapped to its top and it took Liam a full second to translate what he was seeing.

A man's body was fastened to the bed with three wide nylon straps, the kind normally found securing a heavy load on the back of a pickup. One band ran around the corpse's legs, the next around its hips, and the last over its chest. Liam glanced at the man's face and experienced a moment of disbelief.

His lips and the tip of his nose were gone.

The tissue had been raggedly removed, exposing very white teeth smeared with blood, the mouth open in a jaw-breaking scream. Below gaping eyes, a bit of pale cartilage poked from the leveled area where the nose had been. Liam moved around Perring who seemed to be frozen partway into the room.

"Good morning detectives, er, ah—" Toshi said, focusing on Liam.

"You can just call me Liam."

"Sure."

Perring entered the room, her features hardening as she neared the bed and its occupant. Liam took a closer look at the corpse and noticed several long stripes of black and purple flesh that ran the length of each arm and two parallel lines tracing down beneath the strap covering the body's chest. The air in the room smelled like a mixture of excrement and old barbecue. The burnt odor increased the nearer he got to the bed.

"What can you tell us so far?" Liam asked.

Toshi straightened, spinning a pair of tweezers in one latex-gloved hand. "Deceased is Dade Reginald Erickson. Age thirty-five. Single, no children. His housekeeper found him this morning just like this."

"Got an idea on cause of death yet?"

"Looks like some type of poisoning," Toshi said, leaning in over the corpse. "There's extensive chemical burning on the top of the tongue and rear of the throat. It looks like he was force-fed some type of acid."

"Jesus," Perring said.

Liam walked around the side of the bed and saw something plugged into the wall outlet near the bedside table. It was a soldering iron, tip blackened, handle coated with blood. His eyes shifted from the tool to the lines in the cold, white flesh.

"Those are burns from the soldering iron, aren't they?" Liam asked, pointing toward the stripes.

Toshi nodded. "Appears so."

"Pre- or postmortem?"

"Pre."

"Wow," Liam breathed. "That's . . . really something."

"I'll say. I can't imagine the level of pain inflicted by the burns. They're easily third degree. But that's just the tip of the iceberg. Look at this." Toshi slid one finger beneath the chest strap and pulled it down.

A large number four was crudely branded in charred lines on the skin.

"What the fuck?" Perring said.

"My sentiments exactly," Toshi said, glancing at each of them. He let the strap go, partially covering up the blackened symbol. Liam ran his eyes up over the man's ruined face and then back down to the number.

"What did they use to remove his lips and nose?" Liam asked. "It looks like they were torn off."

Toshi let out a grim chuckle. "That's probably the most grisly part of all this. The killer didn't do that. The victim's cat did."

"What?" Perring said.

"That was one of the first things the housekeeper said when she called it in. Apparently the cat was sitting on his chest, munching away when she came up here. Tony had to chase it out of the room and put it in its cage."

"You're kidding," Liam said.

"Wish I was."

Liam stepped back and looked at Perring. Her expression hadn't changed since she'd entered the bedroom. She looked like someone in their first minutes on land after being at sea for months. As he watched, she seemed to surface within herself and glanced around.

"Do we have a time of death?" she asked.

"Around one this morning."

"Any prints yet?"

"No, but we got a rough shoe size from the crushed glass downstairs. Looks like our guy wears either a ten or ten and a half. Other than that he was very careful. We got some hair but I'm betting it's either Dade's or the cat's."

"It looks like Dade was injured downstairs and then came up here," Liam said. "But not under his own power, right?"

Toshi's eyebrows went up. "That's correct. There's a laceration on the bottom of his right foot that's consistent with one of the shards downstairs. It appears he cut himself and then was dragged or carried to the bed and strapped down. Then whoever it was went to work on him."

"The gun is an interesting point though. Do we know if it's Dade's or not?" Liam asked.

"Charlie checked and it's registered to the deceased."

The sound of footsteps came from the stairs and a moment later Tony appeared in the doorway.

"Have you guys been to the neighbors yet?" Perring asked, her voice steadier.

"Yep," Tony said. "The people to the north said they heard fairly loud music start up around nine, but that was it. No vehicles in his driveway or on the street that they noticed."

"Music," Perring said, glancing at Liam.

"To cover up the screams," Liam said. She nodded.

"Tony, I want you and Charlie to scope out the area around the house. See if you can find out where and how the intruder got inside."

"Yes, ma'am."

"Toshi, how fast can you get a toxicology report?"

"Maybe by noon if I put a rush on it."

"Good. Get it to me as soon as it comes in. Liam, let's go downstairs."

They left Toshi to his work, passing his assistant in the hallway with her camera. The kitchen was empty now save for the violent mess on the floor. It was like an artist's representation done in glass and blood.

Perring walked around the glass and made her way to the garage door. Inside rested a new Mercedes, its sleek lines and dark gray color elegant against the barren concrete.

"Nice car," Liam said.

"Lots of nice things here," Perring said, turning back toward the kitchen.

"You thinking the same as me?"

"Why would someone come in and kill this guy but not take a thing?"

"Exactly. His wallet was on the bedside table and his car keys are in the kitchen."

"This had nothing to do with money."

"That's for sure. Someone hated that man upstairs. They took their time with him." Liam moved toward the gun on the floor. He looked at it, then studied the blood trail and the dark splotches in the center of the room. "So the gun's his and he has it out, right? Why?"

"He knew someone was in the house."

"That's my guess. He's upstairs and hears something. Grabs his gun and comes down to investigate. There's a struggle, he loses the weapon and then is incapacitated somehow and brought upstairs."

Perring nodded. "Yep."

"Then whoever it is starts in on him and doesn't quit for the next three or four hours." Liam knelt and studied the bloody handprint on the counter side. Slowly his eyes traveled to the pet cage in the corner of the room and found a large tomcat staring back at him from behind the wire mesh. It licked its chops. "The countdown has begun," he murmured.

"What?" Perring said.

"The countdown has begun," Liam repeated, rising. "What the kidnapper said yesterday. Seemed to me like a strange choice of words."

Perring shrugged. "He was being dramatic."

"There's a number four burned into Dade's chest." He let her absorb what he was saying.

"No. Liam, I hear what you're saying, but no."

"Why not? When's the last time you had a homicide?"

"Two months ago."

"What kind?"

"Domestic disturbance that got out of control. Wife shot her husband after he drank all the beer in the house."

"She may get off for that."

"Stop it! What are you getting at?"

"That there's too many connections here. Two nights ago someone breaks in and takes Valerie. Now this man is brutally murdered and has a significant marking on him that relates to the kidnapping."

"We don't know that."

"We don't know any different," Liam said. "This isn't my show but I think it would be a huge mistake not to find out if there are any connections between Valerie and Dade."

Perring began to chew on her lip and then fumbled for her pack of gum. "You remember whose show it is, right?"

"Of course."

"Good."

The front door opened and Tony entered the kitchen, his face reddened from the chilly air.

"No signs of forced entry anywhere. I'm thinking the killer had a key or knew Dade and he let them in."

"You checked the garage?" Perring asked.

"Yeah. Locked tight."

"They could've snuck in behind his car as he pulled in last night," Liam said, his eyes glazing over.

"Kinda unlikely," Tony said.

"It's been done before," Liam said, coming back to the present.

"Who do we have for next of kin?" Perring asked.

"Mr. Erickson's mother, Stella. His father passed away a few years back. She lives on Park Point but word is she's in the late stages of Alzheimer's. Might not even realize what you're telling her."

"We'll worry about that. I want you and Charlie to go through the rest of the neighborhood. Someone must have seen something, heard something. This guy's not a ghost. Don't call me until you have somebody that will give us a lead. And have Blair do a background check on Mr. Erickson. Send over his record, if he has one, when you get it."

"Yes ma'am." The officer gave them each a nod and left the room.

Perring moved across the kitchen and stared down at the cat. "I don't want you to mention the number on Erickson's chest to anyone else. And do not say anything about a connection between the cases, especially to Owen." She glanced at him over her shoulder.

"I won't."

"Good. Now let's go tell Mrs. Erickson that her son is dead."

CHAPTER 10

They coasted down the winding hill from Erickson's house into the gunmetal morning.

The sun was only a suggestion of light behind the thick cloud cover and the air was full of mist. It didn't so much fall as spun and split around the vehicles, like a premature burial shroud, as they passed.

When Perring checked with Sanders, he told her there had been nothing new. Owen was still sleeping. Yes, he was fine taking care of things until they got back. As they drove, Liam studied the buildings that rose on either side of the car. Many of them were old, their brownstone sides weathered from countless winters. A large hospital loomed on their left, then receded into countless shops, restaurants, and bars, all of them sharing walls beside the cobbled street.

"Coldest October we've had in years," Perring offered as she navigated through the city, ever downward toward the lake. "Snow'll come early."

"Think it will rain today?"

"Did you see the sunrise?"

"Red sky in morning."

"Sailor's warning." She was silent for a time, the occasional shush of the windshield wipers the only sound. "I hate this."

"Informing the family?"

"Yeah. How many times have you had to do it?"

"Too many."

"Never gets easier does it?"

"No."

"You remember your first?"

"We still talking about informing family?" He shot her a half smile and she chuckled. "Yeah. Can't forget it. It was the worst one I've ever had to do."

"I think everyone's first is the worst one."

"Mine was a nine-year-old boy who'd drowned in a river. I was twenty-two. It was my second day on the force."

Perring glanced at him and then back at the road. "Damn."

"Yeah. I've never forgotten the look on his mother's face when she answered the door. He'd been missing for over a day and she knew, she knew as soon as she saw me coming up the walk. She kind of just fell against the wall inside the house and slid down like she'd been shot. I guess in a way she had been."

They turned down a narrow street and crossed an intersection, splashing water from a puddle up onto the sidewalk.

"Mine was a middle-aged man. Fell down a flight of stairs in his house and no one found him for a week. Neighbor called in after the smell started to creep across into her yard. She thought it was his compost heap. She'd complained to the cops before about it. I had to call the guy's daughter who lived in Wisconsin. I was shaking so bad and stuttering, I think she ended up consoling me more than I did her."

Liam nodded. "I think that's why a lot of cops are drinkers, or why a bunch of them eat a gun when they retire. You don't slough those things off. They stay with you and compound over the years until you're carrying around everyone else's grief." He glanced out the window. "Grief is heavy."

"Yes it is."

They hit the bottom of the street they were on and cruised up and over a small bridge that brought them to an intersection. Perring hung a left and they passed trinket shops and restaurants. To the right the harbor opened up revealing dozens of docked boats, their flagged tops bobbing and swaying. Ahead a looming skeletal structure grew up from the street. Its soaring interspersed steel girders were like dried bones of some prehistoric titan.

"I've seen this a few times from the highway but I've never been down to the lift bridge," Liam said, leaning forward in his seat.

"It's quite the tourist attraction," Perring said. "It's one of only a few left in operation."

Liam kept looking up, trying to see the top of the structure as they passed onto it, but its peak was hidden in the folds of mist giving the bridge a ragged appearance as if it had been sheared off in the clouds. The steel grating hummed under the car, then they were on another narrow street, Superior's waters expanding to either side.

"Park Point is pretty unique too," Perring said. There was a hint of pride in her voice as she gestured to the homes they began to pass. "It's basically built on a big sandbar but it's almost like its own city. Residents are pretty insular, lots of old homes, old money."

"Is this connected any other way than the lift bridge?"

"Nope. We call it getting 'bridged' if you get stuck on one side or the other. If it's up, you can only get here by water or air."

"Air?"

"There's a little airport on the end."

"You're kidding."

Perring shook her head. "Not too much traffic there, though. Local pilots, a few private flights, but that's all."

The road curved and Liam admired the stands of trees decorated with dripping leaves the color of fire between and around the homes. Perring slowed the vehicle and turned onto a small side street before angling into a driveway that ran parallel with the shore. They passed through a row of bushes several feet higher than the car and pulled to a stop in a cramped roundabout before a sprawling Tudor house. A white marble fountain in the shape of a cherub spit water in a silver stream in the center of the circular drive. Liam saw a curtain twitch in an upper floor window as they climbed from the car.

Perring rang the mother of pearl doorbell and they listened to a series of musical chimes sound deep inside the house, followed by footsteps. A middle-aged woman with a shock of dark hair plagued by gray roots opened the door.

"Yes?"

"Hello ma'am, I'm detective Denise Perring with the Duluth Police Department and this is Mr. Dempsey." Perring unfolded her wallet to reveal her ID. "We're here to speak with Mrs. Erickson. Is she home?"

"She is but may I ask what this is about?"

"I'm sorry but that's a confidential matter we can only talk about with Mrs. Erickson."

The woman put a hand to her throat in a self-calming gesture before stepping aside to let them enter.

They walked into a cathedral-like foyer lined with plush chairs and wide-leafed plants seated in brass pots. Before them a grand staircase swept upward and divided at a picture window that looked out onto the harbor side of the lake. Everything was burnished copper or stained mahogany. Liam wiped his shoes several times on the mat, eyeing the flawless shine of the floor.

"Mrs. Erickson is upstairs but I'm not sure that it's such a good time to speak with her," the woman said, stopping at the base of the stairway.

"Why's that?" Perring asked.

"She suffers from fibromyalgia and severe arthritis as well as Alzheimer's, and I'm afraid she's not having a good day."

"I'm sorry but we can't wait to speak with her."

The woman eyed them with resignation again. "Very well," she said, and led them up the stairs. Liam gazed out the picture window as they passed it. The dreary haze took very little away from the grandeur of the view. Gentle waves lapped at a sand beach and a tall sailboat shifted on its mooring fifty yards away from a wide dock. The woman turned right at the split in the stairway and stopped before a door painted a flawless white. She knocked softly and a voice drifted from behind the door.

"Henry?"

"No Stella, it's Avery. May I come in?"

"Oh. Of course, dear."

Avery opened the door onto a massive bedroom with walls the color of coffee with cream. The floor was carpeted in white shag and a four-poster bed rested before a window that gave another expansive view of the lake. A woman sat in a wheelchair across the room, watching them from beneath feathery tufts of white hair. Her body was as twisted as an ancient oak branch, head tipped to the side and forward so that her eyes rolled up almost to the whites to follow them as they entered the room. Liam caught sight of two gnarled things that might have once been hands poking from the cuffs of her nightgown.

"Stella, there's two visitors here to see you, okay?"

"Oh, that's nice dear. You could bring us some tea if it's not too much trouble."

"Mrs. Erickson that's okay," Perring said. She turned to Avery. "It's fine really, don't bother."

Avery nodded and headed toward the door. "I'll be downstairs if you need anything."

Perring waited until the sound of Avery's footsteps faded. "Mrs. Erickson, my name is Denise Perring. I'm a detective with the police department."

"Police department? Oh dear."

"Yes. I am sorry to say I have some very bad news about your son, Dade."

"Oh no. I think Henry should be here for this, don't you think?"

"May I ask, who is Henry, ma'am?" Liam said.

"He's my husband." She bobbed a little in her chair, the awkward angle she sat at increasing.

"I see. Well, we've actually already informed him," Perring said slowly.

"You have?"

"Yes ma'am."

"Was he down by his boat? He loves his boat. He's always cleaning it and changing the rigging. I think we'll go out later this afternoon if the weather lightens."

"Yes. That sounds very nice. Now Mrs. Erickson, about what I have to tell you, it will be very shocking."

"Oh dear. What is this about?"

"Your son, Dade."

"Dade. He hasn't gotten into trouble again has he? He and his two friends? Their names escape me now, the golden years haven't been as kind to me as to Henry. His memory is like a steel trap but mine seems to get worse each day." She tried to straighten herself but only slid sideways a bit, her clawed fingers groping at the chair's armrests.

"Yes, like I was saying, ma'am, please brace yourself. I'm very sorry to say that your son was the victim of a home invasion last night. He passed away sometime this morning."

Liam watched the old woman sway forward again and blink, her eyelids so thin and veined that he imagined she could see through them. Her lower lip began to tremble and it appeared as if she were going to try to stand. He stepped forward and bent one knee, coming closer to her level to put a hand on her forearm. Her liver-spotted skin had a dried papery feel and it was chilled, like she had already left her body behind and it was cooling. There was a smell about her. Something that reminded him of the weather outside. It was the odor of softly decaying leaves.

"Mrs. Erickson? Did you understand what Detective Perring told you?"

Stella's eyelids fluttered and she focused on him as if seeing him for the first time. "I need to get my pills. I haven't had them yet today. Henry's out on the boat with our son. Maybe you can speak to him when he comes in. They should be back anytime now. I hope he's not in trouble again."

"Mrs. Erickson—" Perring began, but Liam shook his head slightly.

"What type of trouble was he in before?" Liam asked.

"Oh he and his friends got up to mischief. That was all. Boys being boys."

"What did they do?"

"I'm not sure they did anything. It was all hearsay. Someone accused my Dade of beating up that black boy after the Webb girl died." The old woman shook as she tried to raise her head higher. "But he didn't. He's a good boy, my son. Always helping. He's going to be a lawyer, you know."

Liam held her wavering gaze. "You must be very proud."

She smiled revealing a set of flawless false teeth. "Yes, I am."

Liam nodded. "We're going to leave you be now, ma'am. You have a lovely afternoon, okay?"

"Of course. Henry's going to take me out sailing later. If the weather lightens that is."

Stella blinked rapidly, then managed to get her hands on the controls of her wheelchair. She maneuvered it around so that she could look out the window at the lake, then fell still as if dropping into a slumber. Liam and Perring went out into the hall, stopping once the door was shut behind them.

"God, she has no idea what we just told her," Perring said.

"I think somewhere it registered but she won't realize it until later." Liam put one hand against the wall and stared at the floor before bringing his eyes up to Perring's. "Did you catch all that?"

"About Dade assaulting Dickson Jenner. Yes, I did."

"Did you know about it?"

"No. This is the first I've heard."

Liam opened his mouth but closed it as Avery appeared at the top of the stairs.

"Are you finished? Is she all right?"

"Yes, I think she's fine but I'd like to ask you who her power of attorney is," Perring said.

"Well it's her son, Dade."

"And if something were to happen to Dade? Who would the responsibility default to?"

"To me. Why?" Avery shifted from foot to foot as if the floor were too hot to stand on.

"I'm sorry to have to tell you this Mrs. . . ."

"Lott, Avery Lott."

"Mrs. Lott. It will come as a shock to you but Dade was killed in a home invasion last night."

Avery's hand went to her throat. "Oh no! Are you sure?"

"Unfortunately yes. If I might ask you a few questions?"

The other woman looked shell-shocked, her jaw trembling. "Of course."

"Are you a family member or just a caretaker?"

"I'm, well, my mother was best friends with Stella before she died. After she passed away and Stella's health declined, I started providing home care for her. I've known the family for years." A tear broke free of the corner of her eye and trailed down her cheek.

"I'm sorry for your loss," Perring said. "We won't take up much more of your time. Can you think of anyone who would want to hurt Dade in any way? Someone he'd had a falling out with through business or otherwise?"

"No, not at all. He was always so kind. He'd come to see his mother every other day. It always brightened her up so much when he'd stop by." Avery's face crumpled and she began to cry in earnest. "This is going to be so hard on her."

Perring nodded. "Anything else you can think of that may help us? Anything Dade said in the past weeks that was odd or unsettling to you?"

"No. Not that I can think of."

"Was he very close with anyone? A girlfriend or fiancée?"

"No. He always said he never wanted to get married. 'Being tied down,' he called it. No, he had his work, a few friends, and he loved to sail but that was it."

"Thank you Mrs. Lott. We'll be in touch as soon as we have more information. If you think of anything, please feel free to give me a call directly." Perring handed the crying woman a business card.

Avery began to follow them down the stairs but Liam turned and tipped his head toward Stella's room. "We can see ourselves out. Go ahead and check on her." She gave him a grateful smile and wiped at her face as she made her way back toward the room.

Outside the sky had sunk lower and a light rain fell. Superior was a tumult of hundreds of cresting whitecaps. They hurried to the car and climbed inside, both shrugging off the cold rain from their jackets. Perring drew out her cell phone and dialed as she started the car but didn't put it in drive.

"Blair. Were you able to pull up Erickson's record? Um hmm. Okay. How about the neighborhood?" She listened for a long time and frowned. "Fuck. All right. Do a run-up of Dade's friends and acquaintances at his business and send it over to me. Yeah, we've already been there. Not sure. Okay." She ended the call and sat back in her seat. "Erickson doesn't have a record."

"Nothing?"

"Not even a speeding ticket."

"And the neighborhood canvass?"

"Nada."

Liam stared out the window at the churning water. "Is there someone who's been at your precinct long enough to have arrested Erickson on the Jenner charge?"

"Yeah. Actually Mills might know about it. He was uniform up until two years ago and he's about the right age."

"Worth a try."

Perring drove them through the sodden streets, everything outside the windows the same color as the sky. As they pulled past the squad car positioned at the end of Owen's drive, a fork of blue lightning stabbed the clouds above the lake, crawling away through the gray until it winked out. They jogged to the house. Liam took off his coat, reveling in the warmth and dryness of the entry.

Sanders appeared in the archway and watched them come in. "So?" he asked as Perring neared him.

"I'll fill you in in a minute. Where's Mills?"

"In the bathroom."

"Is Owen awake yet?" Liam asked.

Sanders gazed coldly at him for a moment. "He just came down. He's having coffee in the living room."

"Thanks." Sanders didn't budge from the place he stood. Liam sidled past the older detective, brushing his shoulder with his own. He found Owen standing at the windows in the living room nursing a steaming cup of coffee. New lines seemed to have formed around his weary eyes.

"Morning," Liam said.

"Morning."

"You got some rest."

"Yeah. I think my mind just finally shut down."

"Probably a good thing."

Owen dropped his gaze from the waves and stared into his cup. "I want to apologize for how I acted yesterday. You're right, Valerie needs me now more than ever and everyone is doing their best to help."

"You don't need to apologize. I have no idea how I would cope with what you're going through."

"I do. You'd be out there hunting the bastard."

The thoughts from earlier that morning rose in his mind along with the imagery of the dream. Liam started to reply but Perring and Sanders entered the room, stopping behind the couch.

"How are you today, Mr. Farrow?" Perring asked.

"Doing okay."

"Good. Have you secured the money yet?"

"Yes. It's being wired into three separate banks later this afternoon. I'll have to go and pick it up personally."

"We'll wait on that until the drop location's been determined. We don't want you carrying around two million in cash until we have to."

"While we're talking about that, how is this going to be handled when we receive the details about getting Valerie back?"

Perring sighed. "That's difficult to say since we don't know the specifics yet. But generally speaking we'll arrange the exchange for your wife and comply with all of the kidnapper's demands. When everything is set we'll strategically place our SWAT teams around the exchange site. Depending on who is requested to bring the money, we'll have multiple officers hidden in a crowd if the meeting place is public, and if it's not they'll be seconds away if they're needed. In the event that the exchange doesn't go as planned, because in all honesty we do not intend to let this person walk away with two million dollars, we'll have a small tracking device hidden within the money."

"What if something goes wrong?" Owen asked.

"Nothing is going to go wrong, Mr. Farrow. We're going to take every precaution," Sanders said. "Besides, there's a good chance that we'll get this guy before we ever have to meet his demands."

"Was that where you both were this morning?" Owen said, addressing Liam and Perring. "Following up a lead?" Liam glanced at

Perring, seeing the look in her eyes that was as clear as a shout. *Not a word.*

"It was a possibility but turned out to be inconclusive," Perring said. "But I promise you the moment we have something solid, you'll be the first to know."

"I want to say, you've all been great," Owen said, looking down again. "I'm sorry if I was harsh with any of you yesterday."

"No apology needed," Sanders said.

"Absolutely not," Perring said. "Liam, could you join us in the kitchen please?"

He nodded and left Owen to stare out at the lake as he followed Perring and Sanders into the next room. He poured himself a cup of coffee even though his stomach was a cold and aching hole in his center that demanded solid food.

"I filled Rex in on the situation with Erickson and we spoke to Mills," Perring said.

"And?"

"He didn't make the arrest in the assault case but a friend of his did who's since retired. Apparently shortly after Alexandra's suicide, Erickson and two of his friends accosted Jenner on a road near his home."

"How did they know him?"

"They were a year or so older but went to the same high school."

Liam ticked his fingers off. "So you're saying both Webb girls, Owen, Jenner, and these three guys all went to the same high school?"

"Yes." Liam started to continue but Perring cut him off. "Let me finish."

"Okay."

"Jenner was walking home one evening and they cut him off in a vehicle and beat him pretty badly."

"How badly?" Liam said.

"From what Mills said he spent several weeks in the hospital with a fractured orbital bone, four broken ribs, a punctured lung along with multiple bruises and cuts."

"Holy shit."

"Yeah."

"Who were the other two men with Erickson?"

"Gage Rowe and Marshall Davis. Another couple of kids who ran with Erickson."

"And how did they get off without serving time for the attack? Sounds like they nearly killed him."

"Jenner refused to press charges. His mother was the one that called the police. She showed up just as the three were leaving. Dickson might have died if she hadn't come along right then."

Liam set his coffee down, the interior of his stomach mimicking the lake outside. "Why didn't he press charges?"

Perring shrugged. "I think he knew it was another losing battle. Suppose he figured money would get thrown at lawyers until the kids got off. I'm guessing he wanted to be done with it."

"So now we have Erickson murdered in his home." Liam glanced at the two detectives. "And you're looking at Dickson as a prime suspect, aren't you?"

Sanders shrugged. "Shoe fits."

"Why would he wait this long to get revenge?"

"Finally got up the courage. Who knows? Point is we've got motive out the ass for Jenner to want Erickson dead," Sanders said.

"It doesn't make any sense," Liam said quietly.

"Well it's a good thing you're not in charge of this then," Sanders growled.

"Rex . . ." Perring said.

"No, seriously. You might be a nice guy, Liam, but you're getting too big for your britches. This is our case, not yours, so from now on you keep your opinions to yourself."

Liam bristled but clenched his jaw, keeping his retort from flying free.

"Listen, we need to cool it here," Perring said. "We're all on the same side, let's remember that." She was about to continue when her phone chimed and she drew it out, frowning at the display. "Perring," she said, moving into the dining room. Sanders stalked to the sink and rinsed out a coffee cup before turning to stare at Liam. Liam matched his gaze and refused to blink, neither of them giving in until Perring stepped into the kitchen, a strange expression on her face.

"Who was it?" Sanders asked.

"The station." She looked down at the phone in her hand as if it had just bitten her. "The bartender that provided Jenner's alibi for the night of Valerie's disappearance just came in and changed his story. He said Jenner left well before nine o'clock that night."

CHAPTER 11

Liam paced across the living room for what seemed like the thousandth time.

Perring had departed shortly after receiving the call possibly implicating Jenner, leaving Sanders in charge of the task force once again. The house was quiet save for the constant burble of the coffeepots in the kitchen and dining room. Rain continued to slash at the windows, cutting silver scars across the panes that withered away before others took their place. Liam could hear Owen's voice murmuring in the office off the living room. He'd been on the phone almost constantly since Perring had left, his voice cracking at times.

Liam finally gave up his pacing and eased into a chair, weariness a physical thing hovering over him. The basic sandwich he'd thrown together and wolfed down a half-hour ago was a brick in his stomach. He let his vision grow hazy as the details of the last forty hours washed over him. Erickson and his two high school friends had assaulted Jenner, and now Erickson was dead. He'd done a little research on Gage Rowe and Marshall Davis. Rowe owned three restaurants in town, apparently paid for by some savvy stock investments while he was a young man. The bits of information on the Internet included Rowe's picture in the local paper for donating several thousand dollars a year to various children's charities. He looked like a GQ model with clean-cut good looks and expensive suits.

Marshall Davis was a completely different story. Davis had come from a poor household on the bad side of town and hadn't been able to pull himself out of the life he grew up in. There were six public notices attached to Davis's name in the last five years. Two charges for shoplifting, two for drunk and disorderly conduct, one aggravated assault, and a single class-one drug charge with intent to sell. The latter had landed him in jail for a stint of seven months before he was released. Davis had most likely given the DA a plea in exchange for a suspension of sentence.

A local pariah, two successful businessmen, a drug dealer, and a mayoral candidate's wife abducted from her home.

He put his fingers to his temples and without warning the cold case he'd been working on before coming to Duluth sprang forward from the darkness of his memory. What had made him think of Dennis Sandow's face amongst the whirlwind of facts he was trying to sort? It took nearly a minute for the answer to come to him. Sandow's case was unsolved because something had been overlooked. He was sure of it. There was something in the notes or photos that he'd pored over for hours at a time. It was staring him right in the face. And the same was true of Valerie's disappearance, along with Erickson's murder. There was some detail that connected them, but the more he changed angles and theories, the fainter it became. It was like a fine splinter beneath the skin, irritating but invisible.

Owen stepped into the room and rubbed at his eyes.

"Get all your calls in?" Liam asked.

"Yeah. Pretty sure. Caulston took the longest. He didn't actually say 'I told you so' about Jenner's alibi falling through, but I could hear it in his voice." Owen strode to the nearest chair and sat down as if it were covered with broken glass. He adjusted himself, then sighed, looking through the streaked windows to the lake beyond. "God I hope she's all right," he nearly whispered. Liam glanced at his friend, hovering over what he was about to do before wading in.

"Did you know a Dade Erickson?" Liam asked.

Owen glanced at him and slowly frowned. "Not well. Why?"

"You and Valerie went to high school with him, right?"

"Yeah. He graduated with us. I had one class with him at college. Why?"

"Just curious. Did you and Valerie have any dealings with him on a professional level?"

"No. Liam, what's this about? Why are you asking about Dade?"

Liam hesitated, glancing around. Sanders was sitting at the dining room table speaking with one of the task force members. Liam looked back at Owen and lowered his voice. "Dade was killed last night in his home."

"What? You're joking. Do they have someone in custody?"

"Not yet. It got me thinking that there might be some connection between Valerie's kidnapping and his murder."

Owen's face seemed to lose a little color, his skin matching the gray light that filtered into the room. "What could that be?"

"I'm not sure."

"Could it be Jenner? I know Dade and a couple of his friends did a number on him after Alexandra died."

"I didn't get that impression when I spoke with him."

"But what about the bartender? He said Jenner left way earlier."

"That's just it," Liam said, leaning forward. "Why'd he change his story?"

"Maybe he's afraid of Jenner. Maybe he threatened him."

Liam began to tap his forehead, the metronomic sensation making his scalp tingle. "How about Gage Rowe or Marshall Davis? Did you or Valerie know either of them?"

Owen shook his head. "I think I had a study hall with Marshall in high school. We talked a couple of times but that was it. It was a pretty big graduating class, there was no way to know everyone."

"How about Alexandra? Did she know them?"

"No. She was a year younger than them. Valerie would've mentioned that to me at some point over the years. I mean, Caulston would've been thrilled if Alexandra had been dating any of them, especially Erickson since he was loaded and came from a good family. No, Val would have said something." He looked down at the carpet and seemed to nod to himself.

"I did a little digging on Davis and it looks like he went off the deep end after he graduated," Liam said.

"Yeah," Owen said, absently. "Yeah, I think I heard he got into trouble."

"You wouldn't know where either of them live, would you?"

"Who, Rowe or Davis?" Liam nodded. "No. Not really. Rowe is a friend of an associate of mine though and I heard that he bought a place on the shore about an hour or so north of Duluth. He got the land dirt cheap because an earthquake knocked the house into Superior a few years ago. You might've heard about it. Some horror author owned it, Lance something or other."

"An earthquake? Up here? Weird."

"Yeah, it was in all the papers. Anyway Rowe bought the land and built a big house up there from what my associate said, spared no expense."

Liam was about to ask another question when he heard the front door open. A moment later Perring appeared in the dining room. She looked his way before motioning to Sanders. The two detectives came into the living room as Liam and Owen stood.

"What did you find out?" Owen asked.

"I spoke with Jim Houston, the bartender. It was only him and Jenner in the bar that night and he'd had quite a few drinks himself.

He said that Jenner left before nine p.m. and then returned around one thirty in the morning right before closing. He had one drink and then left before Houston closed up. When the officer came to question him the next morning he told him what he remembered. It was only after sobering up completely that he recalled Jenner leaving for the span of time between nine and one thirty."

"Did he mention how Jenner was acting that night?" Sanders asked.

"He said he was twitchy when he first came in, like he was waiting for something to happen."

"Shit," Sanders said, rubbing his jaw. "You get a warrant?"

"Should have one within the hour."

"What about the basement of the abandoned printing building?" Liam asked. "You're saying Jenner left the bar near his home, drove across town, broke in here, took Valerie to the basement of the building, left her there, and then went back for a nightcap?" Liam glanced around the circle. "Does that sound logical to you?"

"If he's the one that took Mrs. Farrow do you think logic was a strong factor in his mind?" Sanders said. Before Liam could answer, Perring's cell rang and she stepped away to answer it.

"If Jenner had been drinking I guess that would explain the rough way the door was broken into," Owen said.

"Exactly," Sanders said triumphantly, looking directly at Liam.

"There's a chance someone's framing Jenner you know," Liam said. "The bartender's change of story is odd."

"He was drunk as a lord. You ever forget something when you've been drinking, Liam?" Sanders sneered.

"I'm starting to regret giving you those cigarettes, Rex." Sanders's lips curled and he was about to reply when Perring moved back toward them.

"Could I speak with you both in the kitchen?" she said. They followed her into the next room and she shut the open doors leading to the living room before turning to them. "The toxicology report came back on Erickson. There was a fairly high amount of diphenhydramine in his system. It's normally found in over-the-counter sleep aids. Looks like it was concentrated in something he either ate or drank right before he was attacked. The cause of death was a derivative of sodium hydroxide that burned through his esophagus as well as his stomach lining causing massive internal bleeding."

"My God," Sanders breathed. "Do they know where it came from?"

"It's a type of lye that's found in paint stripper used on airplanes and vehicles." She glanced at Liam. "Something a mechanic or a junkyard might have on hand."

"Sonofabitch," Sanders said.

"That doesn't prove that Jenner did it," Liam said.

"Oh what the hell do you want, Liam? A fucking neon sign from God in the sky above the guy's house that says 'he's guilty'?"

"Rex, calm down," Perring said. "Liam, why are you so convinced Jenner isn't responsible?"

"Regardless of being illogical enough to kidnap or murder someone, I don't think a person would take the risk of leaving the victim in a basement overnight and then moving them again in the morning. Why not bring her back to his own house right away? And this bartender doesn't sound credible. He could be lying or doesn't truly remember what really happened at all. And . . ." Liam hesitated, knowing what his next statement would bring him. He didn't care. "Jenner didn't seem capable of any of this when I spoke with him yesterday."

Perring's face fell and she closed her eyes. "You did what?"

"I went to speak with him yesterday morning about Alexandra and Valerie."

"You dumb shit," Sanders growled. "Did you compromise this investigation?"

"No. I just talked with him. He's a drunk and he seems unstable, but I don't think he had anything to do with either incident."

"That's it, Liam. I'm sorry, but that's unacceptable. You stepped over the line. I want you to pack up and leave the premises." Perring's eyes were hard now, two glittering stones in her face. "I've been lenient on account of Mr. Farrow's wishes, but this is too far." Her cell phone rang again and Liam was sure she was going to ignore it and keep berating him, but she stopped, turning away again to answer it.

"What? You're fucking kidding." She put a hand against the counter before sighing. "Which channel? Thanks." She barely gave them a glance as she opened the doors into the living room and approached the large flat-screen TV. Liam and Sanders walked behind her, Sanders shooting a heavy look of disdain at Liam. Perring flipped the television on, clicking through channels until a female reporter with tightly cropped blond hair appeared. She was speaking beneath an umbrella on the corner of a city street.

"—sources tell us that two nights ago Mrs. Valerie Farrow, the reclusive wife of Duluth Mayoral candidate Owen Farrow, was abducted from their residence on London Road."

The screen cut to a large picture of Valerie smiling. She looked younger and Liam realized the news station must have used a photo from her college years or before.

"As of this broadcast the authorities have received a ransom demand of an unknown amount and are in negotiations with the kidnappers. Sources say that former homicide detective Liam Dempsey, who was embroiled in the slayings in Tallston, Minnesota, last year, has been brought onto the case as a police consultant. If any of our viewers have information regarding Mrs. Farrow's disappearance, please alert the police. We'll be on scene relating the unfolding events as they become available in this breaking story. I'm Debra Destin reporting for Channel Four News."

The screen cut to an anchor desk and Perring turned the TV off before tossing the remote onto a couch cushion. Without turning around, she said, "Who else did you speak to, Liam?"

He was at a loss for a split second and then absorbed her question for what it was. "I didn't talk to the press."

"So you're saying there's a leak in our task force?" Sanders said.

"I'm saying," Liam said, pinning Sanders with a stare, "that I'm not the leak."

"Let's book this fucker for obstruction of justice," Sanders said, glancing at Perring.

"What does this mean for Valerie?" Owen asked.

"It means we need to hurry," Perring said, finally looking at Liam. There was no emotion on her face now, only dismissal. Her cell phone chirped and she checked it. "We got the warrant. SWAT's already primed. Let's go." She turned to Liam. "What I said in the kitchen holds, Mr. Dempsey. I want you gone when I come back."

"Wait a minute," Owen said. "I want Liam here."

"He's interfering with the case now, Mr. Farrow, and if he continues to do so he'll put your wife's life at risk. It's final. You can call the chief if you want but the position won't change. Right now we're going to go and search Dickson Jenner's residence. Hopefully he's holding Valerie there and this will all be over in a matter of hours and you'll have your wife back."

"I'm coming with," Owen said, beginning to move toward the door.

"No. You need to stay here," Perring said. "I allowed you to come along on the prior raid against my better judgment. I've done several things in the last few days against my better judgment," she said, glancing coldly at Liam. Without another word, Perring and Sanders left the room, saying something to the task force before heading toward the door. Three members around the dining room table remained seated while two others rose and followed the detectives outside.

Liam unclenched his fists. "I'm sorry, Owen. I didn't mean for things to come to this."

"I know you were trying to help. But maybe they're right. You're very good at what you do, but maybe they can take it from here. I appreciate all you've done, but I can't risk Val's safety either." His voice was hollow. Defeated. "If you want you can stay in town. Maybe Perring will have a change of heart. I know the manager of the Radisson. I could call—"

"It's okay." Liam studied his friend. Owen looked beaten, strained, but there was something else underlying his words. Possibly a sense of relief that Liam was leaving despite what he said? Liam noticed the same strangeness as Owen met his gaze and looked away again.

"You came when I called you like the true friend you are. I know you didn't talk to the press; I know you wouldn't do that to us."

"Thanks." Liam held out his hand and Owen moved past it, embracing him with a rough hug before letting him go.

"Thank you."

A black cloud of disappointment and grief overcame him as he headed for the door, grabbing his overnight bag on the way. He fumed against the sensation of failure as he left the large house, the rain picking at him like a flock of enraged birds. He hadn't done anything that he wouldn't have if he were in charge of the case himself.

Perring and Sanders were on the wrong trail, he could feel it.

And he had a feeling Owen wasn't telling him something. Possibly something crucial.

Walking away from the case wasn't only a stinging nettle of frustration, but it also came with disillusionment. Why was he really here? To help his friend or keep his toes in the water of police work as

Perring had said? Dani's words came back to him. *You need to stay for Owen or for you?* He resented what both women were insinuating, but the evident truth that echoed within him as he started his truck was undeniable. He'd never put his own aspirations above what the actual goal in every case was: to find the wrong and right it. *Until now,* the niggling voice said in the back of his mind.

"Shut it," he murmured as he turned the truck around and drove down the driveway. Rain battered the cab as he pulled onto the street and gave Owen's house a last look in his rearview mirror.

CHAPTER 12

Gage Rowe watched the ghost standing at the end of his dock in the cascading rain.

Of course it wasn't a ghost. He didn't believe in such things. Even with the rumors surrounding the property he'd bought earlier that year, rumors of the prior house that had been swallowed by the lake in an unprecedented seismic event, the stories were just that, stories. His feet had been grounded solidly his entire life. He'd gone to church with his parents but never experienced a divine visitation or vision. He'd witnessed a woman die in a traffic accident but could claim no sensation of her spirit passing him on its way to the beyond. He'd even attended a séance once in college, a stupid gathering of mystics his own age that thought they could summon the dead to speak with them and reveal secrets from the afterlife, but there had been no communication with anything otherworldly. Only a bunch of drunk college students sitting around in a circle surrounded by candles humming some nonsense words under their collective breath. No, to Gage the supernatural wasn't super at all. To him it didn't exist.

But he couldn't deny the lance of ice that slid through his stomach at the sight of the figure standing motionless down on the dock. He'd been cleaning in his office, trying to finally organize business-expense receipts for all three of his restaurants for the year. Candice had threatened to do it herself if it wasn't taken care of by the time she and the kids returned from the long weekend at her mother's, and he didn't want her rummaging around through his office. He loved the woman but she was prone to throw out anything that didn't scream importance. So when he decided to take a break and make a sandwich in the midafternoon, his stomach grumbling the entire way down the stairs, he hadn't noticed the ghost standing on the dock. It was only after pacing to the picture window overlooking the lake and chewing his food that he stopped and stared, the sourdough turning to a soggy mixture on his tongue.

Now he shifted position, trying to see more of the person through the rain, because it was a person. He or she was substantial and didn't fade in or out of reality as he moved from window to window to gain a better view.

"What the fuck?" he said to himself, watching the unmoving figure. He—though he couldn't be sure it was a man—stood with his back to him, completely dressed in black from the boots all the way up to some sort of knitted cap pulled down tight over his head. Simply staring out over the turmoil that Superior had become during the morning hours.

Gage went to the south end of the house and looked out the second floor window that gave a more expansive view of the shoreline. No boat was pulled onto the shining rocks. When he walked to the front door to check the driveway for a car, nothing but layers of dancing rain met him. Cursing under his breath, he moved back to the picture window and froze.

The figure was gone.

His eyes widened and he blinked, sure that the person had simply knelt down or was perhaps sitting in Gage's boat that bobbed beside the dock. He hurried across the kitchen and looked out into the south yard, knowing the intruder would've had to have run up the beach and onto the lawn to have disappeared that fast. Intruder. Now the person was no longer a ghost but a threat to him. He chided himself. It was probably a neighbor's friend. Most likely having wandered through the woods onto his property, probably drunk as a skunk.

Gage stopped at the rear patio door and opened it. Water ran in a steady stream out of the gutter at the end of the covered porch and a gust of chilly wind took a swipe at him as he stepped onto the stoop, scanning the lawn for movement.

Nothing.

"Hello?" His voice died against the onslaught of rain, and all at once he had the overwhelming urge to return to the warmth and safety of the house, to lock the door behind him. Maybe he'd even load his shotgun and stand it in the living room while he had a cup of coffee.

The rope tying the boat to the dock let out a pained creak as a large wave washed into shore. Regardless of the intruder (*stop calling him that*), he needed to check the knots on the boat. He'd let his son Paul secure the craft last time they'd come in from fishing and he hadn't been down to the lake since. If Paul hadn't tied the knots tight enough the waves might loosen them and his twenty-foot Lund would be a useless piece of battered aluminum by tomorrow morning.

Gage gave the yard a last glance, then stepped inside the house to don his shoes and a jacket. He considered locking the house behind him but brushed the thought off. *You're being silly. Go down to the dock and secure the boat. Maybe you'll run into whoever it was down there and you can either run them off or direct them back to wherever they came from.* If all else failed, he could call the local law enforcement in Stony Bay.

The wind shoved him first away from the lake and then toward it like a panicked child tugging at his clothes, unsure of which way to run. The gray waters below the steep hill were nearly black. For a moment he wondered how it would feel to sink beneath them, to have the cold depths close over his head. What would be waiting down in the dark? Surely there would be secrets there both benign and malignant. Every dark place kept its secrets.

He shook himself from his musings, another cold battering of fear rising within him like the waves at the foot of the hill. As he made his way down the wide stairway built into the drop to the lake, the large rocks in the bay beyond the land seemed to rise and fall as well. It felt like they were watching him with a sentience both calculating and unkind.

Gage jogged across the stretch of beach sand he'd had hauled in, his shoes sinking with each step, and hopped onto the dock's decking. The boat surged upward again and he could see now that the closest rope was partially untied. Another few hoists from the lake and the front end of the craft would be free. He'd have to teach Paul the running bowline knot again. As he approached the craft he noticed several shining objects lying close to the end of the dock. His pace slowed and he walked carefully forward, noticing how slick the decking had become. When he neared the end of the dock he stopped short and blinked.

Numerous large fishhooks had been attached to some type of thin cable that had been wrapped around a few planks of the decking. Their wicked-looking shapes were like violent question marks tipped with curved barbs.

"What the hell?" he said to the lake. He was about to kneel down and try to retrieve one of the hooks when he heard something behind him.

He tried to turn, but he slipped on the soaked surface, his tennis shoes going in different directions. A strong hand gripped his jacket, steadying him, and he placed his hand on the arm attached to it before bringing his eyes up to the person's face.

A surge of electricity blasted through his throat as the stun gun crackled beneath his jaw. The last thing he saw was the sky opening into a wreathing halo of white fire that ate everything away into darkness.

CHAPTER 13

Liam sat in his truck, staring at the address on his phone.

He'd turned the windshield wipers off after pulling beneath the canopy of the gas station to fill the truck's tank. Now, parked in the station's lot, the windshield was a solid sheet of water that obscured everything beyond the glass.

He'd told himself that he would simply turn south once the gas had been pumped. He'd repeated the fact as he paid for several sticks of beef jerky and a bottled water inside the store. He'd even drawn his phone out to call Dani and tell her he was coming home. But instead of punching her number and putting the phone to his ear, he accessed the county auditor's website. It was only a matter of minutes until he found the property listed under Gage Rowe's name. The parcel abutting Superior was fairly large by the looks of the aerial photo, and as he scrolled downward on the map, he saw that the closest town was to the south by the name of Stony Bay.

Liam shut the phone off and hit the wipers once. The glass cleared enough for him to glimpse the road heading north, the blacktop gleaming and jumping with the falling rain. A pair of fading taillights rounded a bend further up past the gas station and winked out behind a row of trees.

"Fuck it," Liam said, and put the truck into gear turning the wheel right, away from home.

As each mile marker passed he ignored the abhorrently smug assertions of the voice in his head about his current motives, and instead focused on the information about Erickson's murder. He'd been tortured and then forced to drink an acid that would've taken some time to kill him, causing unfathomable pain in the process. Was there a type of symbolism associated with the violent death? The burns and the acid were definitely related, but why? Burns. Burning. Fire. Immolation from within.

"A reference to hell?" he said aloud. The wipers shushed him. Who had hated Erickson so much that they would sentence him to that type of punishment before death? But of course that was why Liam was traveling north along the edge of the great lake instead of south, wasn't it? Gage Rowe was a friend, possibly a client of Erickson's. And who better to question about the beating Dickson Jenner had received than the man who participated in it?

"You're going to get yourself thrown in jail," he said. "Rowe is going to give you nothing and then he's going to call Perring and she's going to have you arrested. Yep." He gazed out at the unending wash of leaden water that seemed to blend with the sky above. Thick stands of pine trees spread to either side of the road when it curved away from Superior, the green growth blemished only by the sporadic explosion of a red oak or the shimmering yellow leaves of a birch, its white branches like thin bones stripped of flesh. Before long Liam piloted the truck around a broad curve and the town of Stony Bay greeted him. It was picturesque and charming in the way small towns could be. Images of Tallston's quaint businesses and high bluffs began to overlay Stony Bay's streets and buildings and he had to breathe deeply and focus on the road as he passed through the little village, ignoring the tremor that threatened to dominate his hands.

The main street became the highway again and soon he was immersed in the woods once more. It was only minutes before he slowed the truck, glancing at his phone for assurance that he was at the correct drive. A mailbox appeared at the border of the road and he squinted, trying to make a name out on its side but there were only numbers inlaid on the metal. Liam swung into the driveway and idled up its length, a canopy of leaves closing over the top of the truck like a patchwork tunnel.

A house slowly took shape through the burning foliage. It was a modern two-story rambler with a multiple-hipped roofline. A long porch ran across its front and a flawless lawn stretched around the newly constructed home and down to the lake. The view was incredible even with the haze of rain that refused to abate.

He coasted to a stop before the front door, noting the glimmer of several lights behind the panes. He zipped his jacket all the way up and stepped into the weather, his hair matting to his skull instantly. He ran up the steps and shook himself off before touching the glowing doorbell button. He waited. He jabbed the button again and leaned to the side, looking through the frosted glass that lined the doorway. No movement from inside the house. No footsteps coming to meet his call.

Liam stood for another moment in place, then walked the length of the porch to the far right side, glancing in windows as he went. The end of the porch turned and dropped away into a set of stairs leading to a covered patio. He hesitated before climbing down, glancing back the way he'd come as he neared a sliding door on the side of the house. Rain drummed on the roof above him as he approached the entrance, hoping that one of the Rowes wouldn't be stepping out as he lifted a fist to knock on the glass.

He froze.

The sliding door was open several inches.

Liam's hand went to the small of his back and grasped the Sig. He kept it holstered as he leaned his head toward the gap in the door, listening. Turning, he glanced down the hill toward the lake finding the long dock and the fishing boat floating at an odd angle away from it. The rear was the only section tied, its front pointing away from shore and rising high with each wave that washed in. His eyes slid to the end of the dock and the spread-eagled form lying there.

He pulled the handgun free.

Liam crouched and turned in a half-circle, heart already double-timing. The rain obscured the woods to the south. He shot a glance into the house once more, then raced down the hill toward the beach.

His feet nearly slipped from under him twice, moisture flooding his eyes. The only sounds were the hammering waves and the white noise of rain. He flew down the short set of stairs to the beach and crossed the sand to the dock.

A wave broke the boat completely free and it floated toward shore. Liam kept the gun leveled on the form at the dock's end, throwing a glance over his shoulder every other step. He slowed as he came even with what was on the planking and his stomach shriveled with revulsion.

Gage Rowe lay on his back, glassy eyes staring up at the weeping clouds. Large, shining fishhooks were embedded in each of his ears and attached to the dock with wire. Dozens more pierced the muscle of his arms and legs, binding him against the agony that would accompany any movement. But the worst was his mouth. The largest fishhooks curved over his lower teeth and out the bottom of his jaw. Wires ran from them down to his belt and were fastened there, keeping his mouth open in a constant scream. Water pooled around his lolling tongue, mingling with the blood that seeped slowly from the wounds. The man had drowned from the falling rain.

On his pale cheek a ragged three had been carved into the flesh.

A loud screech and a bang jerked Liam's head up from the horror before him and he raised the pistol, almost firing at the fishing boat being tossed against the rocks farther down the beach. He lowered the gun, arms thrumming with adrenaline and fear. Rowe's ears had nearly been torn from his skull from where he'd struggled to rise away from the onslaught of suffocating water. Liam put a hand out and steadied himself on a dock support, his beef jerky rising in the back of his throat.

Over the sound of the waves and thumping of the boat came a grinding whine.

He turned toward it, squinting down the southern border of the half-moon bay. There was nothing visible, but the sound continued, cycling through a quick mechanical hum.

A boat motor trying to start.

Liam ran down the dock and leapt into the sand, his feet finding purchase on the rock wall that lined the bank. He flew up it, scrambling with his hands and feet until he was on solid ground again. He rushed into the forest lining the yard, rain like stinging nettles on his face and eyes. The undergrowth was thick at first, holding him back as he raced beneath the higher trees, but then it lessened, fading to browning reed grass that slithered past his soaked pant legs.

The boat motor wound up again, its cry coming from straight ahead. It coughed once and then fell silent. He ducked beneath a pine bough and ran up and over a rocky outcropping, dropping several feet on the other side. Water splashed up around his shoes, freezing his feet inside. The boat motor made a grinding sound again and it was closer. Much closer.

Liam slowed, gathering his bearings as he wiped his eyes free of water. He blinked, taking in the brightening behind a row of pines that towered above him. Between their trunks he could see the undulations of Superior as well as something else.

The front of a boat.

He eased forward, gun straight out before him, feet making no noise on the wet pine needles. He crested a band of rock and stepped behind the first pine tree, glancing around its side.

The boat was there, bobbing in the waves a dozen yards offshore. A figure dressed entirely in black stood at its helm, pressing a control that caused the whining of the twin outboards attached to the stern. Liam watched the figure's head turn toward the motors and saw that he wore a black cowl that hid his features.

Liam breathed deeply, then stepped out from behind the tree, hurrying between the other pines and out into the open.

"Police! Hands in the air!" he yelled, training the sights on the figure's chest.

The figure didn't hesitate. He swung a pistol upward and fired.

A hot hissing filled Liam's right ear as the bullet sung past him. He squeezed the Sig's trigger and the gun snapped up in his hands. The figure's jacket jumped with the impact and he fell backward, a single hand scrabbling at the boat's steering wheel before dropping away.

Quiet. Only the waves on the shoreline.

The boat clunking up and down in the water.

Liam held his stance, waiting, muscles aching as his vision doubled with moisture and he blinked it away. After nearly a minute he took a step forward, his foot crushing a pile of shells against some rocks.

The pistol came over the boat's gunwale and barked twice.

Liam dove backward, pebbles kicking up near his feet in a shrapnel spray. His hand found a tree trunk and he swung behind it, kneeling and aiming around its opposite side. The figure rose above the gunwale and fired again. Something snapped against Liam's throat and he felt a hot wetness shower his face. He slid back behind the safety of the tree.

He'd been shot in the throat. He was going to die.

Even as he slid his shaking fingers beneath his jaw to feel the damage, the image of Kelly's throat exploding with his bullet flooded his mind, hand clutching her pregnant belly as she fell. How ironic. To be killed the same way he had ended her life.

His hand met sticky pulp and something fibrous. When he held it up before his eyes he saw that his fingers were covered in pinesap and shredded bark. No blood.

Another shot rang out and the ground beside him kicked up as the sound of the motors turning over came again.

There was a pop that wasn't gunfire and the outboards roared to life.

Liam rolled away from the safety of the tree and rose to one knee. The boat was surging away from shore, the figure standing with one hand on the wheel, the other aiming the gun at him. Liam pulled the trigger twice and the boat's windshield shattered. The pilot lurched to the side, the boat following in an aerobatic roll that nearly capsized it. Liam walked out from the woods, firing a round with each step as the boat sped away. One of the outboard's engine cowlings detonated into a shower of plastic, and sparks flew from a steel handhold near the helm. The driver threw a last shot his way that cut the air several feet to his left but he barely noticed. If his count was right, he had one shell left.

He steadied the pistol.

Squeezed the trigger.

The gun jumped, the slide locking open.

The figure staggered, arching his back, but maintained a grip on the steering wheel. *What the hell? That should've dropped him.* The motors screamed as the boat planed out and skipped away over the tops of the waves, its form shrinking, then fading altogether in the drifting rain.

Liam drew out his cell phone and tried to turn it on but the screen remained dark. The rain must've soaked it through his pants pocket.

"Fuck!" He scrambled up the bank and ran through the woods, sticks slicing at his jacket, brambles digging furrows in his exposed skin. He burst into the Rowes' yard and ran straight for the house. Throwing the sliding door all the way open, he skidded on the tile inside the entry, eyes raking the room until he spotted the cordless phone on the kitchen counter. He punched 911 and listened as the call was answered.

"Nine-one-one, what is your emergency?"

"My name is Liam Dempsey and I'm a police consultant. A man by the name of Gage Rowe has been murdered and I've been involved in a shooting with his attacker. I'm calling from his residence north of Stony Bay."

"Okay sir, I've dispatched state police to your location, they're only a few minutes away. Are you injured in any way?"

"No, I don't think so. But listen to me. You need to patch me through to the nearest coast guard station. The assailant escaped by boat and they need to intercept him."

"Okay sir, just stay calm. I'll notify the authorities in your area of the situation."

"No, you don't understand! You need to get a plane and some boats out right now and start searching the water south of my location. The assailant could be going anywhere and we need to stop him before he disappears."

"Sir, I'm going to need you to calm down."

"Goddammit!" He hung up and groped in a nearby drawer, pawing two more open before finding a tattered phone book that might've been years out of date. He flicked through it until he found the police station's number and dialed it. A moment later a male voice answered.

"Duluth Police."

"Hello, this is Liam Dempsey, I've been working with Detectives Perring and Sanders over the last few days. I need you to connect me with one of them."

"Uh, Mr. Dempsey, this is officer Charlie Cross. I was at the, uh, scene this morning."

"Charlie, good. There's been another murder. Gage Rowe is dead. I'm at his house now."

"Gage Rowe?"

"Yes. You need to scramble the coast guard and get a plane in the air. Whoever killed him is driving a boat in Superior."

"What type of boat?"

"It's dark gray and has two outboard motors on the back. A guy dressed completely in black is driving. He's armed and I think he's wearing body armor."

There was the scribbling of a pencil from Charlie's end. "Okay. I'll make the call."

"I need to speak with Perring."

"Not sure she'll answer but I'll patch you through."

"Thank you."

The phone went quiet in his hand. He stood in the kitchen, the continual patter of water dripping from his clothing to the floor. He glanced at the counter where a half-eaten sandwich dried out on a plate.

The line opened to a sigh. "This is Perring."

"Perring, it's Liam."

"Liam, I don't really have time for this."

"Gage Rowe is dead. He was killed at his home and I traded shots with the murderer."

"What? What are you doing there?"

"I came here to ask him some questions about Erickson."

"Liam, I swear—"

"I know, I know, just listen. I showed up here and Rowe was tied down with fishhooks to his dock. He drowned in the rain."

"What? You're not making any sense."

"You have to see it. I can't explain. But the killer was in a boat on the opposite side of the bay. His motor wouldn't start and we exchanged fire. I shot the bastard twice but he's wearing some type of body armor. Before Charlie patched me through I asked him to dispatch the coast guard. If they hurry they can catch whoever it is before he gets ashore." The faint keen of a siren rose in the distance. "The state police are coming. How soon can you and Sanders get up here?"

There was a pause and Perring sighed again. "Sanders is in the ICU right now. He's been shot in the chest. They don't know if he's going to pull through."

"What? What happened?"

"Dickson Jenner shot him."

"Oh God." He closed his eyes as the siren came closer and closer, and a strobe of blue and red lights began to reflect off the tree line.

"We were walking up to the house when he started shooting. I almost got clipped but Rex was in front of me. Dumb asshole wasn't wearing his vest." There was a huskiness to her voice and she sniffed once.

"Why the hell did Jenner do it?"

"We don't know yet and it might take some time to find out."

"Why?"

"Because he and his mother are both dead."

CHAPTER 14

The state police quit questioning him when Perring arrived.

In advance Liam had set his gun and straight razor on the kitchen counter and stood outside the house with his hands on his head. The trooper who came around the side of the house through the rain, gun drawn and pointed at him, was young but professional. He searched Liam and secured him while backup arrived. Three officers guided him to the rear of a cruiser and put him in the back before questioning him. He answered everything except queries that bordered on Valerie's kidnapping. For these he used an old rerouting tactic he'd picked up from veteran cons, bringing the conversation around full circle before repeating his story. The troopers seemed appeased and when Perring showed up, her hair tied back but soaking, they were happy to release him into her custody.

Liam sat in the front seat of her sedan, the rain having tapered off to a steady drizzle. He watched Perring stand beside the crime scene team on the end of the dock, all of them in yellow rain slickers. After nearly a half hour she trudged up the hill and across the lawn to where he waited. When she climbed in the car a draft of cool air buffeted the interior and she stripped away the slicker, tossing it in the back seat. She stared at him.

He waited.

"You're a complete asshole, you know that?"

"Yeah."

"You directly disobeyed a police order."

"I did."

"You broke . . . I don't know how many laws in the last two days."

"Um hmm."

"And nearly got yourself killed in the process."

He nodded.

"Do you have anything to say for yourself?"

"Can I have my gun and knife back?"

"No. Forensics needs them to make sure you weren't in on this whole cluster fuck."

"You know I wasn't."

Perring gave him a long look. "Yeah, I know you weren't."

"And you know I didn't leak anything to the press."

"Yeah. I just got word on the way here that one of the uniforms was seen talking with a reporter earlier today." She put the car in reverse and backed out to the driveway before pulling away from the house. "You better start talking and don't stop until all this makes sense."

"I figured Rowe would know something about Erickson since they were friends in high school and he was involved in Jenner's assault. All I wanted to do was ask him some questions. I never expected to find him like that."

"And when you pulled up, he was . . . where he was?"

"Yeah. One of the damnedest things I've ever seen."

"Tell me about it. What about the guy in the boat? Any ID at all? You didn't see his face?"

"Nothing. Like I said, we traded shots. I hit him at least twice. It just staggered him, then he bounced right back and took off. You hear anything from the coast guard yet?"

"They sent three boats out and took a plane up, but with the weather it was rough going. They didn't find anything."

"Shit." He touched the side of his neck that was still tacky with sap. They rode in silence for a time, the hiss of the wheels on the slick highway the only sound. He finally glanced at Perring. Her profile was haggard, eyes holding deep bags beneath them. "I'm sorry about Rex."

Perring seemed to consider something, then nodded. "Thanks. He's got his family with him now. He'll pull through."

Liam gave her a moment. "What happened?"

"SWAT was in place. We were going up the front stairs, Rex was in front of me. There was a dog going nuts on the deck, barking and snapping like he was going to rip us to shreds. Then we heard a shout, I think it was Dickson's mother. I think she yelled 'no.'. I heard glass break and then the shot. Rex stumbled but stayed standing in front of me. By then SWAT was moving in and Jenner was standing in the living room window with a gun. I remember our eyes locking and his were so fierce, like he was absolutely crazy. He aimed at me but just then one of the team ran around the side of the house and drew his attention. Someone fired and Dickson jerked but got another round off in our direction. There were a few more shots, I don't know how many. Everything went so fast. I was holding Rex on the stairs, trying to drag him back and there was so much blood."

Perring paused and pulled out a deflated pack of gum. She considered it for a second, then exchanged it for a pack of cigarettes in the center console. She pulled one out, lit it, and inhaled deeply.

"Damn that's good," she said. She squinted at the cigarette before staring straight ahead. "Jenner and his mother were dead when we got inside. She must've been trying to pull him away from the window."

"He must have been drunk."

"I think it was kind of a constant state for him."

"He told me he was at the breaking point when I went to visit him. He said he was tired of cops coming around. Maybe if I would've said something . . ."

"Maybe you damn well should have!" He could see the pain outlined in her features. "Maybe it would've made a difference!" Perring drew hard on the cigarette and some of the anger seemed to drain from her. "And maybe it wouldn't have. We were careful; we had the team in place before we ever went up those stairs. It might've been unavoidable."

"You read my file."

"Yeah."

"So you know my partner was wounded too." She nodded once, not looking at him. "I know how it feels, how you wish it were you instead."

Perring swallowed loudly. "It's like a nightmare that won't stop even though I know I'm awake."

"I'm sorry. I do feel responsible."

"You shouldn't have gone to speak to him, but this was how it was going to play out, one way or another. Jenner wasn't ever going to get over what happened. He was always going to have the suspicion and anger hanging over him. I'm sorry that he and his mother are dead. If he hadn't shot at us it would've ended fine. I don't see any other route we could've taken."

"This is the only part of the job that I couldn't stand. The doubt and regret." Liam brushed his neck again then let his hands fall to his lap.

"I owe you an apology, Liam," Perring said, surprising him. "You were right about the connection between the cases. I'd be a fool to deny it now after seeing that three carved into Rowe's face."

"The countdown has begun."

She blinked and took another long drag. "This guy's a fucking psychopath."

"I don't think so."

She shot him a look. "What do you mean? Did you see the same things I did today? Two murders in less than twenty-four hours?"

"But look at the synchronicity of it all," Liam said. "Valerie is abducted two nights ago. We get a ransom the next day. That night Erickson's killed. We find him in the morning. This afternoon Rowe gets a visit. Did I hear the trooper correctly saying that Rowe's family was out of town for the past few days?"

"Yeah."

"See. Planning. Whatever this guy is, he's not sporadic and impulsive. This whole thing's like a clock, each piece working with the next, everything meshing. But what truly worries me is what happens when the clock winds down."

"The countdown has begun," Perring said quietly.

Liam's cell phone rang in his pocket, startling them both. He drew it out, surprised to see the display working again. Dani's number filled the screen.

"Hello?"

"Hey."

"Hi. How are you?"

"I'm okay." There was something in her voice, something that set all his senses alert.

"What's wrong?"

"Nothing, it's nothing. I just . . . had an encounter at the park."

"What do you mean 'encounter'?"

She was quiet for so long he was about to ask the question again when she spoke. "I took Eric to the park today, the one down from the market?"

"Yeah?"

"And there was this guy there. He was sitting on a bench near the street. He watched us come into the park and he just stared for the longest time, but I didn't think much of it. He didn't look dangerous or anything. He was just an average guy about our age. He was wearing a red sweatshirt with a yellow circle on the chest, and I remember it looking really small on him, like he was trying to show off how in shape he was. Maybe he noticed me looking. I don't know. Anyway, after a little while the park started emptying out, but Eric was still playing so I kept reading my book and all of a sudden the guy is sitting next to me on my bench."

Liam's insides squirmed. "What happened?"

"He . . . he was nice at first, just making small talk but then he started saying suggestive things, like he didn't live too far away and I could come to his house for coffee if I wanted and that he had a big TV that Eric could watch while we talked."

Liam gripped the phone, hearing the plastic squeak under the pressure. "Then what?"

"Then he touched me."

"What? Where?"

"On the arm. He kind of let his fingers trail up my arm." Now Dani was beginning to cry. He could hear the tears tightening her voice. "When he did that I stood up to walk away and he ran his hand up my leg and grabbed my ass."

"Sonofabitch," Liam breathed. Every muscle in his body trembled. "What did you do?"

"I turned and backed away and the whole time he just sat there smiling and watching me. I went right over and got Eric and we left. I'm sorry, God I'm being so weak," she said, the tears fully there now. He could hear her wiping at her face. "Thank God Eric didn't see. He could tell I was shook up but all he asked was if I was all right."

"I'm coming home right now."

"No, Liam, I'm fine. It's not like that's the first time some guy's grabbed me."

"It doesn't matter if it's not the first. It's going to be the last."

"It's okay. He was just some creep. We'll steer clear of that park from now on. We can go to the one down from Eric's school."

"Damn it, it's not okay, Dani," Liam said with more vehemence than he meant to. He saw Perring glance at him out of the corner of his eye but he ignored her. "And for God's sake, it wasn't your fault because you looked at him."

Dani sniffled but when she spoke again her voice was stronger. "I know. But I'm fine, Eric's fine. It shook me up, that's all."

"I'm still coming home."

"Don't. As much as I'd love to have you here, stay there where there's a real problem. I just needed to talk to you, to hear your voice."

He closed his eyes. Sometimes he forgot how much she'd gone through in Tallston the year before. How much she'd endured and how truly strong and resilient she was. But the scars on her legs weren't the only wounds she carried. There had been nights when she'd woken him with her own nightmares. She hadn't deserved any of it. And now this. His hands trembled with anger. "I'm so sorry I wasn't there."

"If you had been, you'd be in jail right now."

"But more importantly he'd be in the hospital."

She laughed a little and the sound broke the tension holding him rigid in his seat. "I'm fine," she repeated. "Eric and I are going to make dinner soon; chicken fettuccine Alfredo."

"I still think—"

"I just want to forget about it. There's a million jackasses out there like him but what you're dealing with there is much worse. Valerie needs you more than I do tonight."

"You make me feel so wanted."

She laughed again. "I love you."

"I love you. I'm sorry I wasn't there to help."

"You did help. A lot. I'd better go, I've got a hungry boy here."

"Give him a hug for me."

"I will."

"Call me later tonight."

"I will."

He hung up and stared at the phone for a while, the urge to call her back almost too great to resist, but one thing kept him from doing so. Guilt. Where had he been when she really needed him? Gone. Away. Running off on another case, telling himself that he wasn't doing real police work, while he made every attempt to. He should go home right now, be with the people that truly needed him, simply shut off the inner pull toward any more cases that came across his doorstep. But how would he feel if he left and tomorrow they found Valerie's body? How could he ever look Owen in the eyes again? Or himself?

Valerie needs you more than I do tonight.

He wished he knew if that was true.

"Trouble on the home front?" Perring had cracked her window and lit another cigarette. Liam looked at his phone for a long moment, then tucked it away.

"No."

"I'm having one of the forensic assistants drive your truck back tonight. Your possessions should be cleared by then. You can get going after that."

"I want to stay." The edge in his voice made her glance at him.

"We went through this."

"Perring, who do you have to work this with you? You said yourself that you're understaffed."

"That's not the point. You aren't a cop anymore."

"Exactly. I can do things that you aren't allowed to. I can get information. I can help you."

She made an exasperated sound. "I must be nuts." She dragged deeply on the last of her cigarette. "What are you thinking? Even though I'm by no means agreeing to anything at all."

"I think we should try to locate Marshall Davis because I have a feeling his name is the next on the list. We may even be too late but I don't think so."

Perring nodded. "I'll have Charlie check around the office, see what the word is on Davis."

"There's something else that's really irking me."

"What's that?"

"The bartender's new story. It's off. I didn't like it from the beginning. There's no way to prove he's telling the truth."

"He was drunk, that much was apparent even to the officer that interviewed him the morning after Valerie's disappearance."

"I'm not disputing that," Liam said. "But there's something wrong with how he came back and amended his version of what happened. Is he still in custody?"

"No. As far as I know he went back to his bar."

Liam glanced out the side window at the rain-swept trees. "Then let's go have a drink."

CHAPTER 15

The Cornerstone Bar wasn't on a corner and it wasn't made of stone.

Liam traced the roof's steel peak, taking in the dirty sidewalls that may have once been a rich red but were now stained a dull brown. Water coursed out of a broken gutter on the closest end of the building, pooling and running in a miniature river past a scuffed and discolored security door shut to the weather. A neon *Open* sign hung at an angle in a murky window. There was one vehicle in the muddy parking lot, a rusted Chevy with a bed that canted to the left like a busted jaw.

"The proprietor's chariot?" Liam asked as Perring coasted to a stop before the building.

"Yeah, that's his. Liam, what are you planning on doing here?"

"I'm going to ask him some questions." He opened his door and stepped into the rain. There was still a black manic energy coursing through his veins from Dani's phone call. It was like some intravenous drug that wouldn't leave his system no matter how much he disregarded it. He had felt hints of it before: whenever he thought of Abford, when he'd seen the pictures of the mangled bodies of his brother and sister-in-law, whenever he looked at a cold-case photograph, the victim's eyes beseeching him for justice.

But it was stronger now. So much stronger.

He walked beneath the building's awning, holding the door for Perring, as she hurried from the car, inside.

The bar reeked of stale popcorn and fried food along with smoke. A long, pitted bar stretched away from them and turned at the rear of the building, ending next to a set of double doors. The windows let in pale swaths of light through their filmy panes, illuminating high-top tables that hadn't been cleaned in some time. A digital jukebox waited silently in one corner and what appeared to be a brand new pool table sat in the center of the floor. As Liam shut the door behind them, a broad man with a gray ponytail stepped through the double doors, holding an open beer can and smoking a cigarette. His eyes found them and narrowed as he stepped out from behind the bar.

"What can I do for you, detective?" He said the last word like a slur. Perring walked toward him while Liam moved to the pool table, glancing at the bar's owner as he went. Houston was in his late forties or early fifties, his hangdog face covered in a growth of whiskers that resembled a wire brush. He wore a white leather vest over a long-sleeve button up, and a gaudy gold ring on his left index finger. Liam stopped beside the pool table, running his hand across the flawless, green felt. He fished in his pocket for a moment before drawing out several coins.

"Mr. Houston, we're here to ask you a few questions."

"Already answered all of your questions when I was in at the station house. I ain't got nothin' more to say to you."

Houston and Perring both looked Liam's way as he shoved in the coin bed and the pool balls dropped from inside the table, the clatter echoing throughout the bar.

"Sorry," he said, flashing them a sheepish look. Perring frowned at him and turned back to Houston.

"Sir, we need to go over what you've told us so far. Honestly we're concerned about the change in your story."

"Listen, I told you already, I was drinkin' since there wasn't any customers in that night 'cept for Dickson. We had some shots and I didn't remember until later that he took off and came back. That's it." Liam watched the bartender spin the gold ring around and around his finger as he racked up the pool balls.

"Do you have credit card receipts from Jenner that night?" Liam asked, racking the pool balls. "Maybe something to give us a solid timeline about when he was here and when he left?"

"He paid cash," Houston said, his upper lip curling in a sneer.

"Can you tell me again why the epiphany came to you about Dickson leaving?" Perring asked.

"The what?"

"Epiphany. Why did you suddenly remember he hadn't been here the whole time when you plainly told the officer the day before that he had?"

"Because I was drunk. Ever been drunk before, detective, or you too good for that?"

Liam broke the formation of pool balls with a stroke of the cue. Several dropped into pockets and Houston glanced his way before returning his gaze to Perring.

"Mr. Houston I don't appreciate your tone and if you're unwilling to cooperate with us we'll have to continue this conversation at the station."

"You got no right coming in here and orderin' me around. I told you everything I know. Now I got business to attend to so if you're done, I'd appreciate you gettin' the hell out of my bar."

Liam took a shot at a three ball, letting the cue slide from his fingers and drop to the floor.

"Watch it!" Houston said, pointing at the table. "All that's brand new. You'll be payin' me if that cue's broken."

"Sorry. Lost my grip," Liam said, picking the cue up. "How long have you known Jenner?"

"Since he could drink. Who the hell is this guy, anyways?" Houston said to Perring, pointing at Liam.

"His name is Mr. Dempsey. He's assisting us on the investigation."

"Well if he ain't a cop, I don't have to talk to him."

Perring sighed. "Sir, Dickson Jenner is dead. He was killed in a shooting with police this afternoon."

Houston's face tightened, the lines around his mouth and eyes flattening. "That's too bad."

"It's more than too bad if we find out you aren't telling us the truth," Perring said.

"I don't have to say nothin'. Think I'll call my lawyer and speak with him. In the meantime, I want you two to get the fuck out of here."

Houston took a step toward Perring, towering over her, encroaching on her space.

"Sir, I need you to move back," Perring said, hand dropping to her handgun.

"Or what? You gonna shoot me too? Shoot me in my own bar after I done nothing wrong." Houston swaggered forward, chest nearly touching Perring's face as she retreated another step.

In his mind, Liam saw Valerie tied to the chair in the dank basement, crying through her gag, saw Abford spinning around and taking aim, saw the man in the park running his hand up Dani's leg.

He took another shot and the cue bit hard into the felt. The tip snagged and pierced the green cloth, tearing a six-inch strip across the table.

The sound caught Houston's attention and his eyes flew open wide. "Goddamnit!" he yelled. "You sonofabitch! That's a brand new fuckin' table." The larger man came at Liam, one hand outstretched to grab him by the shirt, the other cocked back in a fist.

In one motion, Liam grasped Houston's wrist and yanked him forward as he snatched the cue ball from the table. He pressed the big man's palm to the felt and slammed the cue ball into the back of his hand.

There was a muted crackling as several bones in Houston's hand broke.

The bar owner opened his mouth to scream but Liam punched him in the throat. The man's cry became a squawk and his eyes bulged, watering instantly. He tried to pull away but Liam grasped him by the collar and twisted the cue ball into his hand at the same time. Houston whimpered and gagged.

"Liam!" Perring yelled, drawing her gun.

"Listen here you lying fuck, I know you're not telling the truth so let's dispense with the bullshit. Sound good?" Houston lurched away but Liam drew him back, leaning more on the cue ball. The bar owner's knees gave out and he slumped to them beside the table. "Sorry, was that a yes?" Liam asked.

"Yes," Houston croaked.

"Good. Why did you change your story?"

"Liam!" Perring yelled.

"Why?" Liam growled. When Houston only gagged again, Liam screwed the cue ball down harder into his ruined hand. The man's eyes began to roll upward and Liam grasped the upper part of the man's ear between his fingers and pinched. Houston retched and vomited on the floor. Liam released the pressure on the cue ball and the bigger man slumped to his side, cradling his broken hand to his chest.

Liam knelt beside him. "That was the beginning of the pain. There's a lot more if you need it."

"No," Houston said, tears flowing out of the corners of both his eyes.

"Then tell us the truth."

"He paid me," Houston wheezed. "He paid me fifty grand to change my story."

Perring stepped closer, holstering her gun.

"Who paid you?" Liam asked. When Houston didn't respond he began reaching for his crushed hand.

"Okay, okay!" Houston nearly screamed. "That girl's father, Caulston Webb, he paid me!"

CHAPTER 16

Liam swallowed the last of the coffee in his Styrofoam cup and crumpled it in a fist.

He glanced down the hallway outside of the room he was sitting in, still not seeing Perring anywhere. The bustle of officers communing in the area adjacent to the waiting room created a constant hum. Phones rang intermittently, papers shushed against one another, file drawers banged shut. All the sounds were so familiar. If he closed his eyes he could imagine he was back in his precinct building in Minneapolis.

He turned and stared out the window at the rain that refused to stop falling. The streets outside shone blackly as a bus hissed to a stop on the closest corner, depositing two men who hurried down the sidewalk, their heads ducked low into their collars. It was nearly six in the evening and the day's events wore on Liam. He rubbed his eyes, stifling a yawn as footsteps echoed down the hallway, drawing nearer. A second later Perring appeared in the doorway.

"So?" Liam asked when she only gazed at him.

"Let's go." She turned and didn't wait to see if he was going to follow. He tossed the destroyed cup into the trash and walked after her.

They went down the stairs to the lower garage where Perring had parked her sedan earlier after spending several hours at the hospital dealing with Houston and the fallout of his arrest. She had dropped him off at the precinct prior and left him to sit and wait while she went through the necessary steps. When they climbed inside she started the car but made no move to put it in gear. Liam waited, picking at the drops of sap that still clung to the skin of his neck.

"You're an asshole."

"Thanks, but you already told me that."

"That was the most irresponsible and reckless thing I've ever seen on duty."

"Tearing the felt on the pool table or breaking his hand?"

She gave him a cold stare. "If I'd known that was what you were planning, I would've never—"

"Yeah and we never would've known what really happened," Liam said.

"That doesn't excuse what you did."

"The purest form of truth is found in violence." He looked down at his hands, rubbing his knuckles. "Is Houston pressing charges?"

Perring gritted her teeth, then grabbed the rapidly dwindling pack of cigarettes. "No. He's more concerned with the charges of conspiracy, obstruction of justice, and making false statements we're slapping on him." She lit a cigarette and inhaled deeply before cracking her window.

"What did you tell the hospital staff about his injuries?"

"The official report says he was resisting arrest."

"Thank you," Liam said. Perring refused to look at him. Instead she smoked, exhaling at an angle out the window. "I knew he wasn't going to talk. And he was threatening you."

"I can take care of myself, thanks."

Liam smiled. "I know, but I felt threatened."

"Bullshit." Perring reached into her coat pocket and pulled out a plastic bag containing his straight razor. "Here. Forensics is done with this. They're keeping your gun for a while longer though."

"Thanks," Liam said, opening and closing the blade before tucking it away.

"Odd thing to carry."

"Not for a barber."

"You're a barber?"

"No, but if you need a haircut I could probably help you out."

"Asshole."

He watched the rain fall outside of the open garage entrance, its meteoric dance in the puddles. "It was my father's. He passed it down to me."

"So he was the barber."

"Yeah."

"Was he pissed that you didn't follow in his footsteps?"

"No. He was proud of me being a cop. Cried when I graduated the academy."

Perring nodded. "Wish my dad would've been like that."

"He didn't approve of your choice in careers?"

"You could say that. I'm not sure he ever spent a full week inside the law. Told me if I became a cop to consider myself an orphan. Needless to say I don't get a card on my birthday."

Liam appraised her out of the corner of his eye but saw no change in her demeanor. He looked forward again and said, "What did Caulston have to say?"

"When they first brought him in he wouldn't say anything but I kept talking to him, goading him a little. He finally broke and admitted that he paid Houston the money, said he was glad Dickson was dead. Probably by tonight we'll have the bank transaction record to back it up." Perring shook her head. "Damn him. The old bigot let his hatred cloud all reason. If he hadn't bribed Houston, Jenner would still be alive right now and so would his mother. The chief said there's going to be a full inquiry into the shooting. He thinks it will be open and shut, but the race issue will be unavoidable."

"Racism is the whole problem here. Jenner was blamed after Alexandra's suicide, not only because he was her boyfriend, but because he was black. If he'd been white the resentment wouldn't have followed him as long. Caulston set this whole thing off, but the groundwork was laid a long time ago."

Perring nodded. "Yeah."

"Does Owen know yet?"

"I called Mills. He's standing in as task force leader until I get back. He said he'd relay it to Owen."

"And there hasn't been any more contact with the kidnapper?"

"None. And the search for the IP address came back with nothing."

"Okay." Liam brought his hand up and began tapping his forehead with a finger. "I think it's obvious who we should speak to next."

"Charlie said he wasn't able to get anything concrete on Marshall Davis's whereabouts. He was registered at a halfway house a month ago but nothing since. He's checking with one of our informants now. I didn't mention it before, but an ounce of cocaine was found in Dade Erickson's nightstand."

"I'd wager his good friend Marshall Davis sold it to him."

"Exactly."

"Was Erickson's phone checked for Davis's number?" Liam said.

"Yeah. So far there's nothing labeled with his name. Erickson must've been erasing the calls after he made them. I'm having his phone records sent over as soon as they're available." Perring drew in one last lungful of smoke before tossing her cigarette butt out the window. "What a cluster fuck. If I don't get an official reprimand for this case it'll be a miracle."

"There's worse things than reprimands."

"Easy for you to say."

"No. Not easy."

She gazed at him for a moment before dropping her eyes to the crumpled cigarette pack. "Rex would give me unending shit if he knew I was smoking again."

"I won't tell him if you don't," Liam said, giving her a small smile.

She returned it. "Deal."

His stomach rumbled and he placed a hand over it. "I hate to be a pain in the ass, but I need to eat."

"Should've had breakfast when I offered."

"Sounds good now."

"There's a place a few blocks away—" Perring began, but her cell phone rang, cutting her off. "Perring," she answered. She listened for a long time, her face darkening. "He's sure? Okay, I'll go check it out. Thanks." She hung up and placed the phone in her lap. "The office just got a call from a pawn store owner downtown."

"Yeah?"

"He says he recognized Valerie's picture on TV this afternoon."

Liam sat forward. "From where?"

"He says that she's been coming to his store for two years."

⌣

Dusk layered the city in shadow as they drove, rain beading and rolling off the windshield. The pawnshop was on a side street attached to a bank, its brick front matching seamlessly with the financial institution. A sign reading *Jewelry-Cash-Gold* was illuminated in flowing script above the doorway.

"Doesn't look like a pawnshop at all," Liam said as Perring parked directly in front of the entrance.

"Good part of town. You should see some of the other places."

An odor of dust as well as a pleasant, electronic chiming met them as they stepped inside. The shop was simple but elegant, its walls a deep burgundy lit by sconces as well as a crystal chandelier hanging from a high ceiling. Glass cases lined three sides of the room. A velvet-covered table was positioned at one corner of the cases and several shining bracelets were draped across an angled display. Behind the table a man read a paperback novel, the cover bent around the back. He had a shock of gray hair, slicked straight back from a tall forehead and a long nose holding up a pair of bifocals. He glanced up as they entered and placed the book beneath the table. Then he was on his feet approaching them, a warm smile gracing his aging features.

"Good evening. How may I help you?"

Perring drew out her ID. "Mr. Sorenson?"

"Yes," the man said, examining her badge before clasping his hands before him like a child.

"I'm detective Denise Perring and this is Mr. Dempsey. You called the station a short time ago saying you recognized Valerie Farrow's picture?"

Sorenson's face blanched and he nodded. "Yes, I'm afraid I did." His voice had a soft twangy, southern lilt to it.

"You're the proprietor, Mr. Sorenson?"

"Yes. I have two other staff but they normally work in the mornings."

"Can you tell us how you recognized Valerie?"

"She's been coming in here for nearly two years I'd say."

"And what were the purposes of her visits?"

"She was a window shopper. She'd come in every other day or so and walk around the store looking in all the cases. She seemed very interested in our jewelry. We have one of the largest selections in the city you know."

"I see. You say she came in every other day?"

"That's right."

Perring shot a look at Liam. "And you're sure it was this woman?" She took out a folded picture of Valerie and held it out to Sorenson. The store owner adjusted his glasses and gazed at the photo for a few seconds before nodding.

"That's her. Such a pretty woman. Is it true what they're saying on the television? That she was taken from her house?"

"I'm sorry but I'm not at liberty to discuss the details of the case."

Liam began walking around the store. He bent at the waist and scanned the rows and rows of diamonds glittering in necklaces, rings, watches. He moved down the display, pausing before a section set off by itself. He stayed there for a beat before returning to Perring and Sorenson.

"Such a shock for something like this to happen." Sorenson was saying. "Even though we're not a small town it's always frightening to hear news like this."

"What time of the day would Valerie typically stop by?" Liam asked.

Sorenson regarded him. "I would say it varied a little but normally she'd come in around ten in the morning. Sometimes a hair before noon."

"Did she ever speak to anyone?" Liam said.

"No. That was the curious thing. She'd come in and say hello, but that was about all. She'd stay for maybe ten minutes and then leave."

"She never asked to try anything on?"

"No, nothing."

"When was the last time she came by your store?" Perring asked.

"I would say it was last week, maybe Tuesday."

"And she hasn't been by since?"

"No, ma'am. I always wondered about her. She had a skittish look to her, you know? Almost like she was afraid of being around people.

She had a hard time holding eye contact whenever we'd ask her if she needed help. She always said no, of course."

"Was there ever anyone with her on these visits?" Liam asked.

"No. She was alone every time."

Liam glanced around the room. "You have a very nice business, Mr. Sorenson."

"Why thank you."

"Do you purchase items from the public?"

Sorenson gave a small frown. "We do, but it's a very low percentage of our retail supply. Mostly we buy wholesale. Fair-trade diamonds and gold, of course. Like I said, we have one of the largest selections in the city."

Liam nodded and looked at Perring who gave Sorenson a tight smile and held out her hand. "Thank you very much for your call and cooperating. Would it be a problem to get the footage of the last time Mrs. Farrow was in the store?" Perring asked nodding at the small camera mounted in the corner of the room.

"Absolutely. I'll have one of the employees e-mail it over."

"That's perfect. Could we get a business card in case we have more questions for you?"

"Of course," Sorenson said, pulling a beige card from his pocket.

"If you remember anything else about Mrs. Farrow's visits, don't hesitate to contact me," Perring said, exchanging his card with one of her own.

"I will. Thank you, detective."

Perring began heading for the door but stopped when Liam didn't follow. He glanced at her and tipped his head toward the street. "I'll be just a minute." Perring's mouth tightened as if she were about to say something when Liam held out his hand. "Only a minute, I promise." She gave him a withering look before moving toward the door and out into the rain.

As the chime sounded again, Liam turned back to the store owner, fixing him with a smile.

"I apologize, but I have a few more questions for you."

Five minutes later Liam stepped into the evening air that was gradually clearing of rain. The streetlights were beginning to turn on, coating the street with a pale orange glow that reflected wetly on every surface it touched. When he climbed inside Perring's sedan she had the heat going and he held his hands out to it.

"What the hell was that about?" she asked.

"Nothing."

"Bullshit nothing."

"I promise I didn't break his hand."

"Anyone ever tell you you're an asshole?"

"Only you."

Perring put the car in drive and cruised down the street before turning in the direction of the lake and lower roads.

"This adds a whole new dimension to the case," Liam said.

"You mean Valerie not staying at home every day like Owen said she was?"

"Yep. If she was leaving the house and going to that jewelry store . . ."

"Then where else was she going?" Perring said, eyes not leaving the road.

"Exactly. Sorenson said that she started coming in about two years ago. That's the same time Valerie's therapist said her overall condition began to improve."

"Well maybe that's the connection. She got the courage to go outdoors and didn't want to tell anyone for fear of failing and regressing."

Liam frowned. "Doesn't fit though. She stays inside for how many years, and then suddenly decides to go for a drive? Makes no sense."

"So what do you think she was doing?"

Liam shook his head and glanced out the window. "At a jewelry store? I have no idea. We need to talk to Owen."

They rode in silence for a time before Perring shifted in her seat and threw him a look.

"Seriously though, what did you say to him?"

"It's just a theory as of yet. I won't say it out loud since I don't want to jinx it."

Perring huffed. "Well please clue me in if anything pans out."

Liam smiled. "I will."

Perring's cell chimed and she checked it, glancing in the rearview mirror before pulling to a stop at the curb. "Charlie got a tip on who Davis has been running with."

"Yeah?"

"A guy named Warren Richard. Looks like he's been in for a couple of small sales of weed, a little meth. It appears that he's been using some of his own product." She turned the phone to him. Richard's picture was from the neck up. He had stringy, dark hair and a hooked nose that curled down to his upper lip. His skin was a pasty white, pocked with meth sores around his mouth.

"Good looking guy. Do we have an address?"

"No, but Charlie said his typical hangout is the Far End Bar on the south side of town. He's been caught dealing outside twice, along with the night club next door."

"Shall we pay him a visit?"

Perring pulled back onto the street and hung a hard right that made Liam's empty stomach cringe. "Let's."

CHAPTER 17

The Far End Bar was a low, slate-colored building with reflective glass set in its front.

Its parking lot was full and several cars were nose to the curb in front of its entrance. As he climbed from the sedan, Liam glanced at the nightclub beside the bar, a place called Zink. A short queue of people waited outside a door guarded by a hulking man wearing a bright yellow security sweatshirt. As he waited for Perring to round the car, he scanned their faces.

"See him?" Perring asked.

"No. Want to wait outside or make a scene in the bar?"

"We don't have time for niceties. Let's go in and get the bastard."

When they were still a dozen steps away from the entrance, the door opened, pouring out a Willie Nelson song along with two men. One was tall and sported a tight, blond crew cut, his face down and lost in shadow. The second was shorter, wearing a faded leather jacket and a sneer on his thin mouth below a hooked nose. Richard was in the middle of saying something to his companion when he spotted them.

He froze, hands sliding into his jacket pockets as his narrow-set eyes flitted from Perring to Liam.

"Warren Richard?" Perring said.

Richard bolted, shoving the taller man at them like a piece of furniture.

Richard's friend tripped and fell toward Liam who caught him before he could connect with the sidewalk. Perring was already in motion, her hand on her weapon as she ran. Richard dashed to the corner of the bar and vanished behind it.

"Get your fucking hands off of me," the man Liam had caught growled. He thrashed in Liam's grip and took a wild swing at him that breezed over the top of his head. Liam kicked him in the side of the knee and pushed him to the ground as he dropped. Without waiting to see where the man landed, Liam jogged to the corner of the bar to see Perring in pursuit of Richard, his lead widening as he ran up the street and cut diagonally to an alleyway.

Liam sprinted across an intersection and onto the next sidewalk.

A couple walking their dog stood aside as he passed, the furry mop on the end of the leash lunging at him with a snarl. Liam sidestepped the dog and kept going, a picket fence flowing by on his right.

His feet hammered the concrete and he didn't break stride as he came to the next corner and curved right, the pavement rising beneath him in a steep hill.

A dry cleaner's brightly lit windows shone across the street, a row of apartments on the opposite side. His legs began to burn with the incline of the ground, his breath a metronome in his ears. Perring shouted again somewhere to the right and he poured on more speed.

Richard exploded out of the alley ahead of Liam and threw a small bag of something beneath a parked car without looking. The leather jacket flapped behind him like a cape and Liam closed the gap between them as Richard darted to the left between two apartment buildings. The heavy, sodden grass soaked Liam's shoes as he poured on the last reserves of speed and reached out, snagging the waving hem of Richard's coat.

Richard cried out and tried to turn but Liam kept moving, whipping the other man around by his jacket. Richard stumbled and fell as Liam released his hold.

The drug dealer slammed into the solid brick of the nearest building and rebounded, air whooshing from him like a punctured balloon as Perring emerged from the gloom.

"Didn't you hear her yelling stop?" Liam asked as Richard straightened. The other man drew something from his jacket pocket and rushed forward without warning, a flash of silver on his knuckles. Liam ducked, throwing a short hook into Richard's ribs. The man groaned but swung his fist backward. Liam caught his arm and locked it tight to his own body.

"Brass knuckles," Liam said, twisting Richard's wrist until the man bellowed and his hand sprung open, releasing the hold on the silver weapon. Liam peeled it from his fingers and dropped it to the ground. "That's cheating."

"Hands up, Warren," Perring said, covering him with her handgun.

"Let me go!" Richard yelled, twisting away from Liam's grip. "The fuck you want with me?"

"We have questions for you," Perring said, stepping closer.

"I ain't telling you shit."

"You better start talking, or we're going to go get that bag of meth from underneath the car down the street and haul your ass into the station," Perring said.

"I don't know nothin' about any drugs."

"Now that's a double negative," Liam said. "So you must know something."

"Fuck you, pig."

"Oh I'm not a cop. She is though and I'd suggest you tell her what she needs to know." The same black energy was running through him again. It hummed in his ears like a broken live wire. His fingers twitched.

"We need to find Marshall Davis. Where is he?" Perring asked.

"Who?"

"Don't bullshit me, Warren. You've been seen together and booked together. We need to find him."

"Don't know who you're talking about. I don't know any Davis."

"You want to do this the hard way? I'll go collect those drugs down there and then I'll haul in your buddy you were going to sell to back at the bar. This is probably your third or fourth offense so I'll be more than happy to ask the DA to lock your ass away for the next three years. But I hate paperwork and I'm sure you hate going to jail, so let's cut this shit and start talking."

Richard's mouth became an even thinner line. "Fuck you, dyke cop."

Liam's hand flashed out and Richard's head rocked back. The younger man brought his fingers to his mouth and they came away dark with blood.

"You fucking hit me! You can't do that! That's police brutality!"

Liam stalked forward. "Told you, I'm not a cop."

Richard threw a punch and Liam lowered his head, taking the blow on the crown of his skull. He heard the other man grunt with pain before he grabbed Richard by the throat and slammed him to the ground.

"Get offa me!"

"You know there's an old wives' tale about getting a bird to speak," Liam said, holding Richard down as he climbed on top of him. With a quick movement he pinned one of the man's arms down with his knee and drew out the straight razor. "They used to say a bird's tongue wasn't shaped correctly to form words. So you know what the answer was?" Liam snapped the blade open and it caught the dull light between the buildings. "They used to split their tongues."

Richard's eyes widened as Liam leaned forward, bringing the razor closer.

"Liam?" Perring said.

"The fuck you doing, man?" Richard said, struggling against Liam's weight. He tried to buck his hips upward, but Liam moved with him, settling more firmly on his chest. With his free hand he grabbed Richard's chin and forced his lips apart.

Liam shoved the straight razor into Richard's mouth.

The younger man's eyes bulged and he made a hoarse mewling in the back of his throat as Liam leaned closer.

"I wouldn't struggle too much, bud, might cut yourself. Or maybe you're like the birds and you need your tongue split. Maybe then you'll talk."

"Liam. Don't," Perring said from behind him. He squinted at Richard and turned the razor over on the drug dealer's tongue so that the edge pressed downward into the soft muscle. Richard moaned a word and Liam tilted his head.

"What was that?" Slowly he withdrew the blade from between the man's bloodied teeth.

"I said I'll tell you!" Richard yelled.

"Start talking," Liam said.

"I don't know where Marshall is. We usually meet up a couple times a week."

"When did you last see him?" Liam asked.

"Three days ago."

"Where?"

"At my girlfriend's apartment. He said he was meeting someone for a deal that night. I haven't seen him since."

"Who was he meeting?" Perring asked.

"I don't know." Liam tilted his head and held the razor in front of Richard's face again. "I swear, man, I don't know! He said he was doing a big deal, that was all he told me. I never got involved with his coke shit, he wouldn't let me in."

"Where was the deal supposed to happen?" Liam said.

"I don't know, I swear, I swear to God."

"Who's his connection in town for his stuff?" Richard shook his head slightly. "Okay." Liam pushed the razor back into the other man's mouth, wiggling it between his clenched teeth.

"Okay! Okay! Shit! Guy named Milo, I don't know his last name. He's big time from what Davis told me. Doesn't mess around with smalls like me."

"Where's he deal out of?"

"Marshall went to a place down by the lake on sixth before, big house made outta white stone. That's all I know."

Tears streamed out the corners of Richard's eyes. Liam stared at him for another beat, then stood, releasing him from the ground.

"Get the fuck out of here," Perring said. "And if you get busted for dealing again I will make it my personal mission to lock you away for the longest the law will allow. Is that clear?" Richard got to his feet and nodded, his tongue running over his teeth and across his lips again and again. "Go!" Perring pointed at the far end of the buildings and Richard spun, tripping once before sprinting out of sight.

"What the hell was that?" Perring asked.

"An interrogation."

"That was torture."

"I didn't hurt him. Not really."

Perring stared at him and shook her head before picking up the brass knuckles. "Let's go."

They walked down the street to the car that Richard had dumped his drugs beneath. Liam knelt and retrieved the small baggie full of white crystals, handing it to Perring as he stood up. They didn't speak again until they were inside the sedan.

"Davis disappeared the same night Valerie was taken," Liam said.

Perring lit her last cigarette and crumpled the empty pack before tossing it into the back seat. "Then we're looking for a corpse."

"Unless he's the one that took Valerie."

"He's a low-level coke dealer. I don't think he'd be capable of pulling all this off."

"I agree, but if he was desperate he might try it. I really hope it is him."

"Why?"

"Because then the person we're dealing with isn't as formidable as he seems." Liam steepled his fingers before him. "But on the other side of the coin if it's not Davis, then he's number two in the countdown."

"Yep."

"And if that's true, who's number one?"

Perring glanced at him. "We can't mention this to Owen."

"He needs to know."

"What? That his wife isn't going to be exchanged for the money? That she's going to be the final victim of a psychopath?"

"It's a pattern. It has been from the beginning. The deaths aren't random, they have meaning."

"And that is?"

"I don't know. There's something symbolic in the way Erickson and Rowe were killed. Erickson was burned from the inside out, Rowe was pinned down and drowned, slowly, I might add."

Perring sighed, rubbing her forehead. "We need a goddamned break here. We need the bastard to screw up. There's no motive linking Erickson, Rowe, Davis, and Valerie other than they graduated together."

"What about someone who wanted to hurt them for the beating they gave Dickson? How about Dickson's father? Does anyone know where he is?"

"I had someone check his whereabouts after we found out about the assault. He's a gas station attendant in North Carolina and was verified at work for the last week."

They fell quiet for a long time as Perring guided the car through the dark streets. Liam caught sight of Superior's vast surface between buildings, the waves like dorsal fins rising in succession.

"What about this Milo that Richard mentioned? Know anything about him?"

"Milo Silva. Rumored to be an exchange point for drugs coming and going out of the ports. He's never been brought up on charges, though."

"He might be able to tell us something about Davis."

"I have the feeling he's going to be leery of talking to the cops. Not a person that likes being put in the limelight whatsoever."

"I can be persuasive."

"Not with this guy. Every person in that house is bound to be armed. You'll get us both killed."

"I didn't say I was going to shove a knife in his mouth."

Perring sighed and turned onto another street. "I must be out of my mind."

"I think you're finally coming around."

"Asshole."

Liam smiled.

CHAPTER 18

The house was made of white, rough-hewn stone and looked as if it had been carved out of bleached bone in the low light.

Liam and Perring stood on the front stoop beneath a heavy awning held up by intricately carved columns and balustrades. Lights were aglow in nearly every window of the sprawling house and soft music trailed from behind the heavy oak door.

"Remember, we have zilch on this guy, no leverage whatsoever. Don't try anything stupid," Perring said as she rang the doorbell.

"We're just here to get some info."

"You make it sound so easy."

He was about to reply when the door opened. A burly man with thick sideburns and wearing an expensive suit glowered out at them. Liam noted the slight bulge of a pistol beneath his left armpit.

"Yes?" the man said.

"Hello, I'm Detective Denise Perring with the Duluth PD, and this is Mr. Dempsey. We were wondering if we could have a word with Mr. Silva?"

"I'm sorry but he's indisposed at the moment. I'd be happy to give him a message."

"We really need to speak with him tonight," Perring said, trying a polite smile.

"I'm sorry. Now if you'll excuse me . . ." The man began to shut the door but Liam put his foot in the way.

"Tell Mr. Silva it concerns a business associate of his that's recently gone missing." Liam kept his gaze level and calm as the man scowled and shrugged his large shoulders. "I'm sure he'll be interested."

The guard shifted his eyes between them. "Wait here."

"We'll wait here," Liam said, talking over the other man. The guard gave him one last look before shutting the door in his face.

"That went well," Perring said, turning to go.

"What are you doing?"

"Um, he's not coming back. We just got the not-so-polite brush off."

"He'll let us in."

"No way."

"Bet you a pack of cigarettes."

Perring returned to the doorstep beside him. "You're on."

They waited for well over a minute, no sounds other than the music filtering through the door.

"Told you," Perring said, beginning to move away again.

"Wait." Liam pointed at the door and a moment later the guard opened it and waved a hand at the interior of the house.

"Mr. Silva will see you."

Liam stepped inside, throwing a grin over one shoulder at Perring.

The interior of the house was lavish, but in an elegant way that didn't shout money, it whispered it. A curving staircase grew from the foyer to an upper hall leading to the second floor. Dozens of oil paintings graced the walls and dark, antique furniture contrasted against the white marble floor that was polished to a mirror finish.

"This way please," the guard said, leading them to the right down a short corridor that opened into a sitting room complete with a mahogany bar and a dozen overstuffed leather chairs beside a crackling fire within a large hearth. "He will be with you shortly."

Without a look back, the guard left them, the clack of his dress shoes echoing back off the stone floor.

"How did you know that would work?" Perring asked when they were alone.

"Curiosity. No matter what type of crime, the ones at the top always want to know what's going on. Thought I'd see if I could pique his interest. Guess it worked."

Footsteps came from the hall and a second later a man appeared wearing a dark pair of dress slacks and a wine-colored, silk shirt. He was tall and well-built with ebony hair swept back from a prominent brow. He was clean-shaven with a dimpled chin and a long nose set below a pair of piecing dark eyes. He paused in the doorway before continuing toward the bar.

"Detectives, good evening. Can I offer you a drink?" Silva's voice was cultured and low with only a hint of a Portuguese accent.

"Absolutely," Liam said, stepping up to the bar.

"No thank you," Perring said, standing beside him.

"What would be your poison, detective?" Silva gestured to the bottles lined up in neat rows.

"What's the most expensive Scotch you've got?" Liam said.

Silva smiled. "That would be the Bowmore twenty-five year."

"Sounds great."

Silva poured two glasses halfway full of amber liquid. "Tell me, what have I done to earn a visit from two of Duluth's finest?"

"I'm actually just a police consultant," Liam said.

"Ah yes, you're both working the Farrow case I assume. Such a sad turn of events for the potential mayor."

"A man such as yourself must be interested in who becomes mayor."

"Politics concern me very little. Such a roundabout way of getting things accomplished. I prefer the direct approach. Besides, politicians bore me." Silva set the glass before Liam on the bar before smelling his own and taking a sip from it. "Sometimes I forget how good that is." Liam took a drink, noting the excellence of the liquor before glancing around the room.

"Very sorry to disturb you this evening," Liam said. "Sounds like you're entertaining guests."

Silva smiled like a shark, revealing very white teeth. "Just a few close friends. But these gatherings can get tiresome."

"I bet."

"Tiresome, just like this conversation. Let us dispense with the politeness of adversaries dancing around one another. What do you want?" Silva said, all traces of humor gone, his face placid and unyielding.

"We'd like to know about Marshall Davis," Perring said.

"Marshall Davis, Marshall Davis, hmm . . . name's not ringing a bell."

"Interesting," Liam said, taking another swig of Scotch. "His contacts sure know you."

"With all due respect, Mr. Dempsey, I don't think you know what you're doing."

"Yeah, you might be right, but I'm guessing the fact that we came here looking for Davis sent a little chill up your spine, didn't it? I mean, how else would we know where to find you?"

"My name and address are in the phone book. I run two successful hauling agencies as well as four art galleries in three states. I'm not exactly hiding. Now, if you'll excuse me I need to be getting back to my guests." Silva set his empty glass down and began moving toward the hall.

"Meant to compliment you earlier on your house as well as your taste in art. Is that an original Caillebotte on the stairway?"

Silva paused at the door and turned back to them. "You're correct. Now I'll give you both thirty seconds to leave my house before I have you escorted off my property, at gunpoint if necessary."

"No need for that," Liam said, swallowing the last of the Scotch. "Wow, that's really good. You've built quite a kingdom for yourself here, Milo. It would be such a shame if someone tarnished it with accusations, and it would be even worse if there were evidence to back them up."

Silva took a step back into the room, the predatory smile gracing his features again. "I'm sorry, Mr. Dempsey, are you threatening me?"

"No, not at all. We just want to know what you can tell us about Marshall Davis, because we will catch up to him sooner or later, with or without your help, and when we do we could ask him all sorts of questions. Some of them might concern you and your business endeavors." Liam set his glass down hard on the bar and the sound made Silva blink. "But of course if you help us now I'm guessing your name won't even come up when we find Davis. Right Detective?"

Perring smiled. "Right."

Silva's jaw clenched and released. "What do you want to know?"

"Where is Davis?" Perring asked.

"I don't know."

"Is he working for you?"

"No. I employed him very briefly a number of years ago but his service was . . . unsatisfactory, so I let him go."

"When's the last time you saw him?" Liam said.

Silva hesitated. "Two weeks ago."

"Where?"

"Here. He came looking for a job but I sent him away."

"What did he say to you?" Perring said.

"Nothing more than the trivial ramblings of an addict."

"So he seemed desperate?" Liam asked.

"Yes. He looked strung out and twitchy. When I told him I had no work for him, he became unstable and had to be shown the door, which is what I insist for you both as well." Silva motioned to the foyer and a moment later the side-burned guard appeared. "Horace, will you escort these fine people out?"

"Yes sir."

"One last question," Liam said before Silva could turn away. "How were you two introduced?"

Silva shifted his gaze from Liam to Perring and back again. "Traz," he said, then moved swiftly out of sight down the hall. Horace approached them both, fingers flexing into fists and relaxing again.

"We'll show ourselves out, thanks," Liam said, walking past the bodyguard. Horace followed them to the door and shut it hard behind them once they were outside. The evening air was cooler, and as they made their way to the car several dead leaves zipped past them, their flight like that of wounded birds spiraling to the ground.

"You owe me a pack of cigarettes," Perring said once they were inside the sedan.

"What? We got inside and spoke to him."

"Yeah but you just made a deal with a major drug importer that I don't know if I can hold up. So, cigarettes."

"I didn't have a choice. He wasn't going to give us anything without a little pressure. To me it sounds like Davis was pretty desperate for a fix. He must've been completely out of money."

"Probably."

"What did Silva mean by 'Traz'?"

"Monica Traz was the big fish in the waters around here before Silva came to town. She was brought up on charges for drug trafficking, extortion, and even murder. Nothing held up in court and the cases were dropped. About twelve or thirteen years ago Traz and twenty of her closest crew were found on her private yacht, anchored four miles offshore in Superior. They'd been hacked to death with machetes."

"Shit."

"Yeah, it was brutal. But it was also a message. About two months later Silva started showing up on our radar."

"So you think Silva was responsible?"

"Definitely. But once again, no leads, no evidence."

"So what did he mean by Davis being introduced by Traz?"

"Not sure."

"Maybe Davis was working for Traz and sold her out to Silva?"

"That's a possibility, but again, how does that help us now? How's it connected to Valerie's disappearance?"

Liam tapped his temple. "I don't know."

Perring put the car in gear and pulled away from the curb. They were quiet for some time before she glanced at him.

"Listen, there's a change of shift coming for the task force in a half-hour, and since Mills is going home for some sleep, I need to be there. You can get something to eat and maybe some rest."

"Sounds good." Liam watched the businesses slide past in the murky light, their windows darkened save for the occasional advertisement lit by neon. "Can I ask you a favor?"

"After all the shit you've pulled tonight? You're asking me for a favor? Really?"

"You said you're having Erickson's phone records sent over, right?"

"Yeah."

"Could you have any information on Alexandra's suicide as well as Davis's background sent along with it?"

"Why?"

"I want to read over it."

"Why?"

"Because you were right."

"About what?"

"The itch never left."

Liam didn't have to look at her to see the tired smirk spreading across her face.

CHAPTER 19

Owen was in the living room, standing at the picture window when they came in, a drink loosely held in one hand.

"Where the hell have you been?" His tone was sharp, his fingers shaking as he set the drink down. When he spotted Liam behind Perring there was a split second when Liam couldn't read his expression, then Owen moved to him, grasping his arm. "Are you okay? I heard rumblings of something happening at Rowe's. They said you were involved somehow."

"Fine. And to answer your question, we were working to get Valerie back."

Owen eyed him for a moment before dropping his gaze. "Sorry about my tone. I didn't hear a thing for hours and then one of the task force members tells me that Jenner and Detective Sanders have been shot. Is Jenner dead?"

Perring nodded. "He was killed after wounding Detective Sanders."

"But he didn't have Valerie?"

"No."

"And there was no sign that she'd been there?"

"No."

Owen turned from them, his long-fingered hands clenching and releasing. "Damn it." He stopped by the window before facing them again. "And Caulston's in custody?"

"Yes," Perring said. "He's being detained for conspiracy and obstruction of justice."

Owen put a palm to his forehead, pressing it there as if he were afraid his skull might come apart. "My God, what's happening?"

"We're not sure yet," Liam said. "But we need to tell you something that might come as a shock."

"After the last two days? Go ahead."

"A pawn store owner identified Valerie today."

"What do you mean *identified*?"

"He called in after seeing the broadcast this afternoon. She'd been to his store, Owen. She'd been going there for almost two years."

Owen's face shriveled into lines of disbelief. "What? No. He was wrong. It couldn't have been Valerie. She was here every day while I went to work. It's not possible."

"He identified her twice," Perring said. "He called it in to the station and when I showed him the picture of Valerie he confirmed it again."

"What pawnshop? Why would she go there?" Owen came forward to perch on the arm of the couch.

"It's the higher end store on Second Street attached to the First National Bank," Perring said. "And we were hoping you could tell us why she was going there."

"What? How would I . . . I had no idea she was leaving the house. I still think there's been a mistake. Maybe someone that looked like her . . ."

"He said he'd seen her personally come in to the store every other day for the past two years," Liam said. "I don't know what this means but we're dealing with something different now that we know Valerie wasn't housebound."

"I . . ." Owen pressed his hand to his head again. "This doesn't make any sense."

In the dining room the phone began to ring.

Liam locked eyes first with Owen then with Perring as Heller stepped into the doorway.

"Mr. Farrow? This could be the call," Heller said.

"Okay, stay calm and collected no matter what you hear," Perring said as they hurried to the dining room, the phone trilling again on the end of the table. Two task force members besides Heller were already at their computers, headsets clamped over their ears. One of them made a twirling gesture to Perring and pointed at the phone. Liam grabbed a vacant headset from the place beside Heller and put it on. Owen approached the phone and picked it up, giving everyone in the room a look before hitting the Talk button.

"Hello?"

"Mr. Farrow, I assume you know who this is?" The same mangled voice growled in Liam's headset.

"Yes."

"Good. Then I'll start off by saying to the officers listening to this call that it's useless to try and pinpoint my location. I'm using a disposable phone that they will find once this call is finished. By that time, I'll be long since departed. Mr. Farrow, I trust you've gathered the two million dollars I've asked for?"

Owen let out a shaky breath. "Yes."

"Good. Understand that if there is any deviation from what I'm about to tell you, your wife will be killed in the most unpleasant way I can imagine, which is saying something."

"You bastard," Owen hissed.

"Let's dispense with the name calling, otherwise I'll have to resort to other methods to get the conversation back on track." There was a pause then Valerie's voice rang out in a short scream followed by several low sobs.

"Don't hurt her!" Owen yelled. "Please, don't hurt her."

"You will deposit the money in a canvas bag and securely attach a neodymium magnet, six inches in diameter, to its top in plain sight. You will then place the bag in the center of the deck of the fishing boat, *The Mare*, which you will contract to leave the harbor at exactly eight p.m. tomorrow evening. The boat will be driven by its captain to forty-seven degrees north and ninety degrees west, then he will receive new coordinates, which is where the money and your wife will be exchanged. If law enforcement is spotted anywhere in the vicinity before or during the exchange, your wife will die. Do you understand the instructions?"

"Yes."

"Good. And one final note. Liam Dempsey, I'm sure you're listening to this. If I see your face again before the exchange, Valerie will die."

The line went dead and Perring looked at Heller who nodded quickly. "We've got a trace. He's at the Duluth East High School."

"That's only a few blocks from here," Owen said.

"Get some cars headed that way," Perring said.

"On it," Heller said.

Liam placed the headset on the table and surveyed everyone in the room. They all met his gaze, then looked away. Owen twisted the cordless phone in his hands, the plastic creaking as he worked it back and forth. Liam rose and went to him, taking the phone from his grip.

"That's where we went to school," Owen said, lowering his head.

"I figured as much," Liam said.

"The bastard's taunting us. Taunting me."

"He's enjoying himself. We need to stick to the plan and we'll get Valerie back safe."

Owen shook his head and when he looked up again a glossy sheen of tears covered his eyes. "What if something happens to her? I couldn't . . ." He seemed to run out of breath and Liam guided him out of the dining room to a chair beside the couch.

"You're doing the best you can right now," Liam said. "You were calm on the phone and now we know when this will all be over. By tomorrow night Valerie will be back in this house."

Owen rocked in the chair like an overgrown child waking from a nightmare. "I keep seeing her, somewhere in the dark with that psycho. She's cold and afraid and I don't want that to be her last moments. I'd gladly take her place."

"I know you would. Everyone does." Liam squeezed his friend's shoulder, trying to pour reassurance into the other man merely through touch. They waited in silence for the next ten minutes until Perring approached them.

"The responding officers found the phone that was used in the school parking lot. We're going to try and get something off the school's camera system but the corner where the phone was discarded was very dark."

Liam frowned. "He must've been driving a car since Valerie was in the background. He had to have driven through one of the well-lit areas to get there. The cameras will have gotten the vehicle on tape."

"In theory," Perring said. "I've already got someone contacting the owner of *The Mare* to arrange the exchange tomorrow. We're also going to question him about any suspicious activity within the last few weeks. Maybe someone hanging around the marina or asking strange questions about the boats."

"The coordinates that he gave, where are they exactly?" Liam asked.

"Over fifty miles out in the middle of Superior."

"What?"

"I had Heller check it twice. It's far enough away from land that a boat, even a small one, will be noticed."

"But if he's making the exchange there, he'll have to be in a boat." Liam tilted his head. "Where the hell is he going to go once the deal is done? There'll be nowhere to run."

"I'm guessing he'll be in something fast, something that he thinks can outrun our boats," Perring said. "I'm arranging for an observation drone to be brought in from the Air Force base in the morning. We'll use that to keep watch on the exchange and have a helicopter ready for pursuit if it comes to that. We'll also have SWAT members hidden on *The Mare* so the moment that Valerie is safe, they'll take the bastard down."

"I don't want her in any more danger than necessary," Owen said. "If he spots something he doesn't like . . ."

"I can assure you that she would be in more danger if we didn't take these precautions," Perring said.

"Why the magnet?" Liam asked after a pause.

"Heller did a quick search and it seems that a neodymium magnet is extremely powerful. One of that size may disrupt a tracking device or any type of electronics within the bag."

Liam paced to the window and back, picking at the last of the sap still stuck to his neck. "He knows who I am," he finally said in a quiet voice.

"Yeah, you're right. How could that be?" Owen said, straightening in his chair.

Perring sighed and dug in her pockets. Liam saw the disappointment on her face and knew she was reaching for a cigarette that wasn't there. "I don't know."

"Yes you do," Liam said. Perring looked at him, freezing as she drew out a pack of gum. "We need to tell him, Perring."

"Tell me what?" Owen asked.

Perring's face was a mask of stone, eyes unblinking. She held the expression, flicking her gaze between Liam and Owen until it finally crumbled and she looked down to the floor.

"We have reason to believe that the individual holding your wife captive is responsible for two murders and another possible disappearance in the last three days."

"What? You mean there was another besides Dade?" Owen asked.

Perring shot a venomous look at Liam but nodded. "Yes. Gage Rowe was killed this afternoon and Marshall Davis's location is unknown."

Owen swayed in his seat and Liam wondered if he might topple out of it. "They're dead?" he asked in a faint voice.

"Yes. Now it's obvious you know about Erickson's murder, but can you tell us anything about a connection between the other two men and Valerie? We know that you all attended high school together."

Owen shook his head. "I told you. Dade, Gage, and Marshall all ran together, but they weren't friends with me or Valerie."

"They ever threaten her or you in any way?" Liam asked.

"No."

"Did they have any enemies they made besides Dickson Jenner or because of the assault they committed against him?" Perring said.

"No."

"Which brings up another question," Liam said. "You told me none of them knew Alexandra but it sounds like the number they did on Jenner after her death was a retaliation of sorts."

Owen ran a hand through his hair. "I don't know, yeah, I suppose they thought they were the knights of the community, taking the law into their own hands. A lot of people believed Jenner was responsible even after Alexandra's death was ruled a suicide."

"So you never heard any rumblings of any other connection between them and Jenner?"

"No, not that I can think of. Why? Are you two trying to tell me something?"

"No. We still think that the person who took Valerie has every intention of trading her for the money. Honestly she wouldn't still be alive if that wasn't the case."

Owen was silent for a moment but when he spoke his voice was low and steady. "I've trusted you both. I've trusted everyone who's working on getting Valerie back. You don't know what's gone through my mind in the last two days, what a future without her looks like. She is my life." He looked at them. "Don't make me regret trusting you."

Liam struggled for something to say but in the end he held his tongue, excusing himself to go clean up. He left them in the solitude of the living room, Owen gazing at the blackened window, Perring hovering between him and her personnel.

The shower was heavenly. Liam turned the water to a near scalding temperature and let it beat against his back. The horizontal scar there always flared bright whenever he was too warm or too cold and this was no exception. He scrubbed at the pinesap on his neck and stared at the tile lining the walk-in shower, letting his thoughts drift. Everything was happening too fast. Events were unfolding like a scroll that had been written years ago, actions and reactions already accounted for and scribed in blood. There was a link between Erickson, Rowe, and Davis, something beyond their ties of friendship. And friendships always have secrets. In this case the secret was something they were being killed for. But what it was might take weeks to become clear. They didn't have weeks. They had hours that were counting down.

The countdown has begun.

Erickson was four. Rowe was three. Davis could be number two. And Valerie . . .

He closed his eyes, letting the water run over his scalp, reminding him with a dull throb of where Richard had struck him. He went back to the moment, pinning the drug dealer to the ground, the razor in his hand, the righteousness flowing through him as if he were a conductor channeling rage from somewhere outside himself. He examined the foreign emotion for a time, approaching it from all sides. He'd never felt that way before, during an investigation. Sure, there had been moments of adrenaline and anxiety as well as jubilation at a discovery, but the feverish burn he felt to inflict pain?

Never.

He didn't want to admit it but it had felt *good* to break Houston's hand, to see the look of terror flood Richard's face as he put the razor in his mouth. It had been exhilarating to know that he'd torn down a barrier full of lies and left the guilty lying in their own misery and fright. But it was more than that, more than exhilaration. What was behind the dark energy was as simple and plain as the waves that beat the shore outside or the wind that pushed them.

It was fear.

Fear was driving him. Fear of the darkness, because he knew what waited there. And when it came for you, there was no fighting it. Fear was pushing him beyond his moral constraints, turning the panic he felt, every time he imagined finding Valerie's lifeless body, into anger that blazed white-hot. It was the fear of who he transposed when he saw her, because it wasn't her face anymore that reflected the pale light of death, it was Dani.

"No," he whispered, and placed his fist against the tiles, pushing hard enough to feel his skin sink into the channels between them.

When the image blurred and faded enough for him to concentrate again, he washed himself and stepped from the shower. He dried off and dressed in fresh clothes that felt soft enough to sleep in. Sleep. The word nearly sent a shiver of pleasure through him but his stomach twisted again with hunger and when he left the bathroom he made his way to the kitchen to find Owen picking at a limp chicken salad.

"Any more of that around here by chance?" Liam asked.

"There's a whole bowl in the fridge. Help yourself."

Liam dished a heaping amount of chicken, lettuce, and cheese onto a plate and sat at the opposite end of the counter. As he began to eat he noticed his handgun resting on top of two file folders partway down the breakfast bar.

"Perring left that for you. She stepped outside to speak with the chief. He dropped by to see how things were going."

Liam nodded. "He's a friend of yours?"

"Everyone's your friend in politics."

"Thought it was the other way around."

"Not when you're trying to get elected."

Liam began to eat and opened the first folder.

A mug shot of Marshall Davis stared out at him, the man's hooded eyes still fogged with whatever substance he was abusing prior to arrest. The edge of a silver crucifix peeked from the top of his collar, only Christ's anguished face and pierced hands visible. Liam scanned the man's legal history. Nearly every charge had to do with some type of illegal drug. Whether it was selling or buying, Davis was an addict through and through. He set aside the folder and opened the second. An array of information on Alexandra's death met him. He chewed slowly as he read, turning page after page of evidence, statements, and finally pictures.

The pictures were always the hardest. At home in his office he kept crime scene photos in a locked drawer for fear of Eric stumbling upon them by accident. The last thing he wanted was for the boy to unintentionally flip through a full-color leaflet depicting crushed skulls, clotted stab wounds, or broken and misshapen bodies of children his age.

Alexandra's pictures were not as gruesome as some he'd seen, but the disturbing air they gave off was, nonetheless, unsettling. There was a collage of shots of her face, close up, her eyes half-lidded and hazed with a film of death. Her lips, no longer red and full of life, were parted, white teeth behind their shrunken slit. She lay on her back, one arm twisted beneath her as if she were caught midway in an attempt to rise. Her neck was broken, distended in a way that nearly made his gorge rise, and a halo of blood spread around her on the cement. He sometimes grew angry at death's portrayal in television shows and movies. A dead body was typically arranged in dramatic fashion with little damage to the victim's face.

In truth there was no beauty or grace in death. It was a cruel, messy, and sometimes violent departure from the world of the living.

Liam sifted through the pictures, setting one aside from time to time as he finished his meal, oblivious to his surroundings until Owen spoke.

"How can you fucking eat while you look at those?"

Liam lifted his head and saw the utter disgust etched on his friend's face. Owen stared at him, upper lip curled, hands smoothing the fabric of his shirt over and over.

"I'm sorry. You get used to it after a time. Callous. I'll bring them in the living room."

"Don't bother," Owen said, brushing past him. A moment later Liam heard the distinctive sound of the liquor cabinet being opened. He sighed and arranged the information back into a pile and shut the folder, the facts and forensic readings all in line with a conclusion of suicide, no apparent discrepancies leaping at him from the pages.

He stood and brought his dishes to the sink, washing them quickly before setting them to dry on a towel beneath one of the windows. He heard someone enter the room behind him and readied another apology, but instead of Owen it was Perring.

"Good, you found those," she said, motioning to the gun and folder.

"Yeah. I guess I'm clear as far as the city of Duluth goes?"

"For now." She gave him a tired smile and leaned against the counter. "They dropped your truck off outside too. The keys are in it." She glanced in Owen's direction. "It really upset him that you asked for Alexandra's file."

"I gathered that, and I understand."

"Find anything of interest?"

"No. Everything seems in order, nothing amiss."

"You still think this has something to do with Alexandra's suicide?"

"Yes."

"Why?"

"I can't say. Maybe it's the photo of Valerie and Owen upstairs in the hall. It's the most recent I've seen of her. She's staring at the camera and looking right through it like it's a window and she's seeing something on the other side. On one hand there's no getting over something like the death of a family member, but on the other, there's never moving on from the moment it happens. I think Valerie never moved on, and when you don't move on, the past catches up with you."

"Regardless, I don't see an avenue for weaving Alexandra's death into the investigation."

"It's at the very center of this. I can feel it."

Liam ambled away from Perring into the living room, leaving Alexandra's folder on the kitchen counter. He hesitated beside a chair across from where Owen sat nursing a full glass of whisky.

"I'm sorry about reading the file in front of you. That was insensitive of me," Liam said quietly.

Owen surveyed him over the rim of his glass then waved the air with it as if shooing an insect. "It's okay. No harm. I just don't see why you keep going back to Alexandra when Valerie's the one missing."

"I told you—"

"And I told you, my concern is for my wife, not her sister." Owen's voice was sharp and laced with alcohol. His eyes shone and Liam held his gaze blinking slowly.

"I'm sorry, Owen. This is how I work. Don't think for an instant that I'm more concerned with Alexandra's suicide than I am with finding Valerie."

"You have a funny way of working."

Liam was about to reply but knew the drunken barrier Owen had built around himself was woven with nothing but anger and resentment. There would be no getting through to him tonight. Instead he sat down and reached forward, drawing Alexandra's diary from the tabletop to his lap. Owen made an agitated sound and got up to cross the room to the windows even though there was nothing to see but darkness beyond them. Liam ran his fingers over the cover of the diary. How many times had Alexandra opened and closed the journal? How many times had she run to it in the grip of utter happiness or despair? It had been a confidant that would not betray her or judge her for her actions or thoughts. The secrets within were her own, precious and unknown in their truest sense even to those who read them.

Liam turned the diary over again, tracing the curving design that flowed across its cover with a fingertip, the embroidered flare upraised but smooth from time. It ended at the spine abruptly and he stared at its edge, a thought flaring into light in the recesses of his mind.

They probably could have passed as twins Alexandra's senior year.

"Twins," Liam said, bringing the diary closer to his face.

He ran his hand over the design.

Half of the design.

"What?" Owen said, not looking at him.

"It's a heart," Liam said, holding up the diary. "On the cover. Half a heart. By itself it just looks like a swooping line but it's not. It's one of two books."

"What are you talking about?" Owen asked finally turning toward him. Liam heard someone approach from behind and a moment later Perring appeared on his right.

"This diary is one of two. If you put them side by side the design on the front would create a heart. They're a pair, one for each sister."

Perring squinted at him and took Alexandra's diary from his hand as Owen came closer.

"Did Valerie have a diary like this?"

"Not that I ever saw."

Liam thought for a minute. "You said Caulston kept next to nothing of Alexandra's, right?" he asked Owen.

Owen shrugged. "I guess. That's what he told us anyway."

"I'm sure anything he did keep, he stored away, maybe in the basement or attic, but he would have known if something as important as her diary was missing if he ever looked, right?"

"Maybe."

"And from judging the man's temper, I'm almost sure he would've been furious at Valerie for taking it. So maybe she was forced to leave her own diary in its place."

"But why would she do that?" Perring asked.

"Maybe at first it was just to keep a connection to her sister, but after a time I think she may have been searching for something."

"For what?" Owen said.

"For the reason Alexandra killed herself."

The room was quiet as Liam glanced from Perring to his friend, gauging their reactions. Owen swayed in place, a thoughtful sourness coating his features while Perring continued to study the pink book.

"I think you're reaching," Owen said, his words slurring into one another.

"Maybe Valerie going to the jewelry store was part of it," Liam said.

"Don't give me that," Owen said. "I know my wife and she wasn't leaving this house. Whoever you talked to was wrong."

"Owen—" Liam began.

"He was wrong!" Owen's jaw set to an edge that cut at the flesh of his face. "This is a wild goose chase you're starting, Liam. You need to focus on Valerie."

"I am," Liam said, his own voice rising. He met Owen's intoxicated stare. "If I'm right, Valerie's diary might have some information that could point us in the right direction. If she had a theory about why Alexandra killed herself, it could tie all the loose ends together. I think Alexandra and the men that were killed in the last couple days have a connection, and Valerie might have known what it was. It might even be the reason she was taken." Liam glanced at Perring. "Who has the keys to Caulston's house?"

"They're at the station, locked up with the other inmates' belongings."

"Can you get me them?"

"No. Liam, I don't think your theory warrants entering Caulston's home."

"You have impunity now that he's in custody. You can okay entry without a search warrant."

"That may be, but I can't leave with no one to pass responsibility to here. There's too much to do before the exchange tomorrow evening."

"Then let me go. Call the station and okay the release of the keys to his house."

"No. No matter what you come up with in that house, it still doesn't change the fact that you're not a cop. I'd lose my job by giving you permission."

Liam stood and looked up at the ceiling. "Then I'll go without your okay."

"Liam, you can't do that."

"You know I'm right," he said, coming closer to her. "Look at me and tell me I'm not." He waited, watching her waver. There was a tipping in the depths of her eyes. She sighed.

"I don't know anything about this," she said.

"This is not why I asked you here," Owen said, setting his drink down.

Liam placed a hand on his arm. "It is though. If I can find Valerie's diary it might give us enough of a lead to locate her. We still have time to get her back before the exchange. We have time to beat this bastard at his own game."

Owen's mouth worked without forming words, the critical lines on his forehead relaxing. "Okay. Do what you can."

"Thank you," Liam said, reaching to gather his coat.

"And you don't have to break in," Owen said, pulling a ring of keys from his pocket and peeling one off. "This opens the front door."

Liam smiled, drawing his friend into a rough embrace before taking the key. "I'll be back as soon as I can."

"I'm going to lay down before I fall down. I think I overdid it," Owen said, giving them both a half smile. "Wake me if anything else happens."

They watched Owen move through the hallway, disappearing from sight on the stairs.

"He's strained to the breaking point," Perring said as she walked him to the entry. "Make sure you don't push this further than he can handle."

"I won't."

"Don't do anything stupid."

"Never."

"And if you get caught, I know nothing about this."

"Of course." He was about to step into the night when Perring spoke again.

"Liam? Be careful."

"Always," he said, closing the door behind him.

CHAPTER 20

Liam swung out of the fast food drive-through and back onto the highway, accelerating to keep up with the late traffic.

The salad had only been an infuriation to his stomach, so when he spotted the arrow promising burgers and fries, he let his hunger guide the car into the parking lot.

He devoured the burger, barely tasting the greasy meat and melted cheese mingling with the flavor of fried onions. The fries followed suit, disappearing in a few handfuls that left his mouth filled with salt and parched beyond belief. By the time he reached the city limits his medium drink was empty and his stomach felt as if a basketball had been transplanted there.

"Shit'll kill you," he murmured as he watched the GPS for the turn that was coming up in less than a mile.

Straiford Heights Road materialized out of the darkness on his right and he swung the truck onto its cleanly paved path. Even with the city only a mile behind, the houses on the street were hemmed in deeply by trees and layers of brush that flared fall colors in the headlights. For every mailbox there was a quarter mile of unblemished land growing untamed. The sight of windows glowing through the shivering tree branches gave him some sense of reality and assurance that there was simple and organized life going on nearby.

The GPS notified him that he had arrived and he nearly missed the driveway in the dark. Caulston's house sat on a rise behind a row of short jack pine. As Liam turned into the approach, the headlights washed the two-story home, giving him a sense of barely contained grandeur. The siding was white, trimmed with dark shutters and long overhanging eaves. An attached garage was positioned on the right while the entryway was built outward into the turnaround, its sides lined with wide windows. Several dormers jutted from the roof, onyx glass within each face.

Liam pulled to a stop and shut the truck off. He sat for a moment in the darkness, watching the house and its corners, the surrounding tree line, the windows. All was still. He stepped from the vehicle and put a hand to his back, reseating the holster and gun before moving up the walk. The key Owen had given him fit the dead bolt, and with a twist the door opened before him.

The entryway was empty save for a wooden bench and a bare coatrack. The grit on his shoes whispered against the clean tile and he wiped them on a rug emblazoned with a word he couldn't make out in the gloom. He shut the door and moved forward, pausing at the junction of the entry and kitchen. The air inside the house was cool and smelled faintly of cedar. Possibly from the sauna where Alexandra had traded her virginity with Dickson's. Liam found a light switch on the kitchen wall and flipped it on.

A grand dining room spread out to his left complete with an enormous hutch lining almost an entire wall as well as a table that would've easily accommodated a dozen people comfortably. A newspaper hung over the back of one chair and a tobacco pipe sat in a small stand on the kitchen counter.

The eerie feeling of being in another person's home uninvited stole over him. He tried brushing it away but it clung to him like a massive spider web. Walking soundlessly around the dining room, he found himself in a great room. A huge suede sectional dominated the floor plan flanked by two overstuffed easy chairs. An enclosed entertainment center stood against the opposite wall. A rectangle of darkness waited beyond the couch and Liam went to it, seeing that it was the basement door after cracking it open an inch. He crept downstairs on the carpeted treads and found a cinema room with rows of stepped seating before a blank digital screen taller than he was. Three doors opened off of the main area and after checking each of them to find only guestrooms, he made his way back upstairs. In the living room again he stopped in the basement doorway.

A sound had met his ears, indistinct and muted.

He stepped to the closest window looking out to the front yard and saw the sweep of headlights fading past the driveway. He stood for a moment, gazing around the dimly lit dining room before continuing through the kitchen to an ascending stairway. Alexandra's possessions must be here, and since there was no storage in the basement, that left the rooms above.

The stairway turned once and emptied out on a landing that held four closed doors. The first revealed the master bedroom and Liam spent only a few seconds glancing at the wide bed and low clothes dresser before moving onto the next door. The second was a bathroom while the third was another guest room, though by the looks of it one of the sisters had definitely occupied it at some point. It was spacious with a generous bay window overlooking the yard and a walk-in closet that would have housed his pickup without trouble. Besides the made bed and two nightstands, the space was empty and held an air of desertion.

The last door opened onto the past.

Liam stepped inside.

The room was laid out nearly the same as the prior space, but where the first had lacked any sense of life, this one was drenched with it.

A few items of clothing were stacked neatly beside a tall white dresser topped with a mirror, a faded picture of Alexandra sitting arm in arm with several friends, on its top. A four-poster bed without a canopy rested in the center of the room and a thick cushion lined the bay window making it a perfect spot for reading or napping on a rainy day.

Liam stood there, gazing around at a life interrupted. The feeling that Alexandra could walk in from the hallway at any moment was so pervasive his eyes kept flicking back to the open door. He moved to the dresser, seeing its top littered with numerous knickknacks and folded notes. A dried corsage attached to an ivory band dangled from a hook on the side of the mirror. It looked as if it would turn to dust if touched. A corded phone sat on the bedside table along with a water glass holding only a dried stain at the bottom, but it was this that gave him the longest pause.

Not only had Caulston been unable to face the memories associated with his daughter's belongings, he hadn't so much as touched an item. Liam was sure that within the dresser drawers he would find clothes folded and waiting, perhaps a pair of shoes beneath the bed.

The room was a ghost's tribute.

He crossed the space and opened the walk-in closet. Rows of clothing hung on hangers and several shoe boxes were stacked below, the fashion undeniably that of a young woman transitioning out of her teens. He moved deeper into the closet, opening an odd box or shifting garments to peer behind them. At the very back was a file box that clashed with every other item around him. It was a police evidence box, the side marked with black ink and the top fastened down with tape. Liam knelt before it, drawing it closer. Two strips of tape at the front had been peeled back and then refastened but they'd given way over time, their initial hold broken. With a fingertip he lifted the lid and looked inside.

A set of clothes was wrapped inside a sealed plastic bag and he recognized them, after a beat, as the garments Alexandra had been wearing at the time of her death. On top of the bag was a sterling silver wristwatch, a black purse, and a set of car keys.

Tucked against the rear of the box was a pink diary.

Elation surged within him as he reached out and grasped it. It felt the same as Alexandra's in his hand and he studied the design on the front, its pattern curving the opposite way of its copy at Owen's house. He tentatively opened the cover, half expecting the pages to be blank, but dark ink met his eyes instead.

He shut the diary, clutching it tightly as he closed the evidence box and slid it back into place. As he shut the closet door, movement flickered out of the corner of his eye and his heart bungee jumped in his chest. He spun to the window, eyes scanning the darkened yard below for what had drawn his attention. Something had moved out there, though he couldn't say what. It had almost been like a blink of light close to the house, perhaps the swing of a flashlight or a reflection off the glass of his truck, there and gone in an instant. He watched for a full minute before stepping away from the window. If there were someone outside, he would be an easy target illuminated behind the glass.

He turned lights off as he moved downstairs, returning to the glass-fronted entryway. He drew out his handgun, making sure a round was chambered before shutting off the last light. His pulse accelerated as he gripped the doorknob and turned it as quietly as he could.

The rattle of dying leaves met him as he stepped outside. Liam kept close to the side of the house, watching for stray shadows to move when they shouldn't. When no attack came and no sound rose above the wind's insistence, he stepped down off the cement stoop and began walking toward the dark form of his truck.

There was a click and the Chevy's headlights sprung on, blinding him in whiteness.

His arm came up instinctually to cover his eyes as the engine keyed on and roared, the truck leaping forward. The instant in which he might have moved was lost in the twitch of his muscles as the truck's grille loomed, shining like hungry teeth.

The impact was explosive.

Everything was pain.

It was as if his atoms were suddenly detonating, beginning with those in his chest and stomach and flowing outward. He was moving backward, the motor growling into and through him, vibrating his fillings. There was a split second of stillness, then he was airborne.

He exploded through the entry windows, their crystalline shattering like ice picks in his ears. He landed on his back and skidded on broken glass, with an exhalation of air that tasted of copper. Caulston's kitchen ceiling was above him, the dead light fixtures spinning, cabinets and stools twisting. He sucked in a breath of air and breathed out again, pain seizing the center of his chest like nothing he'd ever experienced before. He put a hand to his heart, sure that he would feel its raw touch in his palm, as the Chevy's engine flared again outside, the smell of coolant and exhaust noxiously sweet. His chest was whole beneath his coat and as he braced himself with one arm, the kitchen's sickening spin began to slow. He blinked, swallowing a mouthful of blood.

The front entryway window beside the door was gone. Beyond was the looming curve of his truck's hood, one headlight peering inside the house like an enraged eye. As he watched, the engine revved and the truck shuddered but moved only inches before settling once again.

It was lodged on the front steps.

Liam looked down at his legs, ready for the sight of splintered bone winking at him through torn flesh, but besides several tears in his jeans that drooled blood, they seemed intact. He pushed himself up, the agony in his chest and stomach coming down a notch from before.

He had to get up.

If whoever was in his truck decided to come in after him he'd be easy prey. If he were hemorrhaging internally he'd die on his own. Either way if he stayed where he was, he was dead.

With a final shove, he got his feet beneath him, feeling like he was on the last hour of a daylong vodka binge. The floor swayed and he caught himself on the edge of a counter. The truck's RPMs screamed their indignation, then fell lower and lower until silence replaced them completely.

The car door opened.

Liam searched the glittering floor for his gun but it was gone, dropped in the impact along with the diary. He skidded to the corner of the kitchen cabinet, muscles spasming as wetness ran down his back. Something clunked in the entry followed by breaking glass.

They were inside the house.

Liam reached out, grabbing the first thing his hand encountered and pulled the six-inch knife from the cutting block, its blade the brightest thing in the room. He hobbled away from the entry as the crunch of glass came from behind him. Ahead the darkness deepened and he shuffled into a hallway, spitting blood as he felt ahead for hindrances. His fingers brushed the cold steel of a door and he turned the knob.

Liam stumbled down two steps into the attached garage, his feet scratching on the concrete floor. He bumped against a long, low shape in the dark, felt the smooth, cold steel of the car beneath his shaking palm. Gaining his bearings, he sidled around the end of the vehicle, hoping his assumptions were right because if they weren't, there would be no escape.

He crossed the open space of the second empty stall and met the wall lined with garbage cans, several garden tools, a folded tarp.

Where was it?

Where was it?

His fingers scraped against the Sheetrock as careful footsteps treaded down the hall behind him, their stealth barely audible. Liam moved farther to the right, his hand finally finding the side door he hadn't been sure was there. He yanked it open as a shot rang out, a loud bark of sound in the enclosed space. Particles from the wall peppered his face and he lunged forward into the night.

The ground was soft from the rain and he nearly fell, the pain in his legs and chest a constant throb in time with his heart like a lighthouse signal. He ran to the wall of trees lining the yard and plunged into their welcoming darkness, hearing his pursuer exit the garage behind him. His feet were engulfed in fallen leaves, their dried forms pinpointing his location in the dark. He ducked beneath the reaching arms of a pine and began to slide downward as the land dropped away. Small rocks kicked up beneath his shoes, quickening his descent down the hill. He grabbed a small poplar, slowing himself and turning to the left, a semblance of a trail appearing as a lighter shadow in the night. He hobbled down the narrow blade of open ground, fewer leaves crunching with his progress. Chancing a look back, Liam saw a thin line of light sweep the area above him, its glow weak but there.

Coming toward him.

Liam hurried onward until the path twisted in on itself, eating its own tail and ending in a low stand of bramble and towering pines. He turned, gazing up at the hillside but there was no easy route to circumvent the person behind him—he would be heard immediately. The only option was to his right, through the stand of brush and farther down the slope. He pushed into the reaching hands of the thicket, fingernails of thorns clawing at his clothing, holding him back, feet crushing leaves to announce his presence. The woods seemed to want his death as much as his pursuer. He slashed at the brush with the kitchen knife before stooping over, a detonation of pain flowing from his midsection.

Footfalls hammered the path behind him and he dove through a small gap in the forest's defenses gaining an amount of freedom on the other side. The hill began to level and became rockier with blunted heads of boulders protruding from the ground, throwing pools of shadow beneath their bulk. He took several more steps and leaned against one of them, trying to keep his breathing as quiet as possible. His legs burned and the adrenaline was seeping away. He was painfully aware of his energy dipping low into the last of his reserves.

He couldn't go much farther.

The bramble above him cracked and hissed against clothing.

A pale beam of light crept down the hill, falling short of the rock beside him.

Liam swallowed more blood and began to move again, this time laterally across the hill's face. He crawled over a section of pulped rock, willing none of the smallest pieces to move beneath his weight. Ahead a stand of young pine grew in a thick patch flanked by two slabs of granite. Past that the land dropped again, violently this time so that he couldn't see beyond the night's veil. It may have been a descent of five feet or fifty within the void.

He made his way to the copse of pines and crawled beneath the first tree's branches. He had to lower himself to his chest and nearly cried out with the renewed fire that burned there. After crawling as quietly as he could for several yards, he stopped in a natural depression lined with fallen needles and rock. He steadied himself and moved his head, trying to see through the dense layers of pine boughs.

The flashlight beam appeared a dozen paces away.

It wasn't there and then it was, parting the darkness like a knife gash. Whoever held it moved cautiously, pausing every step, waiting and listening. Liam brought the neck of his T-shirt up over his mouth and nose, breathing shallowly all the while hoping the fabric would keep his exhalations from being seen in the cold air.

The figure behind the light began to take shape. He wore dark clothes like those of the man in the boat, the outline of a small pistol in one hand visible as it swung back and forth, covering the area Liam had occupied moments ago.

Liam shifted, wincing at the movement, and rotated the kitchen knife so that he held it point down. The seconds were measured in heartbeats, time speeding up with the throb of blood in his ears. The figure came closer and closer, stepping from stone to stone just as he had done. The light swept his hiding place and he hugged the nearest rock, willing himself to become part of it. The footsteps stopped and Liam risked a look.

His attacker stood ten feet away, head tilted to the side, flashlight off now. The gun panned the surroundings with careful surety, unwavering in its movement.

Liam inhaled and held his breath, ribs screaming in outrage. The muzzle of the gun came even with him and he imagined the searing pain of the shot ripping through him. He wouldn't see the flash until the bullet had already passed through flesh, rending apart anything in its path. He could see his own funeral, Dani and Eric dressed in black beside the open grave. Tears on their faces, flowers in hand, dropping them into the hole where he lay quietly inside the oak box.

The gunman pivoted, taking two steps past the clump of trees where Liam hid. The flashlight came back on and shone down the drop he had noticed earlier. It was a rock ledge overlooking thirty feet of open air. More trees grew farther down, their tops barely visible in the light's glow. The figure stood there, pondering the plunge, breathing softly.

Liam tightened his grip on the knife.

There was no easy way through the trees. The gunman would hear him coming and he'd be lucky if he didn't get hit. But this was the man, right before him with his back turned. This was Valerie's kidnapper. He would wound him, take the gun, then make him reveal where he was holding Valerie. He could do it.

He would do it.

Liam pushed away from the rock without a sound, muscles bunching into knots in his thighs. He gauged the distance to the figure to be a little over twelve feet. Intertwined pine branches partially blocked his way. He would have to be fast. Liam took several quick breaths, vision vibrating in time with his heart. He leaned forward, a downhill skier beginning his run.

And stopped.

Dani's face floated through his mind again. She wore a black veil and her eyes; they were empty save for the tears that clouded them.

The man turned back the direction he had come and picked his way through the rock flow, away from where Liam crouched. He watched his attacker grow fainter until he was only a shadow mixed with the night, his footfalls trailing back in short susurrations.

Liam collapsed into the pine needles, their soft touch like that of a lover. He willed his heart to slow and closed his eyes before cursing himself. No matter the pleadings of his rational mind telling him he might have died or he might have killed Valerie's kidnapper in the attempt to disarm him, a sour pulse of self-disgust continued to beat in his veins. There would be no other chance like the one he'd just given up.

He listened to the night air, its chill invading his coat, cooling the ache in his chest and stomach. Settling deeper into the needles he wrapped his arms around himself, grimacing with the effort. He would listen and wait. If the man came back, he would have to be ready. He would have to be fast. So fast.

His assurances followed him into a fitful sleep glazed with dreams of shadows smiling with shining teeth like the grille of a truck.

CHAPTER 21

When he woke it was still dark and he was welded to the ground.

He thought for a moment that someone had come and driven long spikes through his chest and shoulders, pinning him to the earth, but then he moved and the pain dropped over him in a waterfall of awareness. Every muscle fiber was a rusted strand of wire, his nerves telling him this over and over as he sat up, his air whistling out between his teeth in what normally would have been a scream.

Liam climbed to his feet, supporting himself on a rock and looked around. He must've passed out for a few hours. Dawn was only a suggestion in the east but the feeble light it possessed cast the side of the hill in a ghostly spray of monochrome. Frost encased everything down to the last fallen leaf.

He watched the hillside for five minutes, then climbed from his hiding place. He moved slowly back to the route he'd taken down the incline, pausing carefully at the largest boulders in case his attacker was concealed and waiting above. When no bullets rained down, he climbed upward, his body protesting like a machine left in the rain for years, corrosion on every joint. He tried to control his breathing, his mouth and throat a channel dried to parchment. When he arrived at the wall of brush he'd pushed through hours before, he stopped, hearing a faint sound in the distance.

Someone was calling his name.

He shoved his way through the gap he'd made earlier and hurried as fast as he could up the narrow trail. Near the top he had to pause to catch his breath, and as he heaved in air he heard his name yelled again. It was a woman's voice, not far away and coming closer.

Perring.

Liam grabbed at roots and saplings, yanking himself up the last stretch of hill until he stood on level ground. Caulston's yard was beyond, the blades of grass lit by the spill of headlights. He stumbled and almost fell coming through the last of the trees, halting as he nearly ran into Perring who held out her gun in both hands.

"Liam! Fuck, I almost shot you." She lowered her weapon. "Oh my God, what happened to you?"

"He was here," Liam said, trying to swallow saliva that didn't exist. "He followed me and hit me with my truck." Perring holstered her gun and turned to glance at the odd angle of his pickup still resting on the concrete stoop leading into the house.

"How?"

"Left the keys in it."

"Are you okay?"

"Doesn't feel like it."

"Let me help you." She looped one of his arms over her shoulders and supported his weight the best she could. They crossed the yard to her sedan, which idled behind his silent truck. "When you didn't come back I called your phone and when you didn't answer I came out here." She eyed the damage to the house and swore quietly. "I'll call this in. You're sure it was him?"

Liam drew his arm away from her and limped around the end of his truck, examining the frosted grass. After a minute of searching he bent and pulled his Sig from the ground, tucking it into the holster at the small of his back. He gazed around the area, dropping to his knees to look beneath the pickup before rising with a groan.

"I'm sure," he finally said.

"Why?"

"Because Valerie's diary is gone."

Perring drove through the waking city, lights of other cars shining across Liam's closed eyes as he dozed in the passenger seat. Even as exhaustion tried to drag him beneath the waves of sleep, he returned to everything that had happened the night before, poring over all he could remember clearly. He analyzed the attacker's gait; how he held his shoulders, his height, general build. He hadn't been able to see the exact make and model of the gun he'd carried, but Liam knew it was a compact pistol of sorts, possibly a .380 caliber by the sound of the report in the garage.

"I'm bringing you to the hospital," Perring said.

Liam opened his eyes. "No."

"You were hit by a truck."

"It wasn't going very fast."

"I know guys can be really dumb, but you may be vying for the world title. You're really setting new standards for the stupidity of your gender."

"That's me, always raising the bar."

"Seriously, you need to see a doctor."

"Have a paramedic come to Owen's. I'm feeling better already."

"You're so full of shit," Perring muttered. But when the pulled to a stop at the intersection leading to Owen's home, she turned toward it instead of in the opposite direction toward St. Luke's.

When they arrived, Owen's driveway was packed with vehicles. Most of them were doppelgangers of Perring's sedan but there were several squads and one nondescript conversion van with blackened windows. Inside the house the largest congregation of officers and investigators Liam had seen yet milled around the dining room table. The house smelled of coffee and competing colognes. He and Perring walked into the dining room and dozens of eyes took in his ripped jeans and hunched form. After a moment of silence Heller cleared his throat.

"Uh, detective? We have the final arrangements here from the coast guard."

"Thanks, I'll go over them with you in a second." She turned to Liam. "You go sit down someplace. You look like hell in the light."

"You're such a charmer," Liam said, moving into the living room.

Owen sat on the couch, his face in his long-fingered hands. He looked up as Liam entered the room.

"Liam?" Owen stood and took in his appearance. "Where the hell have you been?"

"I got waylaid at Caulston's. I ran into the kidnapper, or actually he ran into me. I don't know if he followed me or if there were other reasons for him stopping by."

"Like what?"

"Like if Caulston was on his list."

"Why would someone want to kill Caulston?"

"I don't know. Doesn't seem to fit with the modus operandi. I'm thinking it was an ambush for me. We're getting close to the truth, and with Davis still missing it's more likely he's this guy's next target, or he's already been crossed off the list."

Owen stared at him, his eyebrows drawn, taking in the extent of his injuries. "You need to see a doctor."

"Don't say that in front of Perring, I just got her convinced otherwise." Liam moved to sit on the arm of a chair but took in the filth and blood that stained his jeans and thought better of it. "The diary was there, but he took it from me. I'm sorry, Owen."

"Don't be. You did what you could. I can't ask any more of you."

"Did you get any rest?"

"Not much. I bet you're exhausted."

"Getting there. No more contact or demands?"

"None. I think he said everything he was going to say yesterday." Owen turned to the window and the dawning sun across the lake. "This is going to be the longest day of my life. Longer even than the last three. I can't stand the waiting. It's like each minute is a sliver underneath my fingernails going deeper." He glanced over one shoulder, his face so pale he appeared wraithlike in the strange morning light. "Nothing will ever be the same after this, will it?"

Even though it was more of a statement than a question, Liam said, "No, it won't. But that doesn't mean things will be worse. When Valerie is home safe and this bastard is locked up you'll have time to come to terms with what happened. Right now everything's out of focus, but it will get clearer. You'll have each other to make it clear."

Owen looked away and resumed studying the sunrise. Liam watched him for another second before leaning against the closest wall. It wasn't long before Perring stepped up beside him and said, "Liam, the paramedic's here." He nodded, moving to the dining room where a handsome black paramedic with a name tag reading *Paul* waited holding a duffle bag.

"The detective here tells me you're afraid of hospitals," Paul said as they walked toward the main-floor bathroom.

"Not afraid, just hate them. Babies are the only good thing that come out of them," Liam said.

Paul huffed a laugh and motioned to a stool in one corner of the room. "Why don't you take your shirt and pants off and have a seat."

Liam stripped to his boxers, wincing again at the movement of bringing his arms over his head. It felt as if he'd been caught in a car crusher that had relented at the last minute and left him alive. When Paul had donned latex gloves and laid out an array of tools, gauze, and vials, he glanced at Liam's back, letting out a low whistle.

"Damn, man, you got some mileage on you already."

"I guess you could say that."

Paul began to examine the lacerations on his back from where he'd landed on the glass, asking the occasional question every few minutes. There were several deft tugs and then a cool burning as the paramedic applied disinfectant to the wounds. When that was done, he had Liam stand and examined his chest and ribs, prodding painfully at each one with gloved fingers before having him open his mouth then moving onto the shallow cuts dotting the front of his legs.

"Well, you're damn lucky, my friend," Paul said, stripping the gloves from his hands. "The cuts on your back and legs are superficial, you don't need any stitches. You have a lot of bruising on your torso but no broken ribs, though the very bottom one on the left side might be cracked. You got a cut on your tongue that's clotted, won't need any stitches. My official diagnosis is you should take up a different career."

Liam chuckled. "Only thing I know how to do."

"Then be more careful," Paul said, cleaning up his equipment.

"This is me being more careful."

"Then I'd say see my prior recommendation."

Liam laughed. "Thanks for the advice, and the patch up."

"No thanks needed, you take care."

Paul left and Liam locked the door behind him, then faced the mirror over the sink. His hair was in disarray and black half moons hung below his eyes. Dark stubble coated his cheeks and chin. His chest was covered in a purplish hue that yellowed at its edges.

"You look like shit," he said to his reflection.

He dressed as quickly as he could in the last set of clean clothes he'd packed. As he pulled on a warm, knitted sweater there was a knock at the door.

"Yeah?"

"It's Perring. Can I come in?" Liam unlocked the door and she stepped inside, glancing at the pile of his bloodied clothes on the floor.

"I want to hear everything that happened at Caulston's. Start at the beginning."

He sighed and motioned to the toilet. "Mind if I take the throne? My legs are tired."

"Be my guest."

Liam sat and began relaying everything that had transpired, after leaving the night before. He hesitated at the portion of his story where he had faltered instead of trying to apprehend the kidnapper. Perring must have noticed because when he'd finished she said, "You're beating yourself up, aren't you?"

He shrugged. "I missed my chance. Who else do I have to blame?"

"If what you said was accurate, he'd have heard you coming and instead of talking to you, there'd be men hauling your corpse out of the woods right now. You made the right choice."

"Doesn't feel like it."

"When you're a cop all the choices feel wrong sometimes."

He gave her a tired smile. "I'm not a cop."

"Could've fooled me."

"I think I'm just trying to fool myself. You were right, I'm not so sure anymore of my motivations here."

"You want to help your friend."

"I do."

"You want to get Valerie back."

"Yes."

"Then I'd say your motivations aren't something you need to worry about."

He wanted to say more to her. Tell her about the fear that had driven him to threaten and hurt Houston and Richard, but the moment passed and Perring changed the subject. "Paul fixed you up?"

"There wasn't a whole lot of fixing to do."

"Umm hmm."

"No really. He gave me a clean bill of health."

"You're trying to stay on this no matter what, huh?"

"I want to see it through. You'd do the same."

She appraised him for a beat, then nodded. "Everything's arranged for the exchange. There were no leads on anyone asking questions or acting suspicious down at the harbor. The cameras at the high school turned up nil as well."

"How's that possible? He must've been driving a car. He wasn't leading Valerie around on foot."

"I don't know but there wasn't anything on the tape. No one in or out of the parking lot after sunset. I also dispatched a crime scene team to Caulston's house. They should have something for us before tonight. At the very least we'll have a ballistics report on the weapon that he used in the garage."

"Hopefully it matches the rounds collected at Rowe's."

"It would make things easier, that's for sure."

Liam lowered his head and ground one fist into the opposite palm. "If I could've just gotten the diary . . ."

"You don't know that there would've been anything of use in there."

"No, I don't know." He raised his head. "But I can feel it."

"Regardless, it's gone. We have to move forward with what we do know."

"Which is what?" Liam asked. "We know only what we've been allowed to know. We're being led like lambs to slaughter. Don't you feel it?"

Perring's eyes hardened. "I feel like we've done the best we can with what we have."

He wanted to say more, to dig at the wound and open it up fully so that it could bleed. But then he saw her feeling her pants pockets again for cigarettes that weren't there and his anger deflated.

"Any update on Rex?" Liam asked.

A cloud dimmed Perring's features. "He's about the same. Hasn't woke up yet but his vitals have improved. The doctors are hopeful."

"He's going to make it."

She nodded and seemed to come back to herself from far away. "Owen's sleeping now and you should do the same."

"I still need—"

"You need to rest. I'm putting you in charge of Owen tonight when everything goes down." She paused. "There was a complication with the boat we didn't foresee."

"What was it?"

"There is no below deck on *The Mare*. It's a simple trawler with only a small cabin at the front. There's no room to hide a SWAT team anywhere."

"Son of a bitch," Liam said. "He picked it out specifically."

"Yeah."

"Is there any way to modify it to fit the men inside?"

"Not in this short a time. Besides, I don't want to risk him seeing us messing around with the boat before it leaves the harbor tonight. He could execute Valerie simply because he didn't like what we were doing."

"But how are you going to have police presence there? You can't just hand the money over and hope he plays fair."

"We have an army helicopter waiting at the airport that will have a SWAT team on board. They'll be in the air and in contact with the captain of *The Mare* the entire time as well as with our surveillance boat. The moment the exchange is made they'll be there. He shouldn't have more than a two-minute head start."

Liam shook his head. "I don't like it. There's too many variables left open. Too many things could go wrong."

"What would you have me do?" Perring yelled. The acid in her voice startled him. "Tell me, Liam, because I'd love to know where I'm falling short."

He opened his mouth to reply but a knock came from the other side of the door.

"Everything okay in there?" Heller's voice.

"Fine. We're fine," Perring said, opening the door and disappearing down the hallway. Heller stood framed in the doorway as though he wanted to say something, but in the end he simply nodded once and moved out of sight as well.

Liam rose and gathered his things before walking to the living room. Owen stood near the windows but he didn't spot Perring anywhere in the kitchen or dining room.

Exhausted, he sat on the couch and leaned into its soft folds. For a time he searched for another tack that could give them the upper hand when evening arrived, but came up with nothing. The kidnapper had planned this out too well. He reached out and drew Alexandra's diary to him, turning the pages arbitrarily, and came upon the very last passage she had written.

I have to do something to get rid of this feeling. I want to die.

What had she done to escape the fear of losing the person she loved? To what lengths would a young woman go to ensure the future she'd dreamed of? Was death really what she'd chosen, or was there something unseen lurking beneath the guise of the self-inflicted tragedy?

He flipped back to one of the first entries, his eyes happening across the passage about Alexandra receiving the gold bracelet with the cross, from her father. The man who would one day pay a bartender to lie in order to get the justice he thought was due for her death. The strangeness of life was something to behold and never ceased to create unease within him. At the end of the day, no one was safe from the tide of life or what waited thereafter.

He was about to close the diary when the word *cross* caught his eye again.

Cross.

Crucifix.

Church.

"Was the church where Alexandra died the one she worshipped at?" Liam asked, a splinter of thought sticking in his mind.

"No. I don't think Caulston went to church very much after Val and Alex's mother passed."

"Then why did she choose that church?"

Owen shrugged. "It was close to the party she left. I suppose the bell tower was the highest thing she could see."

Liam climbed to his feet, wincing as he did, and began to pace. "There's something there, some significance. Why a church? Why that night? How does it connect to what's happening right now?"

"I don't know. It could be any number of things."

Liam paced past the windows, gradually slowing to a stop. *Any number of things.*

Number.

2.

There was a beat of utter stillness and silence before he jerked with the realization, startling Owen so much the other man flinched.

"What?" Owen asked.

"Where did Marshall Davis go to church?"

"What are you talking about?"

"In his mug shot he was wearing a crucifix. Did he go to church when you were in school with him?"

"I have no idea. Like I said, I didn't know him all that well."

"What's going on?" Perring asked, coming into the room through the kitchen. Liam caught the faint whiff of cigarette smoke.

"We have any background on Davis's personal life? Where he went to church?"

Perring frowned. "No, but I can have Heller take a look. Why?"

Liam walked past her without answering and found Heller sitting at the far end of the dining room table, his glasses pushed up on his forehead.

"Heller, can you dig up some information on Marshall Davis?"

"Sure. I had his file pulled a minute ago—"

"No, not his file, I've read that. I'm talking family history, personal life, that sort of thing."

"Uh, I guess so," He gave Perring a look over Liam's shoulder and the detective nodded. Heller set to typing at his laptop and a moment later sat back. "Marshall Steven Davis, born September second, nineteen eighty to Thomas Gerald Davis and Michelle Farah Davis. Attended Duluth, West Elementary, graduated Duluth East High School in nineteen ninety-nine. There's references to his arrests, public warrants, things like that."

"Nothing else?" Liam asked.

"Not that I see here."

"How about his parents?"

"Liam, what's this about?" Perring said.

"Just look his parents up."

Heller began tapping again and after a minute turned the computer slightly toward Liam. "Mother filed for divorce when Marshall was five, father died four years ago after doing a year stint for breaking and entering. Looks like he had a drinking problem he wasn't able to support."

"Like father like son," Perring said. "I'm not seeing what you're looking for here."

Liam leaned closer to the screen. "I'm not either. How about an obituary for his father?"

Heller typed several keywords in and searched, bringing up the article after a moment. "Thomas Gerald Davis, died May third, two thousand eleven at St. Mary's Hospital. Let's see . . ." Heller scrolled down the short obit. "Grew up south of Duluth, married twice. Marshall's listed as his only child. He held several jobs including freelance carpenter, backhoe operator, and . . ." Heller paused, eyes narrowing.

"What?" Perring asked.

"And custodian for Saint Peter's Sovereign Cathedral."

Liam straightened, eyes locked on the screen. "That's it."

"Holy shit," Perring murmured.

"What? I don't understand," Owen said.

"Marshall's father was a custodian at the church where Alexandra killed herself. He would've had keys to the building and that means Marshall had access too." Liam turned to face Perring and Owen. "I don't think Alexandra committed suicide at all. I think Marshall Davis murdered her."

CHAPTER 22

"Marshall murdered her? Are you joking? They didn't even know each other," Owen said.

"Marshall was obviously an addict, but he also bought and sold. We know he was involved with at least one major supplier in the area and possibly a second. I think he was dealing way back at the end of high school and somehow Alexandra got tangled up in it. Either she was using or she saw something she shouldn't have and Davis decided he couldn't let her live." Liam glanced from Owen's astonished face to Perring who was chewing her lower lip. "He had his father's keys to the church. He must've overpowered Alexandra and brought her up to the bell tower."

Owen shook his head. "There would've been signs of a struggle, some evidence that she was thrown over instead of jumping."

"Not if he was careful," Perring said. "If he knocked her unconscious somewhere else, the trauma to her skull from the fall would've covered up any signs of foul play."

"But what does this have to do with Valerie?" Owen asked.

"I think she knew, deep down, that Alexandra wouldn't have killed herself. At first she suspected Jenner but I think over time Valerie realized he truly loved her sister. I spent five minutes with him and

I could tell," Liam said. "But Alexandra's death crushed her mentally and emotionally for a long time. It must've been recently that she had something to go on and started to dig into Marshall's past. That's why in the last few years she started leaving the house and making progress with her therapy."

"So Marshall caught wind of it and took her?" Owen said. "How would he have the capability? The know-how? I mean, I didn't know him well but he never seemed like the sharpest knife in the drawer."

"Maybe he had some time to plan it, I don't know," Liam said.

"How do Dade's and Gage's deaths fit into this?"

"They might've been privy to some piece of information that could tie Marshall to Alexandra's murder and he decided to eliminate the loose ends."

"But if Marshall isn't number two, then who is? And why go to the trouble to kill them in the way he did?" Perring asked.

"I don't know. Regardless of the motives, one thing's for certain, we need to search the church. It's somewhere he's familiar with, maybe even comfortable at. Who knows, it could even be where he's been hiding out since leaving the halfway house."

"I agree. I'll organize one of the SWAT groups here to go. We should be able to leave in under ten. Heller, find out if there's been mass at Saint Peter's this week. There's a good chance that's where he's been holding her." Perring nodded once at Liam and moved to the entryway.

Owen walked into the living room and sunk into the couch. Liam followed and stopped a few feet away.

"I know this is a lot to take in, but I think we finally have our connection and motive," Liam said. "If Valerie's being held there we'll get her back." Owen merely nodded, his gaze hazy and unfocused. Liam was about to sit beside him to offer another attempt at comfort when Perring entered the room.

"Heller says the church hasn't had regular mass this week since the resident priest is traveling. We'll be ready to go in five."

"I'll be right there," Liam said. He turned back to Owen who was rocking slightly on the edge of his seat. "Are you going to be okay here?"

"Yeah. I'll be fine," the other man replied in a distant voice. Liam watched him for a short span before moving toward the dining room, but Owen's voice stopped him before he could cross the threshold.

"Liam?"

"Yeah?"

"Kill the bastard if you can." Owen still wasn't looking at him, and after a brief pause, he rose from the couch and disappeared in the direction of the upper level.

⌣

Saint Peter's Sovereign Cathedral sat on a knoll on the lower north side of the city. Its grounds were well manicured, the grass still a vibrant green beneath the fallen leaves that dusted the edges of the small clearing the church was built in. The building itself was an imposing structure of dark-red brick. The bell tower rose at least sixty feet into the air, looming over the rest of the building like a solemn watchman.

Liam and Perring pulled to a stop on the nearest street flanking the property and watched the black conversion van hauling the SWAT team roll past to the second strategic position.

"They're going in through the side and rear entrances. They'll make sure the main level is secure before we go up. We've notified the staff and they've locked themselves in their offices. If he's here, I'd wager he's holding her in the tower," Perring said.

"Yep," Liam replied, checking the load in his weapon.

"You sure you're up for this? I don't want you endangering anyone if you can't stay on your feet."

Liam smiled. "Try and keep up with me."

"Asshole."

Perring adjusted her earpiece and squinted at the building. "Okay. We go in one minute. Liam and I will take the front. Two teams, one sweeps the main level and basement, the other heads for the tower. Be safe." There was a muted reply from the SWAT team leader and Perring drew her own weapon before they exited the sedan.

Though the day was bright, a chill hung in the air as they crossed the grounds toward the church. Leaves whipped about their feet in coiling motions and the wind sung through the trees.

They moved faster as they mounted the steps that lined the front of the church. Liam pulled the right side of the double doors open for Perring. She cleared the entryway and he followed her inside.

The interior of the church was blindingly dark compared with the outside daylight. It took the better part of ten seconds before Liam could make out the wide hallway they stood in, graced with statues of various saints.

They moved forward in tandem, Perring taking the left, Liam the right.

Five steps and they were in a vestibule beside a sprawling sanctuary. Dark, curving support beams spanned the high ceilings and a cross, matching the color of the stained wood, held a statue of Jesus tearing himself away from the nails that held him there.

Movement at the rear of the huge space drew Liam's attention, as three SWAT members spread out between several pews, rifles up and sweeping the area. Three more men appeared at the opposite end of the vestibule and streamed toward a large door marked 'Tower.' They clustered around it, the lead team member grasping the doorknob and yanking.

In a split second the team had disappeared through the tower door, and Liam and Perring rushed after them.

A spiral, concrete staircase wound up through the tower's center, the constant turning beginning to make him dizzy as he kept pace behind Perring. The scuff of many boots was loud in the enclosed space and he kept waiting for the sound of a gunshot to shatter the silence. After what seemed like an eternity they arrived at another wooden door identical to the one on the main level. The team ahead of them was already in place, swinging a door-breaching ram.

There was an explosion of splinters and the yells of the team as they rushed inside.

Liam stepped to the side of the broken door, aiming his weapon into the room. His heart hammered in his chest relentlessly, every muscle tense and aching with his injuries.

He nodded at Perring as she swept inside, then followed a second later.

The bell tower was square and not as large as he'd imagined. The brick walls were broken by tall, gothic-arched windows, their openings grated with steel bars he assumed were installed after Alexandra's death. A single brass bell hung silently from an iron stand in the center of the room.

Otherwise the space was empty.

"Damn it," Liam said, lowering his handgun. Perring moved around the room, looking out several of the arched openings before gesturing to the other team members.

"Go assist with the sweep of the basement," she said. The men filed quickly out of the room, their footsteps growing fainter until quiet refilled the tower.

"I really thought they'd be here," Liam said after a moment.

"It was a good hunch, don't beat yourself up."

He squatted down in the southeast corner where something small and yellow lay covered in a slight layer of dust. "Look at this."

"What is it?" Perring asked, stooping beside him.

"Foam earplug. Guarantee Davis's DNA is on it. He's been staying here, using ear protection for when the bell tolls. It's a perfect place to hide, sleep off the end of a high."

"We'll have forensics bag it, but I'm guessing you're right. He was here."

"Damn it," he said again, holstering the Sig. The urge to strike the brick wall was almost overpowering, but he resisted. *So close. They'd been so close.*

"As soon as SWAT's done with the sweep we should get back to the house."

"Yeah." Liam moved to the head of the twisting stairway.

"Liam."

"What?"

"We'll get him."

"I know. I just hope it's not too late before we do," he said, starting down the stairs.

⌣

The rest of the morning coasted away beneath the constant preparations. Phones continued to ring, people moved in and out of Owen's house in a steady flow, and the waves washed against the shoreline in cold, unending repetition.

An all-encompassing fatigue finally settled over Liam in midafternoon, and under Perring's unyielding insistence, he went to lie down on the couch to rest.

His chest ached. The rib that Paul had said might be cracked was the worst, its protestations like a dagger in his side when he moved wrong.

You failed her, the dark interior voice said. It spoke in pointed tones of malice. *You failed Valerie and you failed Owen.*

No.

Yes. You failed her and now she'll never come back home. Dani will be gone forever.

His drooping eyelids snapped open and he shook his head.

Valerie, not Dani. Dani was safe.

When the voice didn't reply, he closed his eyes but was unable to stifle the thoughts of the evening to come, which whirled through his mind in a tempest. There couldn't be a mistake tonight. One false step and Valerie would be lost.

The pain of his body was mollified as his thoughts quieted, sleep's demands nearly irrepressible. He would just doze for a while, if only to resharpen the edge he had lost overnight in the woods. He would drift for just a moment.

As the fatigue became an immovable weight, dragging him ever downward, he heard muted words being spoken by the dark voice like some demonic Gregorian chant. But before they became clear he was sleeping and they faded away into silence.

CHAPTER 23

"Liam. Wake up."

The cocooning sway of sleep parted around him with a blade of consciousness coupled to pain. His eyes came open and he looked into Perring's face. She stood at the back of the couch dressed in a pair of jeans and a dark hooded sweatshirt. Her hair was pulled back in a tight bun and any makeup she had worn in the days before was gone.

Liam blinked and sat up, the muscles in his abdomen filled with broken glass. His head sloshed with the last vestiges of sleep and he shook it.

"What time is it?"

"Six o'clock."

His head snapped around. "You're joking."

"No. I tried to wake you a couple hours ago but you were out cold."

"Damn it," he said, struggling to his feet. The injuries from the night before felt more painful than when he had woken the first time in the woods. His joints fought his attempted movements as if they'd been injected with glue while he slept. He made it to his feet and began loosening them with small motions, stretching taut tendons, drawing out coiled muscles.

"I didn't see the harm in letting you sleep," Perring said. "There wasn't much left for preparation. I got the preliminary report back from the crime scene team. No prints found in your truck besides yours and none in Caulston's house besides his and yours. The slug they dug out of the wall in the garage was a .380. Other than that we have a size eleven boot print."

"That's it?"

"That's it. Guy was careful. No one in the neighborhood heard the shot either."

"Not surprising. The houses out there are pretty well insulated by trees."

She nodded. "We're ready to head down to the harbor now."

Footsteps came quietly from the stairway and Owen appeared a moment later dressed in a pair of dark Chinos and a heavy, tan button-up shirt. His face was still haggard and lined, but the constant weariness had lifted from his eyes, replaced by a frenetic intensity.

"Are we ready to go?" Owen asked.

"Yes. Liam and you will go in your car. The team and I will take the van and my car along with the money. I'm having a man stay behind here in case anything new comes through on the e-mail or phone. Two other task force members will remain with the money on the dock until it's time to go. The rest of us will be in two separate boats positioned several miles out on the lake. We already have eyes on the location of the exchange that aren't visible from the water via the observation drone. An officer will stay with you both at the harbor and give you updates. When we bring her home, you'll be the first one she sees," Perring said, reaching out to touch Owen on the shoulder.

"Thank you, detective."

She nodded, gave Liam a long look, then headed out of the room. They followed her to the yard, past the remaining team member looking stoic at the dining room table, and into the cool fall evening. They climbed into Owen's Cadillac ATS and reversed out of the driveway and fell in behind the somber line of vehicles that Liam tried not to think of as a funeral procession.

They didn't speak as the cars turned at the various stoplights and traveled like water downhill to the street leading to the harbor. They parked behind a large restaurant where a line of caution tape had been hung. A uniformed officer pulled the tape away as they neared and restrung it the moment they were all through. A cruiser as well as two more unmarked sedans and an ambulance sat in the quiet lot. Beyond the lot's low cement wall was a walkway and past that was Superior's water, rippling in icy waves beneath the bobbing boats. The lift bridge stood in severe contrast to the darkening sky that held a coating of dirty clouds threatening rain, its austere structure more skeletal now in the failing light. At the closest dock, a flat-decked boat sat by itself. A grizzled man stood beside the craft holding a yellow rain slicker. He cast the vehicles a wary look before stepping inside a boathouse on the dock.

"Must be the captain," Liam said.

Owen shut the car off and sat back in his seat. "I think so. Perring told me they tried to get a double who looked just like him to do the drop, but they couldn't find anyone who fit the bill. I guess the guy told her he didn't mind helping out. Apparently his son was a cop down in Florida who got killed doing a routine traffic stop."

Liam glanced out the window and watched the boathouse but the captain didn't reappear. Perring stood among a ring of other officers. She pointed to *The Mare* before gesturing to the canvas bag she held in one hand. The heavy magnet attached to the top of the bag shone in a circlet of reflected light.

"Want to get out or wait here?" Liam finally asked.

"Let's get some air before it rains."

They exited the Cadillac and walked to the group of police. Perring was finishing her instructions as they neared.

"Only when I have confirmation that Valerie is safe do we go. The helicopter will move in first and we'll converge on the location to provide support from the water. Everyone has their orders. Any questions?" When no one spoke she glanced around once at the men and women before her. "Everyone be safe and let's bring Valerie home." The group murmured their assent and started toward the docks. Perring turned to them and glanced at the sky.

"You'll be notified by Officer Evans when she's safe. Then we'll retrieve the insurance money."

"I don't care about the money," Owen said. "Just bring her back to me."

Perring nodded and turned to leave. She stepped over the low wall and was moving down the walk toward the water when Liam called out to her.

"Hey, Perring." She stopped and faced him. "Be careful."

A smile twitched her lips. "Always." She continued down the walk and he watched her climb into one of two streamlined speedboats. The motors started a short time later and they watched the two teams idle out of the harbor and disappear below the bridge, which didn't need to rise at all to accommodate their low profiles. Two task force members stood side by side near *The Mare*, one holding tightly to the bag, the other speaking quietly with the boat's captain. The remaining officer leaned against his car, watching the boats until they were out of sight before climbing inside to consult his dashboard computer.

Liam checked his phone. There were two text messages from Dani. He answered them but without much detail since he didn't want to have to explain the prior night's ordeal. There was no reason to scare her more than necessary. He noted the time before tucking his phone away. 6:33 p.m.

Less than an hour and a half to go.

"Let's take a walk," Owen said, and began to move toward the concrete path beside the harbor. Liam gave the officer and his car a look before following.

The wind that coasted off the lake held a bite to it that nipped at the exposed skin of his hands and face. Gulls soared overhead in a constant turn of feathers and black eyes searching for food. Farther down the shore, two-foot waves buffeted the massive rocks that made up the waterline, the sound like a crowd of voices shouting as one. Owen had turned onto another path that joined the first. It led away from the shops and restaurants that lined the harbor's side and hung close to the channel leading out beneath the bridge to open water.

Liam watched Owen as they walked. The cool weather had cleared most of the people from beside the lake and driven them into the warmth and comfort of the buildings whose lights had begun to turn on against the lowering night. Owen looked straight ahead, his gait easy and smooth, indicative of the runner he was. His hands were in his pockets and his lips kept moving soundlessly as if he were forming a sentence then letting it die on his tongue.

When they were a stone's throw from the lift bridge, Owen stopped and leaned on the half-wall, his eyes focused across the water to the structures lining the peninsula of Park Point. Liam took a position beside him and mirrored his stance. He gazed at the long strip of land and wondered if Stella Erickson had realized that her son was dead yet, killed in his home by someone harboring a hatred deeper than the depths of the lake before them. Perhaps the disease that plagued her mind and robbed her of her memories was now a blessing. A barrier that kept out the knowledge that she was truly alone and that her son would never again come to visit her in the quiet room that would be her sanctuary and prison until she died. And what of Gage Rowe's family? Where were they tonight? Wherever they were, they were surely held in the sharp-fingered hands of grief. They too had lost everything in the last twenty-four hours. Such a small span of time to have something so elemental taken that the world would never be the same again. But life was like the waves that lapped the shore: at times bringing something with them but always taking something away.

"Do you believe in karma?" Owen said, breaking him from his reverie.

"I believe in the past. And that the past echoes. If that's what you're talking about, then yes."

Owen didn't turn to him but continued to stare across the water. "Echoes. Yes. That's more fitting I guess."

"Are you okay, Owen?"

"No. I don't think I am. But I will be when Valerie's back home."

The hollowness of his voice made the hair stiffen on the back of Liam's neck. His friend sounded like a corpse that had been recruited by some morbid ventriloquist. "They'll bring her back. You'll see."

Owen pushed away from the wall, his eyes clearing somewhat from the faraway look that dominated them. "I rented a boat this afternoon," he said.

"What are you talking about?"

"I need to be out there, Liam. I can't just sit here waiting for them to bring her in. I want to be there if something goes wrong."

"Owen, no. Perring has this under control. We tried very hard to get Valerie back before we were forced to this point, but now that we're here we need to let things play out. If you get involved the exchange could go wrong."

"I'm not going to interfere, I just want to be ready in case something happens. If the bastard that's holding her hurts her . . ." His words failed him and he swallowed. "I asked Perring if I could ride along with them and she told me no, but I need to be out there, Liam. And I need you to come with me."

Movement caught Liam's attention and he flicked his gaze to it. *The Mare* was idling toward the bridge. It was time.

"I can't. It's too risky."

Owen stepped back, scrutinizing him. "So you're a coward."

"It's not me I'm worried about."

"Please, Liam. I'm begging you."

He was about to reply when the sharp bark of a car horn came from the street leading to the lift bridge. Liam glanced toward the sound and saw the crossing arms slowly coming down to cut off traffic from either side of the bridge, red lights blinking as they dropped into position. A car honked again, this time longer. Liam traced the length of the bridge. His vision snagged on a lone figure moving across the expanse.

The person was dressed in a baggy black jumpsuit two sizes too large, hands bound in front and a black hood drawn tightly over their head.

Long blond hair spilled from the back of the cowl and over her collar.

Even as Liam tried to calculate what he was seeing, Owen was turning, following his gaze. There was a beat of absolute stillness, a crystalline clarity to the evening air and a silence that became a hum in Liam's ears. Owen drew a deep breath in and then expelled it, yelling one word.

"Valerie!"

"Owen! Wait!" Liam reached out to grasp his friend's shoulder, but he was already gone. He ran across the walkway and vaulted the concrete wall, stumbling on the opposite side. Liam ran after him, throwing a look at *The Mare* as it approached the bridge. Now he could make out the profile of the captain within the wheelhouse, the canvas bag sitting directly in the middle of the empty deck.

Liam sprung up and over the wall, landing with less grace than Owen had managed, and the slight pause in his movements had given his friend all the time he needed. Owen was a runner, and he used his skill now. His lanky form leaned forward, tearing across the ground toward the entrance to the street beside the bridge. Liam sprinted after him, but even as he ran he saw he was losing ground to Owen's longer legs. The figure on the bridge trundled along, her movements drunken and unsteady.

Something was wrong.

He could feel it. The cold knowledge flared in a burst of panic within his stomach. He had to notify Perring or one of the other task force members. But they were all out of earshot. Liam fumbled his phone from his pocket as he ran, barely keeping hold of the plastic casing. Owen had made the street, his wife's name coming from him in frantic cries that rebounded off the building's sides. Liam lost sight of the stumbling figure on the bridge as he neared the sidewalk and raced up its path. Owen's feet slapped the pavement ahead of him as the other man ducked below the crossing arm and continued toward the bridge. Something about his hurried movements triggered a memory in Liam's mind. The way Owen ran, how he held his shoulders, his head tipped forward nearly below them; it was like trying to recall a half-forgotten dream.

"Owen! Stop!" Liam yelled again, reaching the street. The mane of blond hair fluttered behind the hooded woman as she left the bridge's structure and wobbled onto solid pavement. *The Mare*'s horn blasted from the channel, making Liam's eardrums flutter.

Tucking the phone away, Liam drew his gun as another car honked farther back in the waiting line of vehicles. He tried to hold a bead on the woman as Owen reached her.

She swayed once and began to fall.

Owen leapt forward and caught her weight before she could hit the street.

Liam ran, gun out, breath burning in his lungs.

"Owen, no!"

Owen cradled the figure, sobbing his wife's name as he drew the hood up and off.

The hood fell away along with the blond wig, revealing the stricken face of Marshall Davis. His mouth was open in an *O* of pain and a large number two was carved raggedly into the skin of his forehead.

"Owen!" Liam yelled, a dozen steps separating them.

A snarling crack filled the air and Davis's head snapped to the side, his skull exploding in a spray of bone and brain matter. The bullet whined off the road beside Liam.

Owen looked up in a daze, still clutching the twitching corpse.

"What?" Liam heard him say.

Owen's head rocked back as the second shot ripped through his left eye and out the back of his skull.

"No!" Liam yelled, managing to snag the collar of Owen's shirt as he tipped backward. Liam knew he was dead before he began to drag him to the side of the street, but he did so anyway, the whole while keeping his eyes on the bridge, watching for movement. A shot ricocheted off the blacktop beside him, buzzing furiously away. He'd seen the muzzle flash. It was coming from the pilothouse built into the upper middle portion of the lift bridge. A door swung closed on the small building's side as *The Mare*'s horn bleated again.

The entire middle section of the bridge began to rise.

Liam looked down at the ruined face of his friend. Gently, he laid Owen on his back, making sure he was completely on the sidewalk and out of the street. He rose, rivers of adrenaline flowing through his veins, sweat pouring from his skin in waves. He raced along the sidewalk while trying to stay out of the pilothouse's line of sight in case the shooter was still inside. The bridge trundled up. A ten-foot gap between it and the road.

Twelve.

Fourteen.

Liam reached the restricted area where the bridge's structure footing began. He crouched but continued moving until he reached a set of stairs. The stairs ran in switchback fashion within the outer frame of the bridge all the way to its top. Above him enormous chains rattled and a gargantuan counterweight composed of concrete descended. *The Mare* chugged ahead, nearly drawing even with the bridge.

Liam lunged forward and up the first set of stairs, his knee clipping a guardrail painfully. His feet clanged on the steel as he ascended, turning at each platform before rushing up the next stairway. The bridge and its walkway glided upward above him. He would have to get above it and then leap to it before it passed. It would be his only chance to get onto the bridge. Vertigo made grabs for him at each turn, the elevation increasing until the ground became a shrinking pinwheel below him.

Still he climbed.

The walkway was barely above his head.

Up another flight.

Directly beside him.

Another flight. He was above it.

Without thinking he swung himself over the side of the next platform, the steel railing so cold in his hand.

Then he was in a free fall. Iron girders flew past as the rising walkway barreled toward him, the wind howling in his ears. He landed with a force that jarred his teeth and sent lightning strikes of pain shooting through his feet and up his shins, detonating in his ribs. He rolled forward, the concrete biting into his shoulder as he flipped onto his feet and skidded to a stop.

Ahead, halfway across the rising bridge, a figure stood on the walkway. He was garbed in the same dark, bulky body armor as before. In his hands was a contraption composed of a spool and two handles. From its bottom a bulbous object protruded. Beneath the bridge, *The Mare* chugged through the channel slowly. When it was almost directly below them, the figure twisted the handles of the apparatus and the oblong object dropped free of its casing. Liam watched as it fell, connected to the device by a thin strand of cable. It banged loudly onto the deck of *The Mare*, skidding backward as the boat continued through the water.

As the opposite end neared the canvas bag, it leapt up, snapping together hard with the neodymium magnet. The man on the bridge twisted his hands again and a loud whirring came from the mechanism.

The bag of money rose off the boat's deck and glided upward, the spool humming as it was reeled in.

"Stop!" Liam yelled, rushing forward, gun outstretched.

The man didn't turn. Instead he produced a pistol from thin air and fired a shot down the walkway without taking his eyes off of the approaching bag.

The bullet buzzed past Liam's shoulder and he dropped into a crouch, firing twice. Sparks flew from the handrail beside the figure as the canvas bag came into view. The man drew the bag over the side and in one deft movement, uncoupling the two magnets from one another. He dropped the reeling apparatus on the walkway, firing shots as he backpedaled. Liam rolled to the side, returning fire as the gunman turned and fled.

The center of the bridge lurched to a stop, well over a hundred feet above the canal. Somewhere in the distance sirens began to wail.

Liam regained his feet and ran after the figure who had reached the far end of the bridge. He fired another running shot that clipped the gunman's right shoulder, making him stagger forward.

Without faltering, the figure leapt into open air toward the nearest bridge support platform.

He landed on its edge, colliding with a guardrail before flipping over it. Liam reached the end of the bridge just as the gunman swung over and hooked his hands and feet onto the sides of a steel ladder that ran the length of the structure. The man gazed up at him for a split second, eyes peering through two slits in the mask. Liam fired, cutting the air where the man's head had been a moment before.

He stepped to the end of the walkway and looked down. The gunman had slid most of the hundred feet down in seconds using his gloves and boots as buffers against the friction of the ladder's sides.

"Dammit," he swore before taking a step back and launching himself across the gap. He landed solidly but the hand that grasped the rail slipped free as if it had been doused in oil.

Liam teetered above the hundred feet between him and the canal, stomach slopping with the surety of death.

As he began to tip backward into nothing, he snagged the rail again, this time his fingers holding fast. He dragged himself to safety, not giving in to the weakness that buffeted his legs. There would be time later to consider how close he had come to dying.

He threw a look over the side of the platform and caught movement below. The gunman had jumped the last ten feet to the street on the Park Point side, the bag still clutched in one hand. Liam spun away and sped down the steps. How many flights until he reached the bottom? How much time would he lose? A thought dawned on him then, Perring's words coming back to him from their first visit to the peninsula. There was nowhere to go. The bridge was no longer a viable route onto or off the island the killer had created.

He had played them, right from the beginning until now. The concerto of violence as well as the false exchange for Valerie's life had been brilliantly composed. But now he had trapped himself in the process, and Liam would make him pay for the mistake.

Down.

Down.

Down.

Dizziness buzzed in the top of his skull and he tried to control his breathing as he came closer and closer to the bottom, throwing looks over the railings whenever he came to a vantage that gave him a view of where the killer had dropped. When he was thirty feet above the street, the rough howl of a small engine met his ears and he stopped, peering over the platform.

A compact dirt bike shot out from a small side street beside the bridge, the man garbed in black astride it. He swung a right and raced away toward the far end of the island. Liam cursed again and rushed down the last flights as a sickening realization hit him like a hammer to the stomach.

There was an airport at the end of the point.

He was going to fly away.

Liam leapt down the last flight of stairs and hopped the guardrail beside the street. The long road stretched away from him, the fading form on the bike growing smaller and smaller with each second. The neighborhood was quiet, sidewalks empty. Nothing moved. Liam glanced to his left, seeing that only one vehicle had gotten "bridged," as Perring had put it, when the lift went up. It was a small truck, possibly a Ford Courier, with fender wells rusted so high he could see the engine behind the front wheels. A teenager with rampant acne stared out at him, first at his face, then at the gun in his hand. Liam ran to the driver's door and yanked it open.

"D-d-don't kill me!" the kid said, hands up and eyes bulging behind a pair of wire-rimmed glasses.

"Get out," Liam said. The kid slowly unbuckled himself as if at any moment Liam would change his mind and put a bullet through him right there in the middle of the street.

Liam leapt into the driver's seat, dropping his gun in his lap, and threw the truck into reverse. He made a quick turn and hammered the rattling truck into first gear, rear wheels screaming beneath the rotted bed. The window was a crank and after two revolutions the glass lodged and wouldn't go down any farther. With a yell of frustration, Liam jammed his elbow into the gap and shoved as hard as he could. Something clunked inside the door and the window dropped out of sight. In the distance he heard the teenager screech a curse.

The bike was already out of sight around the first bend in the road, but Liam poured on the speed, shoving the gas pedal to the floor each time he switched gears. Houses flew by, parked cars tight to the curbs became blurs of color. He glanced down at the speedometer but wasn't surprised that it was broken, the needle pinned at zero.

"Couldn't have been a beamer," he muttered, slamming the shifter into the highest gear. The engine rose to a vibrating scream beneath the hood and steam began to pour from beneath the wheel wells. He took a sharp bend hard, rubber shrieking against blacktop. Ahead the dirt bike came into view, rounding a corner and out of sight again. Liam gripped the Sig in his left hand and punched the clutch, tagging the brake with his other foot as he skidded around the bend. When the bike came into sight again it was much closer, and the killer threw a look over one shoulder as Liam brought the gun out the window and pulled the trigger.

The shot was deafening and the bike wobbled. The figure hunched lower, pouring on speed again as he leaned into a curve.

Ahead the land widened, the trees expertly placed in yards and surrounding properties vanishing. Superior became visible on either side, large swaths of sand running from its edge up to the street and a parking lot set before a chain-link fence. Sodium arc lights were lit high above several low buildings behind a gate that was open a few feet. Beyond, the outlines of planes stood dormant and dark, like scattered and forgotten playthings of some giant child. The single brake light on the bike flared for an instant then went dark as the killer raced forward through the narrow opening in the gate.

"Ah shit," Liam said resignedly as he punched the gas and braced himself.

The Ford slammed into the gate.

Metal shrieked and glass peppered his face and arms as he closed his eyes. When he opened them, the truck had whipped sideways, the gate conformed to the front end as if it had been welded there. He jammed the brake pedal down and the vehicle shuddered to a stop, inches before the sidewall of the closest building. Liam shook himself, sending glass cascading to the floor from the shattered windshield, and wrenched his door open.

The tarmac was cool and wet with patches of oil between cracks in the concrete teeming with quack grass. He stepped behind the truck's bed in time to see the bike and its rider coast around the side of a large hangar and out of sight.

Liam rounded the quiet vehicle and ran as fast as he could past the building on his left, the windows lit but without movement behind them. He swung left into a broad alley between what appeared to be a maintenance building and a tall hangar. Besides the sound of his breathing and footsteps, there was only silence. A wind sock snapped atop a pole as he came even with the end of the hangar and he drew a bead on it out of instinct before running on. The sound of sirens still keened behind him, but much fainter now so far away from the bridge. He sprinted down another narrow passage between two lower hangars and paused at the end. Trying to quiet his breathing and hammering heart, he leaned out, one eye peeking from behind the hangar's corner.

The dirt bike lay on its side a dozen yards away before a small, streamlined single-engine plane. The aircraft's closest door was open and the gunman hung half-in, half-out of the fuselage. He turned suddenly back toward the path he had taken around the largest hangar, seemed to listen for a beat, but there was no sound beside the wind caressing the beach beyond the airport fences. The gunman focused again on his task.

Liam stepped out from behind the hangar and made his way silently across the space separating them.

Forty feet.

Thirty.

Twenty.

He stopped, raising his pistol, and the killer stiffened, straightening in the doorway.

"Why'd you do it, Valerie? Why'd you kill Owen?" Liam said.

The figure turned slowly, head cocked to one side, and took a step forward away from the shadow thrown by the plane's wing. One gloved hand reached up and shoved the mask away, revealing the angular lines and blond hair framing Valerie Farrow's somber face.

"I thought my warning would mean something to you, Liam, being that I was threatening the life of your friend's wife."

"It did mean something. It meant I was getting closer to the truth."

"You don't have even the slightest perception of the truth. When did you realize it was me?"

"The moment Owen took Davis's hood off on the bridge."

"Then the guise worked pretty well, even against you," Valerie said, unzipping the coat she wore. Liam aimed down the barrel of his pistol and took a step forward, but she merely let the coat fall to the ground with a heavy clunk. She stood tall and straight, wearing only a dark, long-sleeved T-shirt above the bulk of her armored pants. "You gave me quite a few bruises the other day at Rowe's house. Even with the armor, bullets still hurt. But that's true of everything, isn't it? No matter how well we guard ourselves, something always manages to get through and cause damage."

"You need to put down any weapons you still have and come with me, Valerie."

"Do you think after all I've been through that I'm going to go quietly back and be judged by the same people who overlooked what happened to my sister? Do you really believe that?"

"But you've already taken justice into your own hands, haven't you? You killed them all. Davis murdered Alexandra and Erickson and Rowe must've been involved somehow, right?"

At the mention of her sister's name, Valerie's austere facade wobbled slightly in the low light like a fragile wall in the path of a hurricane.

"It was the bracelet, wasn't it?" Liam continued, lowering the gun a few inches. "That's why you were in the jewelry shop nearly every day. You were looking for it."

"They took it from her that night," Valerie said in a dead voice. "Davis to be exact. He was a klepto even then. Power and money, that's what it was always about with those three. Barely out of high school, they always wanted more." She gazed at him and now a sheen of tears coated her eyes. "Davis came up with the plan since he had contacts that were drug suppliers. He and Rowe were poor but they knew the right people, all they needed was a solid way to transport whatever their suppliers were moving that week."

"So that's where Erickson came in. His parents owned the shipping line," Liam said.

Valerie nodded. "He provided the space, unbeknownst to his parents, on whichever ship was traveling to the East Coast. He also invested in the product and made a nice amount with each shipment."

"Was Alexandra using? Is that how she got involved?"

"No. It was love that killed Alex in the end. And that's the saddest thing about this all."

"What do you mean?"

"Alex was madly in love with Dickson Jenner, and when he wanted to hold off on marriage until they were older, she got impatient." Valerie looked over Liam's shoulder and her gaze grew distant. "She was always like that. She'd want to do something, and even if it required years of practice and skill, she'd insist on doing it herself, her own way. She'd rush in without considering all the consequences." Her eyes slid to him again. "And that's what happened the night she died."

"'I have to do something to get rid of this feeling,'" Liam quoted, and Valerie looked as if she'd been struck. "What did she do, Valerie?"

"She called Dade Erickson since he was the richest and most arrogant person she knew, the complete opposite of Dickson. She asked for a favor, to go on a date somewhere public where people would see them together and Dickson would catch wind of it. She thought that by making him jealous it would force him into proposing. Alex and Erickson were supposed to meet up at a party but he never showed. Alex left, but on the way home she spotted Erickson's car near the docks. She walked right into the middle of a drug deal." Valerie's face darkened, the line of her mouth flattening to a razor blade. "They grabbed her and the suppliers they were dealing with threatened to kill them all if they didn't take care of her."

"So Davis had the key to the church."

"Yes."

"And they took her up to the tower and threw her over the side."

"Like she was a piece of trash," Valerie spat. "But they had help that night too. There was one more person with them who wanted in on the fast cash they were making with the shipments. Someone who already had money like Erickson but wanted more."

Liam felt his gorge rise as tumblers began to fall into place within his mind. The hand holding the gun trembled.

"His name," Valerie said in almost a whisper, "was Owen Farrow."

Liam shook his head. "No. That can't be true. Owen was a good man."

"He was a liar and a murderer!" Valerie screamed. "He lived in that house with me every day, knowing that he was the cause of what was eating me alive!" She shuddered with rage and grief. It poured off of her like heat that Liam could feel from where he stood. "They all told me he was there that night. All of them confirmed it when I made them talk and tell me what they did to her. Owen was beside them when they hurt her, brought her to the church in the trunk of Erickson's car, when they killed her . . ." Valerie's voice cracked on the last word. "He walked away and then found me months later and moved in like the predator he was."

The tarmac seemed to be rotating beneath Liam's feet. He clenched his jaw, forcing the world to stay steady around him. "How did you do it? How were you able to leave the house?"

"About two years ago I had a breakthrough of sorts. It wasn't so much the therapy as it was a realization. I knew deep down that Alex would never kill herself. But even knowing that, knowing that her killer was still out there, didn't break me from my prison, it only walled it in closer. You have no idea what I went through in that house, alone most days just trying to get by. It crippled me to the point of no return."

"You tried to kill yourself."

She nodded. "I thought it was the only way out. But as I was lying there, waiting to slip into the nothingness, I saw her, I saw Alex." Valerie swallowed. "She was older, and beautiful, and so happy. She was . . ." Her voice failed her again and she blinked. "She was holding a baby. And I knew then that I was seeing what could have been. I was seeing the life that was taken from her." Valerie composed herself. "When I recovered I started forcing myself to go outside, no matter how afraid I was. I would go a dozen steps from the front door one day, and thirteen the next. I did it until I was able to get in the car and go to the gas station. For some reason it seemed important not to let Owen know I was leaving. Looking back, I think it was fate. The one thing that kept driving me was the only option I had that the police hadn't fully investigated."

"Her bracelet," Liam said. "It had the scratch on it from when she fell as a little girl."

"Yes. When they found her in front of the church, it wasn't around her wrist. I knew it was the longest shot in the world, but it was all I had. I monitored every online jewelry auction I could find, and after I was able to leave the house, I visited every pawn and jewelry store within fifty miles almost every day of the week. I knew that the bracelet might've been lost in the struggle or maybe whoever had taken it already pawned it. I knew there was next to no chance, but without the hope of finding it, the walls would have closed in for good. As I searched, I started tutoring myself in the skills I would need to do what would have to be done, if I ever found the bracelet. I started learning how to shoot a gun at a gravel pit outside of town. I worked out, kept in the best shape that I could. I took private flying lessons from the elderly man who owned this plane behind me. When I got my license I bought it from him. I started funneling money aside to pay for all of the things that would be an eventuality.

"I found the bracelet in a nasty little pawn store on the west side of town about three weeks ago. The owner didn't want to tell me who had brought it in, but when I bribed him he sang like a bird. It was Davis of course. He wasn't smart like Rowe who invested the cash they made from the shipments. Davis was on hard times, addicted to meth and a number of other things. He must've been desperate to sell the bracelet. I think he genuinely valued it as a trophy, a keepsake from that night. Bastard."

"So you set up the meeting with him on the pretense of buying drugs. And you kidnapped him, didn't you?"

Valerie nodded. Somewhere to the west the first beat of a helicopter's rotors rose like distant thunder. "First I staged my own abduction. At that point I was simply going to kill Davis, but of course what he told me when I had him strapped down to a table changed all that. I wasn't looking for one person; I was looking for four." Her face changed, the angles becoming sharper, crueler. "I made them suffer. All of them. I let them feel a little of what I'd gone through over the years. The burning inside, the feeling of drowning in open air, the insanity that constantly lurked at the edge of my mind. Oh, I made them understand. My only regret is not being able to do the same to Owen. I hope he knew it was me right before that bullet went through his rotten brain."

"So you set up the ransom in order to start over once you were finished."

Valerie nodded. "I knew I'd never be able to come back to my old life. Through my work I knew how to edit a video and manipulate it to look as if someone were holding me. That was the simple part. It was only after the first hour of working on Davis with a propane torch that I knew I didn't ever want to return to who I was. Through their agony, I was reborn. I'm not the woman who hid for nearly a decade inside her own fear anymore."

"I can see that." Liam glanced to the side, trying to spot any approaching boats or the helicopter that was coming closer with each second. "Dickson Jenner is dead, along with his mother. Did you know that?"

The briefest flicker of regret crossed her face. "Yes. I'm sorry that they're gone, but it's not my fault."

"You put this all in motion. You could have gone to the police with the bracelet, had them handle it."

Valerie laughed and it was a cold sound in the evening air. "I saw how they handled Alex's case the first time. I told them her bracelet was missing, but they did nothing to find it. My father believed me, but even as powerful as he was, there was nothing to be done. No, they had their chance. I wasn't going to let them interfere in the justice Alex deserved."

"But you were willing to go beyond that, weren't you?" Liam said, raising the gun again. "You nearly killed me twice because I was in the way."

"Twice?" Valerie asked.

"You almost shot me at Rowe's on the shore and you tried to run me down with my own truck at your father's last night."

"I was defending myself at Rowe's, but I wasn't at my father's last night."

"You're lying. I saw you. You followed me into the woods. You were going to kill me for finding your diary."

Liam studied the confusion that crossed her features, trying to identify a flaw in her act. There didn't seem to be one.

"I have no reason to lie to you now, Liam. I did shoot at you at Rowe's, but I swear to God I wasn't at my father's house last night."

Above the trees in the direction of the city, a helicopter appeared. It hovered over the bridge as sirens grew louder and louder, their cries mingling like the voices of wolves.

"You need to let me go. I don't know you well but you seem to be a good man."

"That's why I can't let you leave."

"Let me ask you this, and answer truly from the depths of your soul: if it had been someone you loved thrown from that bell tower, what would you have done?"

Liam blinked. The black rage that had reared its head over the last days rose again within him at the thought. He saw the man in the park that had groped Dani, the smile on his face as she hurried away from him.

"Empathy is one thing, but truly imagine what you would do if someone precious was taken from you. How far would you go to make sure they were avenged? At what point would you stop and let fate dole out justice?" Valerie's voice was lower now. She'd taken a step toward him. "You know deep inside that those men got what they deserved, including Owen. You know that."

Liam watched her, studied the lines on her face that shouldn't be there. The ones that were created solely by long suffering. They were road maps to a pain he hoped he would never truly understand. He felt a tipping within him, scales tilting that balanced every decision he'd ever made of any consequence.

Time slowed around them.

The sounds of sirens, the helicopter, even Superior's waves faded away. There was only this woman and a choice. Nothing else.

"I'm sorry, Valerie. I can't let you leave." His voice was unsteady when he finally managed to say the words. The muscles in his arm holding the gun quivered.

"I won't go back. You know I can't. Please, let me go. No one will ever know what happened here."

"I'll know," he said slowly.

She nodded, as if she'd already guessed what he'd say. "I'm not sorry for what I did. I wrote a full confession and mailed it to the police department this afternoon. I put everything in the letter, including the bracelet. I didn't want to leave any doubt. Doubt is a poisonous thing. Remember that."

Valerie moved in a blur of motion. Her hand flew behind her back and drew out the pistol that was stowed there.

"Don't!" Liam yelled, flexing his knees, his finger tightening on the trigger.

Valerie whipped the pistol up and fired.

Liam jerked the trigger.

Their dual reports shattered the stillness of the airport.

A hole appeared in Valerie's shirt below her throat followed by a dark stain that spread outward, flooding the fabric with blood. The pistol fell from her hand and clattered on the concrete near her feet. She took a faltering step back, a tremulous smile on her lips.

She crumpled against the side of the plane, leaving a bright red slick on its white paint as she slid down and fell on her back.

"Dammit!" Liam said, rushing forward. He knelt at her side, putting a hand beneath her head. Her hair had come slightly undone from the tight weave she'd had it in and it tickled his arm as it fluttered in the wind. Her eyelids flickered and some clarity came to her gaze as he crouched over her. Her lips trembled and opened, a rasp coming from her throat.

"Don't talk. I'm gonna get you help, okay?" Liam said, digging for his phone. As he drew it out, one of her hands fell on his wrist, pushing the phone away. He looked at her and with the last of her strength, Valerie gave a small shake of her head. She took several shallow breaths, each one less than the last. A wet sound almost like a sigh came from the wound in her chest. She looked up at him, past him, through him, as her eyes took on a haze that deepened with each second. She shivered once and was still, her hand dropping from his arm.

Liam swallowed the solid lump in his throat and looked up at the sound of cars approaching as well as the swell of boat motors from the direction of the lake. He placed two fingers over Valerie's vacant eyes, and drew them shut to the deepening October night.

CHAPTER 24

Liam stepped off the hospital elevator and strode down the hallway, looking for the room number the nurse at the station desk had told him.

He switched the small bouquet of flowers to his opposite hand and slowed as he came to the correct door. As he reached out to knock, it opened, revealing Perring who stopped in the doorway.

"Hi," he said, stepping aside to let her through.

"Hi." She glanced down at the flowers.

"They're for Rex. How's he doing?"

"Going to make a full recovery."

"And how are you?"

"Busy. Still slogging through paperwork. If I'm walking funny it's because I have the chief, the mayor, and half the city council up my ass."

Liam couldn't help but laugh. "The paperwork is one thing I don't miss."

"Yeah, I bet."

They stood for a moment, an awkward silence stretching out before Liam handed her the flowers. "I'll let you give him these. You don't have to tell him they're from me."

She took the bouquet from him. "He's got a pretty different opinion of you now. He hates flowers though, so maybe I'll say they're from the department."

"Good idea."

"How are you doing?" Perring asked after a pause.

"I'm fine. Healing nicely. I'm heading home from here, looking forward to seeing my family. I just wanted to stop and say good-bye."

"Is it wrong that I'm not real sorry to see you go?"

He laughed again. "I won't hold it against you." He fished inside his coat for a moment and pulled out a sheet of folded paper. "I wanted to give you this," he said, handing it to her.

"What is it?"

"It's a ballistics report I requested yesterday after I found a pistol tucked beneath the mattresses on Owen and Valerie's bed. It matches the bullet they dug out of Caulston's garage wall."

Perring looked up from the page. "What?"

"It was Owen, Denise. He snuck out of his room the night I went to find the diary. I had Heller check his phone records. He called a cab service shortly after I left and again in the early morning hours after I lost him in the woods. He must've known that something in the diary would lead me to the truth about Alexandra's death. I think Valerie may have written something about the bracelet and that would have been the key to it all. He was willing to kill me to keep the secret."

"Did you find the diary too?"

"No. He must've destroyed it or hidden it somewhere. Who knows if it'll ever turn up. But there was something else. Owen had rented a boat and wanted to go out on the lake during the exchange for Valerie."

"Yeah, I remember you saying that."

"Do you recall they found a long folding knife in his pants pocket?"

"Yeah. Why?"

"I think he was going to try and kill me once we got out into open water," Liam said, watching the surprise wash over Perring's features.

"He thought I was still a threat, even with the diary gone. And he was right. He knew me well enough to know I wasn't going to give up on Alexandra's case no matter what the outcome with Valerie's situation. I think he was going to stab me and throw me overboard then say that I slipped and fell in. I would have sunk to the bottom of the lake. And Superior never gives up its dead."

Perring shook her head in disbelief. "I never would have guessed he was capable of that, or of any of the things he did. I could have sworn he truly loved his wife."

"I think he did. I think maybe he regretted what happened to Alexandra and on some level his marriage to Valerie was a form of retribution in his eyes."

"Paying for his sins?"

"I don't think he ever would've paid for them, but in his mind that might've been what he was trying to do."

"To think that he'd kept that secret for over sixteen years."

"Sometimes the things that people hide grow stronger with time instead of lessening. Sometimes they take over completely."

Perring sighed. He could hear almost a week of fatigue in that one sound. "This will go down as the most twisted case in our department. We've already had several offers from the big news stations to do exclusives about Valerie. I've never seen an orchestration like that. The way she planned it, it was . . ."

"Brilliant," Liam finished for her.

"Yes. For lack of better words. She made us all look like fools."

"She did. But you and your team handled the case admirably. There was nothing you could've done different."

"We did things by the book. But I can see now that some things have to be found outside of the lines. You have to be willing to go there, though."

Liam gazed at her, a slight coolness settling over him with her words. "Yes you do," he said quietly.

"And to think if her bullet had hit you, she would've gotten away with it all: the murders, the money, everything."

Liam shook his head. "She never intended on killing me."

"What do you mean?"

"When she went for her gun she knew I had her beat. She fired the shot well over my shoulder."

"She wanted to die."

"I think so. I guess we'll never know for sure, though." They stood silent for a moment, each wrapped in their own thoughts, until Liam reached inside his pants pocket and drew out a pack of gum, holding it out to her.

Perring laughed and shook her head. "No thanks, I'm trying to cut back."

Liam raised his eyebrows. "And no cigarettes?"

"None. And I'd appreciate it if Rex never found out that I smoked the rest of his pack."

Liam mimed a key turning at his lips. "Not a word from me."

"I think that's a blessing in more than one way." A grin tugged at Perring's mouth.

Liam held out his hand. "Good-bye detective."

She shook his hand. "Good-bye Liam."

He walked quickly down the hall. When he was nearly at the elevator Perring's voice stopped him.

"Liam."

He turned. "Yeah?"

"You're a damn fine cop."

He smiled and stepped into the elevator as it opened. "You're a better one," he said as the doors closed, Perring's smile the last thing he saw.

It was early afternoon when he pulled into the farmhouse. The sight of his home waiting there in the glory of fall foliage left him nearly breathless. The field beyond was golden with swaying grass, the few trees that surrounded the house had flared into even deeper reds, yellows, and oranges of varying shades in the short time he'd been gone. The sound of gravel crunching beneath his tires was a melody he could've listened to for hours.

He'd barely shut the truck's door and retrieved his bag from the backseat when Eric barreled around the pickup, slamming into him with a rib-crushing hug.

"Liam! I missed you!"

"Missed you too, buddy. Ouch, you gotta go easy on me. I'm a little sore."

"Sore from what?" Dani said, following the same path Eric had taken to him. The boy stepped aside and made an exaggerated sound of disgust when Dani pressed herself against him, kissing him hard on the lips. He kissed her back, wrapping an arm around her waist while waving dismissively at Eric who made another vomiting sound.

Dani finally broke away, a smile lighting up her face. "So glad you're home."

"Me too."

"Now what were you saying about being sore?"

"Nothing. I'll show you later."

"What?"

"Never mind. Let's go inside."

They spent most of the afternoon catching up with one another on what had happened since Liam had left a week ago. Dani made cups of tea for all of them and they sat around the kitchen table with the smell of the fresh bread from the bakery he loved permeating the air. He breezed through an overview of the case without mentioning the murders or any of the horrific details that had taken place, his gaze speaking to Dani over the top of Eric's head in the silences. When they were finished talking Dani rose and went to the cupboards, pulling out pans and several cans of organic tomato sauce.

"I'm making stuffed manicotti for supper," she said, throwing a look over her shoulder. It was his favorite of all the meals she had cooked for them.

"That sounds wonderful. Do you need help?"

"No, why don't you relax for a bit. Take a nap or something."

"Can we go to the park, Liam?" Eric asked, bringing his empty cup to the sink and rinsing it. A heavy cloud of fatigue still hovered over him from the past week, but the enthusiasm in the boy's voice was infectious. "Pleeeeease?" Eric intoned, drawing out the word. "Daryl and Christian from the team are going to be there." The boy nearly danced in place with excitement and Liam chuckled, pointing toward the front entryway.

"Get your glove."

"Yes!" Eric yelled, running to the front of the house.

"You sure you're up for that?" Dani asked from beside the counter.

"Just wait until later and see how much energy I have," he growled leaning in for another kiss. She giggled and shoved him away.

"Get going, Mr. Dempsey."

"Yes, Miss Powell."

They drove through the late autumn air with the windows down. The respite from the biting cold of Duluth raised Liam's spirits even further as they wound through a small neighborhood, the wide expanse of the park and brown dirt of the baseball diamond coming into view. The park's grass still held its green color, which only highlighted the gold leaves dotting the stretches beneath several ancient oak trees. Eric and Liam played catch for the better part of a half hour before two skinny boys wearing baseball jerseys approached on bikes, yelling Eric's name as they raced toward the unoccupied diamond. Liam watched them go, a portion of his heart with them in the unburdened happiness of youth on a fall afternoon, the other, greater part, full of pride and a pure contentment at simply being able to see them enjoy it from afar. For a moment all his worry drained away, the horror of how Valerie's case had turned out less overwhelming. Even the simmering anger and fear quieted watching his son play in the autumnal light. He could almost imagine it had been something he had dreamed.

Trying to hold on to the contentment, Liam turned, searching for a park bench to rest on until Eric and his friends were finished practicing drills they'd run a thousand times. He began to move toward the jungle gym and swing sets but froze in mid-step.

A man about his age sat upon the farthest bench wearing a too-tight red sweatshirt with a yellow circle on the chest. He was leering at a mother who was bent over, helping her daughter pick up several toys from a sandbox nearby, his eyes locked on the taut jeans covering the woman's ass.

Liam didn't know he was moving until he was beside the bench.

"This seat taken?"

The man's eyes were still on the young mother slowly walking away with her child, a crooked smile pulling at one corner of his mouth. He was exactly as Dani had described him. Average looking with a blond crew cut that accentuated his sharp nose and bright blue eyes. He was well-built; hard pectorals pulled at the fabric of his sweatshirt, and his thighs were thick within his designer jeans. He glanced at Liam as the mother and daughter moved farther away.

"What?" the man asked.

"Good," Liam said, sitting down. The bench was built for children, perhaps three middle schoolers. It didn't accommodate the bulk of two grown men well, especially when Liam widened his legs and leaned forward, bracing his elbows on his knees.

"Hey pal, I'm not into what you're sellin', you catch my drift?" the man said, inching slightly away from him despite the threatening tone in his voice.

"Oh I know what you're into," Liam said, gazing out across the park's clearing. They were alone save for Eric and his two friends tossing ground balls to one another in the distance.

"What did you say?"

"I said," Liam replied, slowly sitting upright and turning to face the blond man, "I know what you're into. You're into coming to public parks and harassing women. You're so pathetic you think this is the best place to get a date or pick up fun for an hour back at your place."

"What?" The man's incredulousness was so potent, he actually tilted his head to one side. "I don't know who the fuck you are, pal, but—"

"No," Liam interrupted, scooting closer. "No you don't know who I am. But I know you. I know you walk here from your house just down the street. You've come here often enough for me to have witnessed the filth that you are and followed you home. I know where you sleep."

The second before the man threw his clenched fist, Liam whipped a hand to his throat and pressed his thumb behind his earlobe. The pressure he applied made the man wince, but he was strong and seemingly stubborn, so he tried to follow the punch through anyway. Liam caught his fist and turned it, the man's fingers opening as he pushed harder below his earlobe. Snatching the man's index and middle fingers, he twisted, hearing the knuckles pop under the pressure.

"Ah, fuck!"

"Shut up and listen to me," Liam hissed. "I'll be watching all the parks you go to from now on. I have nothing better to do. If I ever spot you in any of them again, the next time you'll see me will be in the middle of the night, standing over your bed." He bent the man's fingers back farther, eliciting a hoarse whimper. "Do you understand me, you piece of shit?"

"Yes," the man croaked.

"Good. Now get the fuck out of here."

Liam shoved him. Hard. The man rolled from the bench onto the ground, gagging. He stayed there on his hands and knees for several seconds, then drew himself upright and jogged away, casting a watery glance at Liam as he left.

Liam wiped his hands on his jeans as if they were dirty, letting the overpowering rage drain away. He tried to regain the peaceful feeling he'd experienced minutes ago as he watched Eric expertly catch a fly ball, but it was only a memory.

The manicotti was fantastic. They dined beneath the warm glow of the kitchen lights, the smell of garlic, Parmesan, and pepper permeating the air. Dani had opened a bottle of cabernet sauvignon, and two large glasses stood beside her and Liam's plates. When dinner was finished they sat in the living room, watching a movie until Eric's head began to slip forward on his neck, his eyes closed to slits.

"To bed, young man," Dani said, switching off the TV. "You've got school in the morning." She stood and made her way into the kitchen. Several dishes clacked together as she loaded the dishwasher. To Liam's surprise, Eric didn't put up an argument but simply lifted himself off the couch and walked to the doorway only to come back to stand by Liam's side.

"What's wrong, buddy?"

"Nothing. I'm glad you're home."

He reached out and squeezed Eric's shoulder. "Me too."

"I worried about you while you were gone. I don't like it when you leave, especially without saying good-bye."

"I said good-bye while you were sleeping," Liam said, sensing a deeper disturbance in the boy's words. "I'd never just leave."

Eric nodded. "I had a bad dream while you were gone."

"What was it about?"

"I don't want to say it."

"Why?"

"Because it might come true."

"I promise it won't."

"You can't promise about dreams." Eric gazed at the wood floor. "You can't control them."

Liam sat forward and took the boy's hand in his own. "Whatever you dreamed, it was only that, just a dream. Good dreams can become goals, they're things to work for in real life. But if something bad happened in your dream it's because you were worried about it. Are you still worried about anything?"

The boy seemed to mull this over for a time before slowly shaking his head. "Now that you're back, I guess not."

"Good. You can always tell Dani or me about anything that's bothering you. You know that, right?"

"Yeah."

"We'll always listen to you."

"I know."

"Good. Now listen to me, go brush your teeth."

Eric gave him a half smile and rolled his eyes. Liam listened to him cross the kitchen and tread up the stairs to the bathroom. He remained on the sofa for a while, relishing the feel of being home, so close to his family. It warmed him in a way that he hadn't felt since he'd left after Owen's phone call. He gazed out of the darkening window. The brown field grass had darkened with the fading light. It was like a black sea beyond the house, stretching away into infinity. Liam let himself drift for a time, thoughts like icebergs veiled in fog passing him by. He stood from the couch and moved to the fireplace beside the TV. After a minute he had a small blaze burning within its alcove, the flames dispelling some of the chill he'd felt when Eric had mentioned his nightmare.

"I was just going to suggest a fire," Dani said. She held their wineglasses, which she'd refilled, and sat down beside him, her shoulder brushing his.

"It's always nice in the fall."

"Umm. So are you going to tell me?" she said.

"Tell you what?"

"About all the things you didn't say concerning the case. Like why you're holding yourself like you're going to fall apart when you walk."

"I'm trying to be more graceful."

She shook her head. "Jokes only get you so far."

He sobered somewhat and took a sip of wine. "I know."

"Tell me."

He glanced at her. Those words. Over a year ago they'd lanced the festering poison he'd been harboring inside. He began to speak, telling her of the details he'd left out over the phone, all the while staring into the flames that danced across the wood like capering sprites. When he'd finished she sat quietly for a time, only drinking from her glass.

"I'm sorry I didn't tell you everything right away," he said. "I didn't want you to worry."

"I worry every time you leave for a case."

"I know."

"But you still go anyway."

He sighed. "Yes." He weighed his words for a time before setting his glass down. "You were right."

"About what?"

"About why I stayed to help Owen. I wanted to find Valerie and help bring her home safely, but I also wanted to stay for me. Police work is all I've ever been good at, Dani, it's all I've known. Being on a case, hunting someone who's committed an atrocity, there's something about it that draws me. It's like you and your art."

"But it's not." Now there was anger in her voice. "My art won't get me killed."

"You've never painted that bad a picture."

"Liam . . ."

"Sorry. I understand, and believe me when I say I don't want danger in our lives any more than you do, but you can't ask me to give up my passion."

The light had fallen farther and now the flickering of flames was the only thing that lit the room. Dani sat like a stone beside him. He waited, knowing he could say nothing else to sway her.

"I'm afraid of losing you."

"I know. I . . ." He paused. "I didn't tell you what Valerie asked me right before she died." Dani turned to him, her features soft in the low light. "She asked me what I would have done if it had been someone I loved, outside that church. But I already knew. She asked me to let her go, and I wanted to, Dani, I wanted to. Because inside I knew that those men deserved what they got, even Owen. Especially Owen," he added. "I've imagined what I would do if I were to lose either you or Eric, and it scares me. I scare me." He swallowed and looked at the floor between them. Finally, Dani put a soft palm to his face, bringing his gaze back to hers.

"You're a good man with a good heart. It doesn't matter what you wanted to do, it matters what you did. You tried to bring her in and she forced you to make that final choice." When he didn't reply she continued. "You're not going to lose us." She leaned closer and kissed him gently. "And we don't want to lose you."

"You won't," he said. But his assurance only went so far and it didn't touch the darkness within him, coiled now and sleeping. He knew there was more than one way to be lost.

"Let's go to bed," Dani said, rising. She pulled him up with her and they moved toward the stairway. He silently went over and over the series of events that had brought him to the walkway of the bridge so high above the cold waters of Superior. He felt a deep failing coating him, like an oil covering his skin that wouldn't leave, no matter how many times he showered or bathed. It was the guilt of being unable to foresee what would come, unable to define or arrange the past into a coherent whole that could be read and understood. He thought of all the cold cases awaiting him, those eyes in the photographs pleading for justice, and he knew the weight he felt was the remorse of lives lost and patterns unseen.

He paused on the first stair, Dani rising above him. His fingers tightened on the banister, eyes unmoving as he stared.

Soft music drifted down from Eric's stereo in his room. The notes raising the hairs on the back of his neck.

Patterns unseen.

Notes.

Dani noticed that he'd stopped and turned to look at him.

"What's wrong?"

"They're song notes."

"What are you talking about?"

"Dennis Sandow. It can't be." Liam moved quickly to his office, his heart beating faster with each step. He flipped on the light once inside, the cool air flowing past him like a ghost that had been trapped there. He sat down at his desk, hands shaking as he opened the locked drawer and found the correct file, pulling out the crime scene photo. He barely registered Dani coming to stand behind him as he turned the picture sideways.

Dennis Sandow's body lay in bright contrast of color. The crushed grass beneath him was a brilliant green, reflective of spring's height, when the father of two had been slain. The gravel road at the edge of the picture was a deep brown, its hearty tone darker with the light rain that had fallen earlier that morning.

And the blood was almost iridescent, its color a presence in and of itself.

"It's not possible," Liam whispered, tracing the wounds on the body.

"What is it?" Dani asked.

"It's the Composer."

"What?"

"He was a serial killer almost a decade ago when I was still on patrol. One of the lead detectives, his name was Galen Faust, headed up the Composer's case. The killer targeted men between the ages of nineteen and thirty. He killed five men in a year. His calling card was a series of papers that he would send to the police station. Each one was sheet music with several notes on it. He'd carve the notes in the men's skin and then press the paper to the wounds to make the symbols."

"That's horrible."

Liam nodded, not looking up from the photo. "He was writing a symphony in their flesh. He would send the paper and then dump the body somewhere that it was easily found. Galen Faust closed in on him in late 2005, but the Composer set a trap for him. Faust became his sixth victim. After that he disappeared and there were no more killings." Liam brought the picture closer, looking at the design the knife had carved in Sandow's chest and stomach. Originally the wounds had appeared crude and without alignment, simply violent slashes that connected at certain points. But now with the page sideways he could see the notes within the carnage, the gunshots being their heads.

"He's back," Liam said. A chill ran through him that had nothing to do with the lower temperature of the office. He stared at the picture for a long time and when he came back to himself, setting the photo down, he was alone. After a glance toward the open door, he sent an e-mail to his friend Michael Diver, lead detective of the homicide division in Minneapolis. With the e-mail delivered he sat in the wake of the realization. He hadn't specifically worked on the Composer cases, but he knew them well, and Galen Faust had been a friend. The ticking of the old clock outside the room became all that he could hear as his eyes unfocused and he stared at the photo on his desk.

After what seemed like hours, he stood and tucked the picture away, locking it again in the desk drawer. He turned off the lights downstairs and climbed the treads to Eric's door. The boy slept facing away from him, only a slice of light from the hallway illuminating the tuft of hair poking from beneath the blankets, the rise and fall of his breathing. Liam watched him for a time, then moved down the hall to the bedroom on the end. Dani was under the covers already, her position a carbon copy of Eric's. A small bedside lamp was the only light in the room. He knelt on her side of the bed. She didn't roll over though he sensed she wasn't sleeping yet. It amazed him, the small ways they'd come to know one another in even the short time they'd been together. He could tell by her breathing if she was asleep or not, by her tone of voice if she was upset about something, by how she looked at him over dinner if she wanted something later in the darkness of their room.

"Dani, I'm sorry, it just came to me. I couldn't ignore it," he said quietly, placing a hand on her shoulder. She didn't pull away, but neither did she turn toward him. "I can guess how angry you are after what we just discussed. The revelation about that case could've come at any time, but it came tonight. I can't control it." He thought he heard her sigh but couldn't be sure.

Liam glanced around the room, spotting his travel bag near the bathroom. He leaned across the distance and snagged it, pulling it toward him. There was a solid knot in his throat now as his hand fished inside his bag, moving clothing aside by touch, searching. Even with the shock of recognizing the Composer's handiwork, an excitement unlike anything he'd ever experienced before began to flow through him, a giddy river that made his muscles weaken, his heart quicken its pace.

"I know you're angry, and I respect that. Maybe soon I'll find a way to turn off this thing inside of me that wants to be a cop again. Maybe I won't. I can't promise you anything except that I love you so much it leaves me speechless sometimes." The emotion in his voice siphoned off the volume of his words until they were a whisper. He'd never felt more terrified or more alive in all his life.

"Mrs. Dempsey, look at me."

Dani rolled over, squinting at him. "What did you—" But she stopped talking as she saw the small velvet box in his hand. Liam opened the lid, revealing the solitary diamond set in the silver ring that he had picked out in the jewelry store in Duluth after Perring had exited. Mr. Sorenson had been delighted when Liam asked him about engagement rings and even more so when Liam knew exactly what type of cut and setting he wanted. Even with the lack of light, the large stone's many facets flashed, aided by the trembling of his hand.

"Liam, wha—" she began again, but her eyes glistened and she sat all the way up in their bed, one hand covering her mouth.

"I guess I got ahead of myself calling you Mrs. Dempsey. I should have asked first." He cleared his throat and brought one knee off the floor, leaving the other down. "Danielle Margaret Powell, will you do me the greatest honor I can ask for and be my wife?"

Dani's laugh was choked slightly by her tears, but the word that she uttered next was one of the most beautiful he'd ever heard her say.

"Yes."

ACKNOWLEDGMENTS

As always, so many wonderful individuals to thank. I truly couldn't have written this book without the help of the following people.

Thanks first to my wife, Jade. You are always so willing to listen when I just need to tell the story out loud to get past roadblocks. Your love and support is why I'm doing what I'm doing. Big thanks to Dave Campbell and Richard Shaul from the aerial lift bridge department in Duluth. You both were gracious, helpful, and extremely knowledgeable about the workings of the bridge, which added so much depth to the story. Thanks to my editor Kjersti Egerdahl for your unending belief in my work. Thanks to Jacque Ben-Zekry who never ceases to provide support and encouragement. Thanks to my agent Laura Rennert for all your work and expertise, so glad to have you on my side! And thanks to the amazing people at Thomas & Mercer who are passionate about books and love getting them out into readers' hands.

ABOUT THE AUTHOR

Joe Hart was born and raised in northern Minnesota. Having dedicated himself to writing horror and thriller fiction since the age of nine, he is now the author of nine. When not writing, he enjoys reading, exercising, exploring the great outdoors, and watching movies with his family. For more information on his upcoming novels and access to his blog, visit www.joehartbooks.com.